K

Love Me Tender

WHEN I FALL
IN LOVE

Love Me Tender

JANICE HANNA

summerside
PRESS™

Summerside Press™
Minneapolis 55438
www.summersidepress.com
Love Me Tender
© 2010 by Janice Hanna

ISBN 978-1-60936-017-7

Scripture references are from the following sources:
The Holy Bible, King James Version (KJV).

All characters are fictional. Any resemblances to
actual people are purely coincidental.

Cover design by Chris Gilbert | www.studiogearbox.com

Interior design by Müllerhaus Publishing Group |
www.mullerhaus.net

*Summerside Press™ is an inspirational publisher offering fresh,
irresistible books to uplift the heart and engage the mind.*

Printed in USA.

DEDICATION

To my stepmom, Jeanene Hanna, who fell head over heels in love with Laguna Beach and taught the rest of us to do the same. And in memory of my dad, Billy Hanna, who invited us nearly every summer to join with friends and family in that heavenly oasis for a season of refreshing. I can still hear the waters of the Pacific even now.

SCRIPTURE

I know thy works: behold, I have set before thee an open door, and no man can shut it: for thou hast a little strength, and hast kept my word, and hast not denied my name.

REVELATION 3:8

Chapter One

TOP BILLING

Teen girls across America anxiously await the release of Bobby Conrad's new movie, First Kiss, *which opens this Friday night. A majority of the girls interviewed by this reporter plan to see the film this weekend. The draw? Bobby Conrad, of course. The quintessential boy next door. Blue-eyed, muscled, and tanned, he's every teenage girl's dream-come-true, and the envy of many a pimply-faced, pale-skinned boy.*

According to those interviewed, Bobby's smooth-as-silk voice only adds to his charm. The proof? After his highly touted performance of the movie's theme song on The Ed Sullivan Show *this past Sunday night, stores across America sold out of the 45 in record time. Pun intended. Teen girls flocked to get their copies of the romantic ballad, wreaking all sorts of havoc along the way. Doo-Wop Records is scrambling to keep up with the demand. This outcry from fans has only served to boost interest in the movie. Good news for producers on both sides of the equation.*

Early reviews of the film are mostly favorable, with only one critic noting slight inconsistencies in the plotline. Still, we can safely assume that viewers won't be paying much attention to the writing. With Bobby Conrad's face front and center on the big screen, one would have to conclude that he could deliver his lines in pig latin and still win over the female viewers. Women of all ages have fallen head over heels for this wholesome crooner-turned-actor. And First Kiss *will only make them love him more. So, what are you waiting for, ladies? Grab your friends and neighbors...and let's go to the movies!*

— *Reporting for* Hollywood Heartthrob *magazine, "On the Big Screen" columnist, Cinema Cindy.*

* * * * *

Sweet Sal's Soda Shoppe, Laguna Beach, California, 1957

"Bobby Conrad is the yummiest thing since rocky road ice cream."

Debbie Carmichael turned as her younger sister broadcast her thoughts on Hollywood's latest heartthrob.

"Have you *ever* heard anyone with a voice like that?" Becky Ann continued, speaking to a group of her friends. "It's positively scrumptious. When he opens his mouth to sing, I could swoon!"

The other girls who'd gathered in the back booth of the soda shop went into giggling fits at this proclamation. They chimed in with their thoughts, their high-pitched, giddy voices layering like the pickles, onions, and tomatoes on top of the Sweet Sal's Cheeseburger Deluxe.

Debbie couldn't disagree with her sister's assessment of Hollywood's latest golden boy. Indeed, Becky Ann had hit the nail on the head with her over-the-top description of Bobby Conrad. And nearly every girl in America would agree, at least those who read *Hollywood Heartthrob* magazine or watched *The Ed Sullivan Show*.

The velvety strains of Elvis's new song, "Love Me Tender," filled the soda shop. Oh, how Debbie loved the tunes on the jukebox. She enjoyed listening all day long as she worked. Balancing a tray of sodas, malts, and shakes with one hand, she approached the girls' table.

Joining in the conversation was inevitable. She could no more avoid this topic than she could leave the whipped cream and cherry off a banana split.

"If anyone would know the scoop on Bobby, it's Becky Ann." Debbie grabbed the chocolate shake with her free hand and passed it to the first teen in the booth. "My little sister has memorized nearly every article in *Hollywood Heartthrob* over the past couple of months, and our bedroom is filled with posters of Bobby. I can hardly see the walls." She laughed and passed out the rest of the drinks—two Coca-Colas, one cherry phosphate, and a strawberry malt.

Becky Ann continued to sing Bobby's praises. "Who needs *walls* when you've got Bobby?" She released an exaggerated sigh. Her gaze shifted upward and her eyelashes fluttered like two butterflies taking flight. "He's the last thing I see when I go to bed at night and the first thing when I wake up in the morning. Sometimes I imagine he's right next to me, saying, 'Wake up, Becky Ann. Let's grab a couple of burgers and head to the beach. I want to spend the whole day with you and only you!'"

A collective sigh went up from the group.

Debbie couldn't help but laugh. "And then she comes downstairs to the soda shop and turns on the jukebox, which is how they *really* spend the day together."

Becky Ann rolled her eyes. "For now, maybe. But I'm going to meet him in person someday, Debbie. Just you wait and see."

Yes, you will, if I have anything to do with it. Debbie wanted to speak the words aloud, but didn't. Not yet, anyway.

"I would pay a million dollars to see those gorgeous blue eyes up close," Becky Ann's best friend, Martha Lou, said. She leaned her elbows on the table in unladylike fashion. "I'm going to Hollywood to audition for his next movie."

"You are?" All the girls let out a squeal.

Debbie could hardly believe it. "But, how?" she asked. "Do they let you just waltz in there and try out?"

"I'll figure that out." Martha Lou sighed. "If it's not an open audition, I might need to get an agent. Mama is looking into that for me. She thinks I've got what it takes to make it. But all of this is going to take money, and so far I've only saved three dollars and twenty cents."

"And she's going to spend all of that on cherry phosphates!" Debbie's brother chimed in as he passed by the table on his way to mop up a spilled soda under the adjoining booth.

Debbie laughed, but Becky Ann didn't seem to find the humor in his remark. "You're just jealous of Bobby's baby blues, Junior. Admit it."

"Sure I am. Sure I am." His gaze narrowed. "Let me ask you one question, li'l sis."

"All right." Becky Ann shrugged and took a sip of her Coca-Cola.

"Six months ago you girls were in love with Elvis Presley, correct?"

"'Love Me Tender' is the cat's meow," Becky Ann said with a dreamy-eyed look.

Debbie glanced at her brother. "You have to admit it's a great song. And Elvis is a one-of-a-kind."

"Of course." Junior nodded. "I agree. But I'm trying to make a point. You're fickle, Becky Ann." He looked at the other girls now. "All of you are. A couple of months after your Elvis-a-thon, you switched gears and fell in love with Troy Donahue."

"He was brand new on the scene," Becky Ann argued. "That's why."

"And he's *so* cute," Cassie Jenkins, one of the younger members of the group, sighed.

"I can't argue with the girls there, either." Debbie shrugged. "Have you *seen* Troy Donahue?"

Junior groaned. "Of course. His signed photo is on our wall." He turned back to Becky Ann. "Correct me if I'm wrong, but after your brief romance with Troy, you wrote Pat Boone a letter, declaring your undying love. Am I right?"

Becky Ann sighed. "I don't expect you to understand, Junior. You're a boy."

"No, he's a *man*," Debbie argued. "He's eighteen years old."

"Yes, I'm a *man*." He paused and his gaze shifted for just a moment to Martha Lou. "Not that anyone around here seems to notice." Muttering something indistinguishable, he walked off with the mop in hand.

Debbie's heart went out to him. "Poor Junior." As she spoke the words, everyone looked Martha Lou's way.

The dreamy-eyed teen took a sip of her cherry phosphate and leaned back against the booth. "What?" she asked after a few moments of awkward silence. "What did I do?"

"It's what you *didn't* do, silly." Debbie laughed. "You're supposed to fall head-over-heels in love with our brother, and apparently you haven't been paying attention to the signals he's been sending."

"Oh." Martha Lou looked perplexed. Her gaze shifted to Junior, who continued to mop. "Well, maybe if he had Bobby Conrad's gorgeous blue eyes, I'd consider it."

This, of course, led the girls right back into a discussion about their newest heartthrob.

Debbie had to admit—if to no one but herself—that Bobby's

scrumptious eyes had captivated her too. Many times she'd awakened to those luscious pools of blue staring right into her very soul. In those moments, she could almost imagine him crooning one of his tunes just for her. And why not? Bobby was closer to her age, anyway. The latest issue of *Hollywood Heartthrob* listed him as twenty-one. She would turn twenty next month, on the third of August.

Across the room, the song on the jukebox changed. When the familiar beat of Bill Haley's popular song, "Rock Around the Clock," came on, smiles lit the faces of the girls in the booth. Well, all of them but Becky Ann. She was still too busy talking about Bobby to notice.

"I can't believe *First Kiss* is finally releasing." Becky Ann clasped her hands together and placed them over her heart. "I've dreamed of this moment for weeks." She looked at the others. "You're all going, right? The first showing at The Palace is at five-fifteen on Friday afternoon. Be there, or be square."

"I'm going to get there at three o'clock to get in line," Martha Lou said. "If I don't get a ticket, I'll just die."

"I'll be there," Cassie echoed.

"You coming with us, Debbie?" Becky Ann asked.

"Of course." She couldn't stop the smile that erupted. "I wouldn't miss it for the world." In fact, she'd been looking forward to the movie's release just as much as the younger girls had.

"Did you see him on *The Ed Sullivan Show* last Sunday night?" Becky Ann asked. "Talk about dreamy. And when he sang "First Kiss," I just knew those words were meant for me. I went to Frazier's and bought the 45 first thing Monday morning."

"I'm so jealous." Martha Lou shook her head. "When I got there, they were sold out."

"No problem," Debbie said. "When you girls are finished with your sodas and shakes, you can all go upstairs and listen to Becky Ann's record."

"The lyrics are out of this world," her sister added. "This is his best song, by far. And you'll never guess what's on the flip side."

"What?" all the girls asked at once.

"Bobby…singing the song in Spanish. You've never heard anything so beautiful."

Debbie grinned as her sister went off on yet another tangent about Bobby's sultry singing voice. The other girls hung on her every word.

Well, all but one. Ginny Anderson leaned back against the seat, arms crossed at her chest. Nothing new there. Ginny wore a serious expression much of the time. In that respect, she took after her father, Everett Anderson, who happened to hold the mortgage on the soda shop. Thank goodness Ginny hadn't inherited his crankiness. Just a slow, calculated way of looking at things.

"I don't understand you, Becky Ann," Ginny said at last. "What's the point of falling in love with someone you'll never even meet? It's such a…a waste of time. Give me a real boy any day." She corrected herself right away. "Er, man. I'm nearly twenty now. Boys are a thing of the past, and so is giggling about Hollywood stars we're never going to meet." She reached for her chocolate shake and took a long sip.

"Who says we're never going to meet Bobby?" Becky Ann argued. "Laguna Beach isn't that far from Hollywood. It could happen. You never know. Bobby might be driving down the Coastal Highway right now, on his way to Sweet Sal's Soda Shoppe to see me in person."

"You're such a dreamer, silly girl," Ginny said. "You always have been."

"She *will* meet him…if I have anything to do with it." Debbie's hand flew to her mouth as soon as the words escaped. Had she really just said that out loud?

"What do you mean?" Junior stopped mopping long enough to ask.

Debbie released a breath and tried to think of a way to fix this. She didn't want to give away her idea just yet. Not with so many things left to figure out. Still, if she had her way, Becky Ann and the others would, indeed, meet the heartthrob in person. "Oh, I have a few tricks up my sleeve," she said finally.

"Debbie, are you saying that Bobby Conrad might come here, to Sweet Sal's Soda Shoppe?" Martha Lou paled and nearly dropped her soda.

Debbie wasn't sure whether to nod or shrug. She finally decided the shrug would be a safer bet. "I've been thinking of asking him to do a benefit concert."

Ginny didn't look convinced. "Do you think he still does things like that, now that he's a big movie star?"

"Well, there's no way to know for sure unless we ask," Debbie said.

"I just can't imagine what it would be like to have him here." Becky Ann's eyes grew wider by the moment. "That would be a dream come true!"

From across the restaurant, Debbie heard her mother call out her name. She turned and gave a little wave. "Be right there, Mom." Looking back at the girls, she winked. "Say your prayers, girls. I've got to wait till just the right time to pop the question."

"Oh, pop the question!" Becky Ann used these words to drift back into a conversation about what it would be like to have Bobby Conrad propose. And Debbie used them as an excuse to scurry off to the register to see what her mom wanted.

As Debbie reached the front of the store, her mother gestured to a group that had just entered. Debbie had been so busy gabbing with the girls that she'd somehow overlooked the jingling of the bell at the front door. A family of four waited to be seated.

"Welcome to Sweet Sal's." Debbie grabbed some menus and led them to a booth.

The woman, who looked to be in her late thirties, paused to stare at the photos on the walls. "Oh my. Look at all those autographed photos of movie stars."

"We've had quite a few come through over the years," Debbie said.

"Like who?" the woman's husband asked. "Anyone we would know?"

"Oh, sure. My mother can tell you." Debbie gestured for her mom to join them as the family took their seats. She arrived in short order and Debbie introduced her. "This is my mom, Sally Carmichael. Everyone around here calls her Sweet Sal."

The woman smiled. "I wondered if the shop was named after a real person."

"I'm very real, I assure you." Debbie's mom laughed. "Some days, more real than others. So, what can I do for you fine folks?"

"They want to know about the photos on the walls, Mom," Debbie said.

"Yes, have you actually met all of these people?" The woman pointed to the wall with the framed photos of Gregory Peck, Frank Sinatra, Audrey Hepburn, Lucille Ball, Desi Arnaz, Ozzie and Harriet, and several more.

"Oh yes," her mother said. "Many of the stars own homes in Laguna Beach or Dana Point. Quite a few stop by as they go back and forth to L.A."

"How perfectly wonderful. Well, I can see why they would. This place is great. And what darling waitress uniforms. Very cute." She gestured to Debbie's red-and-white-striped dress.

"Folks call us the Peppermints," Debbie explained. She straightened her crisp white apron then made sure her cap was on straight.

"They're just precious. Truly. I can't wait to tell my friends back home about this diner. It's so…so California!"

Debbie smiled at the family as she handed out the menus. "Our special of the day is the beef stew. And just so you know, Sweet Sal's is famous for its shakes and malts, so save room."

"Save room?" The woman chuckled. "Why don't we start with a couple of chocolate shakes? Can we share?"

"Of course. I'll bring extra straws." Debbie headed to the front of the store on her mom's heels. As they reached the register, another round of laughter erupted from Becky Ann's booth at the back of the room.

"What do you suppose those girls are up to?" Debbie's mom asked.

"Oh, you know how it is. They're gaga over Bobby Conrad. Can't wait for his new movie."

"I wouldn't mind seeing that movie, myself," her mother said. "I wonder what your father would say if I told him. Can you imagine?"

They both laughed and glanced back over the open counter to the kitchen area where Debbie's dad worked flipping burgers.

"I heard that, Sal," he called out. "And just so you know, I'm not a fan."

Debbie laughed. "I'm sure Bobby is a great guy, Pop. Just like every other guy that age."

"Most twenty-one-year-olds I know don't live in mansions in Malibu," he said. "And they certainly don't drive cherry red Corvette convertibles."

"I'll bet if he showed up in that car and offered to let you drive it, he'd win you over." Debbie flashed a smile.

For a moment, her father's eyes lit up. "Hmm. Maybe. I'd never turn down a ride on the Coastal Highway in a convertible." He slapped the bell. "Order up!" he hollered. "Bossy in a bowl with a cup of moo juice."

Debbie lifted her empty tray and reached for the bowl of beef stew and the large glass of milk. As she headed over to table five, she found herself daydreaming. What would it be like to ride with Bobby Conrad in his convertible with the wind whipping through her hair? Would he want to stop off at the beach afterward to watch the sun set and steal a few kisses? She was lost in the possibilities, a wave of hope sweeping over her.

"You okay, kid?"

She looked up as she heard her customer's voice. Everett Anderson. Ginny's father. The town's most infamous banker was rarely cheerful, even on a good day, but he looked particularly cranky today.

"Oh…oh, yes sir." She nodded. "Just thinking."

"Humph. Better watch it. You almost dropped my stew. I want to eat it, not wear it."

"Sorry." She passed the bowl off to him with an apologetic smile. Dropping plates of food would never do, especially at Mr. Anderson's table.

On her way back to the register, Debbie paused to look through the large plate-glass window at the front of the soda shop. The neon SWEET SAL's sign flashed, its red, white, and black colors beckoning all to stop in for a hot meal or a cold malted.

On the other side of the busy Coastal Highway, brilliant white sands sparkled under a bright midday sun. The cool blue waters of the Pacific still held her spellbound, even after all these years. They seemed to stretch out forever. If she closed her eyes, she could almost hear the waves crashing against the rocks.

Most of the kids her age spent their summers swimming and talking about what the next semester at college would be like. Sometimes she longed to join them. But helping Mom and Pop with the family business took precedence now. Ever since her father's heart attack last spring, things had been different, and not in a good way. They'd had the usual share of financial challenges—keeping up with the mortgage, for instance—but Pop's health struggles loomed largest of all. Debbie did her best to trust God, but some days fear wriggled its way up her spine.

What would they do if something happened to Pop?

No, she wouldn't think about that. She couldn't. Her father would get well, and the shop would be a success, in spite of the competition from that new fast food joint, McDonald's. Those golden arches might sway a few folks, but no other restaurant in the world could hold a candle to Sweet Sal's burgers and fries. No, the real deal was here to stay. No doubt about it. And Pop was here to stay, too, as long as he took care of himself. She would make sure he did.

Debbie stared at the huge expanse of water across the street and whispered a prayer for her father. For weeks, she'd prayed for an answer, and now she truly believed the Lord had given her an idea to make everything better. If she had her way about it, the Carmichael family would struggle no more. Pop could even retire, if he wanted to. Or just work in the back office like the doctor had suggested.

A noise startled her back to attention. Debbie turned and saw that her father was trying to move the jukebox to sweep underneath the edges.

"Pop, you shouldn't be doing that." She ran to him, her heart thumping out of control. "Remember what the doctor said? You're supposed to be taking it easy."

"Frankie Carmichael, taking it easy?" He laughed. "That doctor doesn't know me very well, does he, Sunshine? This shop depends on me giving a hundred and ten percent."

Yes, but giving a hundred and ten percent is what landed you in the hospital with a heart attack in the first place.

She wanted to say the words, but didn't dare. Besides, they wouldn't do any good. It would be a better idea to transition into a conversation about teens and music. That way she could lay the foundation for her plan, the one she would present later tonight when they went to their apartment above the shop.

"Did you hear that ABC is going to kick off a new television show for teens in August?" Debbie tried to sound nonchalant. "*American Bandstand.*"

"Yes, I heard that show from Philly was going national," he said. "Who's hosting it?"

"Some guy I've never heard of. Dick somebody."

"Well, I wouldn't get too hooked on him, one way or the other. *Bandstand* has done pretty well on the local level, but I wouldn't imagine taking it national is the best idea. Blink your eyes and this one will be gone."

"Maybe." She shrugged again. "But it sounds like fun to me."

"Fun?" He sighed. "I remember fun. Had a lot of it, back in my day."

Debbie gave him a sympathetic look. "We still have fun together, Pop."

"You're right, Sunshine." He smiled. "And there's plenty of it ahead."

"Thanks for the reminder." Debbie kissed him on the cheek, and her father responded with a quick hug before heading back to the kitchen.

She glanced at her reflection in the glass one last time, finalizing the plan in her mind. That done, she tried to picture herself through Bobby Conrad's eyes.

Hopefully, when he came—and she had no doubt he would—he wouldn't just fall for her family and their quaint soda shop.

He would fall for *her*, too.

Chapter Two

WALK OF FAME

Move over, Rover. It's getting crowded in here. Southern California is seeing a new influx of starry-eyed wannabes. They're coming from small towns, big cities, rural farms, and university campuses. Some have even made the jump across the Big Pond, hailing from towns in England, France, Italy, and beyond.

Most arrive with little more than a couple of nickels to rub together, but they share a common goal: to make it big. From audition hall to audition hall, they sing, they act, they dance, they perform. Night and day they work tirelessly to prove they've got the goods. A few succeed, but many end up tucking their dreams into worn duffle bags and shuffling back home.

Who are these starry-eyed wonders? They're parking lot attendants (James Dean), beauty contest winners (Debbie Reynolds), college grads (Pat Boone), radio performers (Doris Day,) journalism students (Troy Donahue), accordion players (Connie Francis), store clerks (Bobby Conrad), and self-proclaimed mama's boys (Elvis Presley). In short, they represent every conceivable slice of Americana and beyond.

The Golden State, as always, throws wide her arms and welcomes these weary travelers, offering the promise of dreams-come-true. This promise, as always, is sprinkled with generous layers of pixie dust, which seem to cast an unrealistic spell, clouding the vision of

23

incoming stars and starlets. They're just foolish enough to believe they're the next big thing...and we're just foolish enough to give them a chance to prove it.

— *Reporting for* Hollywood Heartthrob *magazine, "Man About Town" columnist, Sunset Sam*

* * * * *

Paramount Studios, Los Angeles, California

"Johnny Hartmann?"

Johnny startled awake. His gaze shot to the middle-aged man with the clipboard in his hand and the pencil stuck behind his ear. The fellow's thin black wisps of hair stood up on top of his head, making him look a little odd. And speaking of odd, that pale yellow sweater vest really took the cake. Was it some sort of costume? Why, back in Topeka, a guy would get tossed in the creek for wearing something like that. Or worse.

Johnny yawned and stretched, trying to wake himself up. "I'm Johnny." How long had he been sitting in that chair, anyway? Long enough for his backside to go numb. He rose and tipped his head to the right and then the left to get rid of the stiffness in his neck, finally coming awake enough to respond.

"This way, kid," Yellow Vest said.

Johnny followed the man through a door marked CASTING. Once inside, he saw several other guys who'd been waiting with him earlier in the hallway. He found it strange that they were all still here.

Yellow Vest introduced Johnny to a couple of older men sitting in directors' chairs, gesturing first to the man on the right. "This is Ryan Cooper, producer of *The Road to Nowhere.*"

"Nice to meet you," Johnny said.

Mr. Cooper grunted in response.

"This is Edward Landers, our director." Yellow Vest pointed to the man on the left. "These gentlemen will be hearing your audition today."

Johnny turned his attention to the director, who looked distracted, irritated. He didn't look like someone Johnny would want to cross. Not today. Not any day, in fact.

"Hartmann?" the producer asked as he glanced at Johnny's audition form. "Is that your real name?"

"Yes, Mr. Cooper." Johnny nodded. "Hartmann is my real name."

"Sure it is. Let's start with the song."

"Song?" For a moment, Johnny panicked.

The producer's brows shot up. "Why the shocked look, kid? Didn't you realize you were auditioning for a singing role? This is a musical, ya know."

"Oh, sure. I sing. But I'd feel more secure with a guitar in my hand. Wish I'd brought mine, is all."

"Not a problem," Cooper said. "We have one. What can you sing for us?"

"Hmm." Johnny fingered the beautiful wood on the gorgeous black Stella guitar that Yellow Vest passed his way. "I'm pretty comfortable with Elvis's new ballad." As his fingers rippled across the strings, Johnny realized at once the beautiful instrument was out of tune. He took a moment to correct that, finally getting the sound he wanted.

"Interesting," Yellow Vest said to the director. "This kid's the only one who noticed."

A rustling from the other guys in the audience alerted Johnny to the fact that his competition sat nearby. Had they all sung in front of each other? Was the director saving the acting auditions till after the vocals? How did this work, anyway?

For a moment, he wanted to toss the guitar, hop back on the bus, and head back to Topeka. After ushering a silent prayer heavenward, though, his nerves calmed. *I know You've brought me here, Lord. We can do this...together.*

With the guitar tuned, Johnny took his place on the stage, settling onto a barstool they'd provided. Thank goodness he didn't have to sing into a microphone. No, this simple setup would work just fine.

He strummed the first few chords for "Love Me Tender," relaxing at once. If Johnny Hartmann knew anything, it was a good ballad. And he'd never heard a finer one than this. From the moment Elvis had crooned this tune on *The Ed Sullivan Show*, Johnny had been captivated.

He closed his eyes as the words began. Before long, he found himself caught up in the music, forgetting all about his surroundings. Nothing like a good song to transport you away from your troubles. And how wonderful, to sing of a love that would last a lifetime. He knew such a thing was possible. His parents were living proof that love could remain steady and strong through the many changes of life. Still, he hoped to experience that kind of love firsthand. And singing the words to this song made him believe that one day he might.

About halfway into the chorus, Yellow Vest cut him off. "Thanks. That's enough."

Johnny opened his eyes and abruptly stopped playing. "W–what? That's it?"

"Sure, kid." Mr. Cooper scribbled a few words onto the paper in his hand. "We can tell you've got the goods." He whispered a few words to Yellow Vest. "We want to hear you read. Get a script." He pointed to a stack of scripts on a nearby table.

Johnny grabbed one.

"Page thirty-two," Yellow Vest said. "You know what part you're auditioning for, right?"

"Uh, yeah," Johnny said, feeling more like a scared schoolboy than a grown actor. "It's a small part about…"

"There are no small parts, Hartmann," Mr. Landers interrupted, sounding agitated. "Only small actors. Got that?"

He got it, all right. Johnny flipped through the script until he came to page thirty-two.

"Any time you're ready." The director settled back in his chair.

Johnny fumbled with the pages. "Excuse me," he said at last. "What is the character's name, again?"

"Bucky Jones." Mr. Landers gave his watch a glance. "His lines start about halfway down the page."

"How do you want me to play him?"

"Hartmann, are you an actor, or aren't you?" The tips of the director's ears turned red.

"Well, yes…" He'd starred in a couple of high school shows, after all.

"Then act. Just do whatever comes naturally. This is your audition, not mine!"

A couple of the guys in the audience chuckled. Johnny swallowed hard and took a deep breath. He began to read, trying to sound confident. "I'm sorry, Bessie May, but I have to tell you how I really feel. Your father is a lousy, no good…" Johnny paused, staring at the script in disbelief.

"Is there a problem, Hartmann?" Yellow Vest asked.

"Uh, yeah," he stammered. "I, uh…" How could he say it without sounding like a preacher's kid from Topeka? "I can't say these words."

"You mean you can't pronounce them?" Mr. Cooper's brow wrinkled.

"No, it's not that." Johnny tried to hide the tremor in his voice. "I can't say them because…"

"Speak up, kid."

"Because they're swear words." There. It was out. Surely this guy would understand. And since when did Hollywood movies have swear words in them? Other than *Gone with the Wind*, anyway. Was this some sort of new trend? If so, they could give the part to someone else. He'd never forgive himself for using language like that in a movie…or in real life. Real men didn't curse.

"Kid, where are you from?" The producer stood and took a few steps his way.

"Kansas."

"Kansas?" Mr. Cooper crossed his arms.

"Yes."

"Well, do us all a favor, son."

"Sure," Johnny said. "What is it?"

"Follow the yellow brick road all the way back home. You're out of your element here." The producer yanked the script from Johnny's hand, and a roar of laughter went up from the other actors.

Johnny's heart plummeted. "But sir…" He couldn't argue with Mr. Cooper. The guy had hit the nail on the head. Johnny was out of his element for sure. But going back to Kansas wasn't an option, at least not yet. Not when he hadn't even landed one role. How would he ever live that down? And what about the dream God had placed in his heart to use his gifts to make a difference in the world?

"Thanks for stopping by," Mr. Cooper said. He turned to face the others in the crowd. "Ballard, Joseph, and Miller. You three can stay. The rest of you are free to go now."

A group of guys pushed in behind Johnny. A couple of them made snide comments, but he did his best to ignore them. Instead, he glanced one last time at that beautiful guitar and sighed. Maybe the next audition would go better. If he got a next audition.

"Don't let the door hit you on the backside on your way out, fellas," Yellow Vest said and then laughed.

Johnny bit his lip to keep from responding. His mother's words, "If you can't say something nice, don't say anything at all," ran through his head.

He led the pack out into the hall and dropped into the same chair he'd started in. He needed time to think. Time to come up with a plan. Once these other guys cleared out, he could do just that. Sure, he could go back to the YMCA. Spend a few more nights. His money would last a couple weeks, maybe a bit longer. But if he didn't get a part soon, he'd have to wait tables. Or park cars at one of the restaurants.

He thought about what that would be like. Parking cars wouldn't be a bad gig. Why, he'd probably meet some pretty big stars that way, too. Maybe they could open a few doors for him, introduce him to some people in the industry. Stranger things had happened, right? And besides, if the Lord was in this—and Johnny felt sure He was—then divine appointments were to be expected. Today's audition was just a stepping stone. A learning experience. Nothing lost, nothing gained. One more notch on the belt of courage.

A man's voice rang out, interrupting his thoughts. "So, Johnny Hartmann from Kansas."

Johnny looked up, noticing the fellow's flashy blue jacket and slicked-back hairstyle. "Y–yes?"

"So, you're a good boy, then."

Johnny paused a moment before responding. What was it with these people? Why did they insist on making fun of folks like him? Were they allergic to wholesome, clean-cut guys from Kansas? He shrugged, unwilling to give this man any ammunition.

"Oh, I didn't mean it as an insult, son," the stranger said. "On the contrary." He reached into his pocket and came out with a pen and a scrap of paper.

"I see something in you, kid." He began to scribble something on the paper.

"You do?"

"Sure. I was in there when you sang. Heard the whole thing. I think we need more kids like you on the silver screen."

"Really?"

"Sure. And I haven't heard a voice like that in a long, long time. They were right when they said you've got the goods." The man finished writing on the paper then passed it to Johnny.

"What's this?" Johnny asked.

"My name and number, kid. You're gonna need it."

Johnny glanced at the paper then shifted his attention to the stranger, who settled into the chair next to his.

"Listen, let's cut to the chase," the fellow said.

"O–okay." Johnny pressed the scrap of paper into his pocket.

"I'm an agent. The name's Jim Jangles. You can call me Jim." The man extended his hand. "Put 'er there."

Johnny hesitated just long enough for the stranger to grab his hand and give it a shake.

"If you want my opinion, there's plenty of room in Hollywood for good boys," Jim said. "Bobby Conrad is proof of that. Who needs bad boys, anyway? We've already got James Dean and Marlon Brando. They've cornered the market on bad. Anything else would just be a copycat, anyway."

"R–right. So…" Johnny's words drifted off. He wanted to ask this guy the obvious, but didn't dare.

"You want to know why I'm here?" Jim asked.

Johnny nodded. "Yes sir."

"Yes sir. I like that. You're not acting. You really are a good kid," Jim said.

Johnny couldn't figure out how to respond to that.

"I'm here because I know talent when I see it." Jim smiled. "You need an agent, son. These open casting calls are getting fewer and further between, and the competition's fierce, especially with so many young actors entering the scene. You need someone who can go to bat for you. Lead the way. Someone to prove that you've not only got the goods…you're also unique. Different."

"And you're that someone?"

"Sure. Why not? You're something else, kid. I know a talented singer when I hear one, and you've got a great face, too."

"I do?"

"Of course. The girls will love you."

Johnny couldn't help but smile at that revelation.

"Son, you could be the next Frankie Avalon," Jim said.

"Frankie Avalon?" Johnny echoed. "Really?"

"Sure," Jim said. "Or Pat Boone, even!"

"Pat Boone?" Johnny could hardly believe that comparison. "Wow."

"Of course, you might just be another Horace Hinkley." Jim raked his fingers through his hair, looking none-too-pleased.

"Horace Hinkley?" Johnny shrugged. "Who's that?"

"He's a kid from Sheboygan who didn't take my advice. He's currently working at a filling station on Sunset, pumping gas and waving at the stars as they drive by. A far cry from crooning tunes and lighting up the big screen, wouldn't you say?"

"Yes." Johnny paused, deep in thought. "So, you really think I need an agent?"

"I do."

"And you're the one I need?"

"I am." A hint of a smile lit Jim's face.

A wave of peace washed over Johnny as he extended his hand. "Okay. You're hired."

Jim shook his hand then swept him into a fatherly hug, one that made Johnny miss his dad more than ever. For a moment, he paused to imagine what his father would think of Jim Jangles, or the very idea of hiring an agent at all.

"You're not going to regret this, kid," Jim said. "We're going to go a long way together, you and me."

"I'm counting on it, sir."

Jim slipped his arm over Johnny's shoulder. "You got a ride? Where are you staying, anyway?"

"Oh, I…" How could he explain that he'd taken the city bus from the YMCA and planned to return the same way? If the busses were still running this late. He hadn't thought about that.

Jim gave him a pensive look. "So, that's how it is. You need a place to rest your head? My wife won't mind if we put you up for a little while."

"Really?"

"Sure, why not. My son, Toby, will love the idea. You can share a room with him. If you don't mind bunking with a nine-year-old."

Hearing about Toby brought a catch to Johnny's throat. He missed his kid brother something awful.

"That'd be great, Jim," Johnny said. "If you're sure your wife won't mind."

Jim laughed. "Trust me, she's probably already got an extra place set at the table. She knows I'm at an open audition today. I often come back with a stray."

A stray. Johnny sighed as he thought about that. He'd never pictured himself as a stray. The word put him in mind of a prodigal. He had to wonder if his parents and friends back home saw him that way. Possibly. Until this moment, Johnny had only seen himself as a hopeful actor and singer, one who wanted to use the gifts the Lord had given him to bless others. And one who could share his faith with those he met along the way.

"Theresa's making meatloaf." Jim led the way toward the door. "Don't want to keep her waiting."

"No sir."

As they walked across the expansive parking lot to the car, Johnny thought about how quickly things in his life had changed. Why, in just a matter of minutes, he'd gone from being ridiculed to having an agent.

A real, slicked-back-hair-flashy-suit-wearing agent. From Hollywood. Who could beat that?

"You okay, kid?" Jim asked as they reached his blue sedan.

"Me?" Johnny paused from his thoughts long enough to respond. "Sure. How come?"

"Well, you're smiling to beat the band. Wonderin' what's going on in that head of yours."

"Oh." Johnny paused, a little embarrassed to be caught with his head in the clouds. "Well, to be honest, I was just thinking that I haven't been this excited since I got my Roy Rogers lunch box."

Jim's laughter rang out across the parking lot, causing a couple of people to give them curious looks.

"Kid, when you make it big, I'll buy you *ten* lunch boxes. Twenty, even."

"With a picture of Trigger on the front?" Johnny asked, feeling like a kid again.

"You betcha." Jim slung his arm over Johnny's shoulder once more. His smile convinced Johnny—if only for a moment—that all was right with the world. Well, at least the world of Los Angeles, California. How things fared in Topeka, Kansas…well, that was another matter altogether.

Chapter Three

SPINNING TUNES

*They're rockin' and rollin,' hoppin' and boppin,' twistin' and shoutin'
all across the country. Who, you ask? Teens. From soda shops to living
rooms, slumber parties to beachside hangouts, they're tuning in to hear
those addictive Billboard hits. Excitement has never been higher, and
neither has the volume.*

*Parents are stuffing their ears with cotton balls and wondering
what happened to the big band sounds of yesteryear. Artie Shaw.
Benny Goodman. Where are they? They've faded to the background,
crowded out by young, hip artists like Billy Haley and his Comets,
The Platters, and Little Richard. This ain't your grandma's music. Not
even close. But today's teens are diggin' it, and that's what matters
to record producers. They're taking their cues from those calling the
shots...your kids.*

*So, parents, where are your teens? At their local record stores, of
course. And gathered around transistor radios, snapping their fingers
and tapping their toes. They're singing along with Elvis, Pat Boone, and
the like. They're also gearing up for the nationally syndicated* American
Bandstand, *which is sure to be a success, if this reporter's predictions
are accurate. (And since when has Hepcat Harry ever been wrong about
something music related?)*

Wake up and smell the vinyl on the 45, Mom and Dad. Sharpen those record needles and stock up on earplugs. Your teens are setting the trends for the future of entertainment in the US of A. Like it or not, they're here to stay...and so is their music.

— *Reporting for* Hollywood Heartthrob *magazine, "Jukebox Jive" columnist, Hepcat Harry.*

* * * * *

About fifteen minutes after Debbie finished supper with her family, she walked into the living room in search of her father. She found him seated on the divan, reading the newspaper.

"Pop?" She glanced at the television, more than a little curious. "It's time for *Dragnet*. Did you forget?"

He waved a hand and continued reading.

"But Pop, you never miss that show. It's your favorite."

"Sal!" he called out, as he lowered the newspaper. "Sal, could you come in here for a minute, please?"

Debbie's mother entered the room looking a bit frazzled. "What is it, Frankie?" She wiped her hands on her apron. "I'm trying to clean up the supper dishes so I can get back downstairs to help Junior with the evening crowd. We've got a packed house tonight." She glanced at the television, a look of concern registering in her eyes. "You're not watching *Dragnet*?"

"No, I can't think about that right now. This is important." He pointed to the newspaper. "It says right here in this paper that gas could someday cost fifty cents a gallon."

Debbie gasped. "W–what?" She took a seat on the arm of the divan and glanced over Pop's shoulder at the article in the paper. Sure enough, the headline touted the possibility that gas prices could someday rise to unbelievable levels.

"Fifty cents a gallon," her father repeated. "Can you believe that?"

Debbie's mother sat next to him and shook her head. "Frankie, that's impossible. It must be a misprint of some sort."

"A man would be better off leaving his car in the garage," he sputtered.

"At that price, who could afford a car, anyway?" Debbie asked.

"We need to stop taking this paper. It's nothing but foolishness." Her father flipped the page and pointed. "Says in this article here that some scientists think it's possible to put a man on the moon by the end of this century. A man on the moon. What do you think of that?"

"Foolishness, dear. Pure foolishness." Her mother rose and gave him a kiss on the forehead, then headed back to the kitchen.

As Debbie took a seat in the chair across from Pop, she tried to work up the courage to talk to him about her idea. Unfortunately, Becky Ann thwarted her plan. The sixteen-year-old entered the room wearing her prettiest skirt and blouse. Her bright red lipstick was a close match for her new hair color, Miss Clairol's Sunset Red.

Their father took one look at her, folded the paper, and rose. "Becky Ann, where are you going?"

"Hey, Pop! Why aren't you watching *Dragnet*? It's Tuesday night."

"Don't avoid the question, Becky Ann," he said. "Where are you going?"

"I'm going downstairs to the soda shop to jive with my friends. Don't be such a worrywart. It's so old-fashioned."

Debbie held her breath, wondering how Pop would respond

to such sassiness. Oh, if only Becky Ann would stop being such a…
well, a teenager.

"I'll show you old-fashioned!"

Their father drew near, but Becky Ann didn't appear to be paying
attention. Instead, she checked her reflection in the tiny compact mirror she fetched from her skirt pocket.

"Parents, honestly." She smacked her lips together, the bright lipstick now smearing over her teeth. So much for looking like she wore
the stuff all the time.

"What do you need all that lipstick for?" their father asked. His
gaze narrowed. "And what have you done to your hair? It's…it's red!"

"Finally! I thought you'd never notice!" Becky Ann giggled and
turned in a circle to show it off. "You like it?"

"You…you dyed your hair?"

She gave him a kiss on the cheek then winked. "Only my hair-
dresser knows for sure."

Pop's face turned red. "Sal!" he called out. "Sal!"

Debbie's mom reappeared, dishtowel in hand. "Yes, dear?"

He pointed to Becky Ann. "She *dyed* her hair."

"Well, I know. I helped her with it when we came up from the shop
earlier. Isn't it lovely?" Debbie's mom tucked the dishtowel into the
waistline of her apron and fussed with Becky Ann's long red mane.

"Lovely?" Pop's eyes widened. "You think it's lovely? What has
happened to this world we live in? I tell you who I blame it on. It's that
crazy fellow, that, that…Elvis…Elvis…"

"Presley, dear," their mother said.

"Elvis *Presley*! He's completely corrupted our kids. As if we didn't
have enough to worry about. The whole planet could go up in smoke

tomorrow, thanks to the Communists. And what does my daughter do about it? She dyes her hair! *Dyes* her hair."

Debbie fought the sinking feeling that tried to overtake her. With so many distractions, she would never get to talk to Pop about her plan. Would Becky Ann's hair really spoil the whole thing?

"Frankie, remember what the doctor said about your blood pressure. You need to stay calm." Debbie's mom picked up the newspaper, folded it, and tucked it under her arm.

Debbie watched her father, who sat in silence for a moment. She breathed a sigh of relief when he reached for the large remote control and pressed the button. After a loud click, the television began to warm up. A few seconds later, the screen filled with the familiar faces of the *Dragnet* stars. Pop settled onto the sofa.

"No more talk about the Communists," he said. "I'm going to watch my show now."

"Good idea. It'll be therapeutic." Debbie's mom gave him a kiss on the forehead. "Would you like me to bring you a cup of coffee, dear?"

He grunted a "Yes," his eyes never leaving the screen.

Debbie didn't budge from her seat, even as Becky Ann slipped out the door to head downstairs. She would sit through as many television shows as necessary to find just the right moment to approach Pop.

Before long, she found herself caught up in the familiar police drama. Then, as the clock on the wall chimed the half hour, another show began.

About halfway into *The Texaco Star Theater*, Pop lowered the volume on the TV. "Okay, honey. You win out over Milton Berle. Tell me what you want to talk about."

Debbie startled to attention. "W–what?"

"Don't act so surprised. You've been sitting there for over an hour waiting to talk to me about something. I know you well enough to know you've got something on your mind. You might as well tell me."

"Ah." She grinned. "Well, now that you mention it."

"What is it?" he asked. "You need an advance on your paycheck? Want the day off to hang out at the beach with your friends? Want me to add something new to the menu?"

She laughed. "All of those things sound good, but they're not what I had in mind."

"What is it, Debbie? Spill the beans."

She rose and joined him on the sofa. "Pop, I've been worried about you."

His brow wrinkled. "You know what the Bible says about worrying. It won't add a minute to your life. Better to trust God than to worry."

"I know," she said, "but it's not always easy. I see how hard you work."

"'In all labor there is profit.'" He quoted the familiar verse from Proverbs, one he lived out every day and one he repeated often.

"Well, yes," she agreed. "But I liked Dr. Perry's idea about you working in the office and leaving the cooking and cleaning to the rest of us. If we didn't have to worry about finances, you could relax. We could hire a couple of extra cooks."

"I have a feeling you're cooking up something right now, so just spill it."

"Pop…" Debbie rose and began to pace the room. She finally paused and gazed into his eyes, hoping to keep her tears at bay. "Pop, we've been running behind on the mortgage ever since you got home from the hospital. Mom told me."

His gaze narrowed. "I wish she hadn't burdened you with that, Sunshine. It's not your problem."

"I know, but I'm glad she did." Debbie paused. "I knew the medical bills were high, but I had no idea about the mortgage until she told me. I wish I'd known sooner so I could have come up with a plan."

"A plan?" He looked concerned.

"Yes." She waited a moment to ask the next question, choosing her words carefully. "Is…is that why Everett Anderson keeps hanging around the shop? Do you think he's going to…"

"To foreclose?" Her father sighed. "I don't know, honey. He's been concerned about the money from the get-go, and I know he's really nervous that we're not caught up yet. I got a letter from the bank just this week." He paused. "Not really a threat, but close. If the man was a believer, I'm pretty sure he'd be more understanding."

Debbie shook her head. "If he'd walked a mile in your shoes, he would be more understanding, too. Obviously he's never been through a crisis, or he would know it takes time for things to get back to normal."

"Well, I think we'd stand a better chance if McDonald's hadn't built their new place so close by," her father said. "Not that I mind a little competition. I think it's healthy, in fact. But folks like to try new things, and McDonald's is the new kid on the block."

"We might be the old kid, but we're still the best," Debbie said. "And we're going to prove it. We're going to do something else, too."

"What's that?" he asked, his brow now wrinkled.

"I think it's high time we did a benefit. Folks have been talking about it for months. They're all concerned about you."

"A benefit?" He did not look convinced. "What for?"

"To pay off the mortgage on the shop so you can take it easy."

"Pay off the mortgage?" He laughed. "Get it caught up, you mean."

She shook her head. "No, I want to pay it off. Otherwise, we could get behind again, if…." Debbie shook her head, unwilling to think of the "ifs."

"Honey, we owe eighteen thousand dollars on the mortgage. What kind of benefit is going to raise that kind of money?"

"The kind where Bobby Conrad comes to town and sings on our stage at Sweet Sal's."

"What?" He slapped himself on the forehead. "Have you caught Bobby Conrad fever, too?"

She decided to avoid the question by going a different route. "It's not about what I want. It's about what those teen girls want. They want Bobby. And if we could get him to come and sing a few songs, we could take donations from the people who attend. And think of the sales. We'd sell hundreds of burgers and fries and such in one afternoon. People would come from all over Orange County and beyond. It would be fantastic."

Her father's gaze narrowed. "And just what makes you think Bobby Conrad is going to come here to do this concert?"

"I don't know if he will. But I'm sure we could ask…if we had some sort of connection." She gave her father a pleading look. "You know folks, Pop. You could call in a favor, couldn't you?"

He paused but said nothing for a while. When he did speak, his words surprised her. "You're really concerned about your old dad, aren't you, sweetheart?"

She nodded.

He kissed her on the forehead. "I still say you don't need to worry, but it does my heart good to know you've been thinking about me." He sighed. "And I'll be honest with you. The idea of working in the office and leaving the cooking to other people is tempting."

"I knew it. But why didn't you say so before?"

He shrugged. "You're young, honey. You wouldn't understand. When you get older, you don't want people to know that you feel… old."

Debbie laughed. "It's not like you're ancient, Pop. You're only… what? Forty-eight?"

"Forty-nine," he said. "But who's counting?"

They both laughed. But even as they did, Debbie thought back to that awful day last spring when Pop had collapsed in the kitchen. The event replayed in her mind over and over again, like a scene from a bad movie.

On that horrible day, she'd feared she might lose her father. Even now, she blinked back tears as the possibility settled in.

"So, let's go back to talking about this Bobby Conrad idea," her father said. "I might know his agent."

"W–what?" Debbie looked his way, stunned. "Why didn't you tell me?"

"What's to tell? I know a lot of people. Folks come and go from the shop and I get to know them. Nothing new there."

"So, do you think you could ask him if Bobby could come?" she asked. "Performing at a benefit concert would be really good for his reputation. And the television reporters would love it, too."

"Probably." He patted her arm. "I'll make you a deal, Sunshine. You talk Becky Ann into dying her hair back to its original color, and I'll consider calling my old friend and asking him to come down for a visit."

Debbie sighed. Of all the things to ask. Becky Ann would be plenty miffed at the idea of dying her hair back to its original blond. On the other hand, she would squeal with delight if she heard that Bobby Conrad might really be coming to Sweet Sal's Soda Shoppe. Surely that would be incentive enough.

Debbie sprang to her feet, more determined than ever. "Pop, you've got yourself a deal. By tomorrow morning, all of your offspring will be blond once more, or my name isn't Deborah Marie Carmichael."

"I hope you're right," he said. "Because right now Becky Ann's hair is redder than Bobby Conrad's convertible…and that's pretty red!"

Debbie laughed. "I promise. Not sure how I'll do it, but I'll do it."

With a spring in her step, she headed for the door, excited for the day she could tell the others the good news.

* * * * *

Johnny sat in the front seat of Jim Jangle's sedan as they cruised up the highway to an unfamiliar part of town. "The Great Pretender" played on the radio, and he pondered the words, realizing they hit a little too close to home. What in the world was he doing in California, halfway across the world from Topeka? Oh yes, chasing his dream. Following his heart.

"Thanks for stopping by the Y to pick up my bag," Johnny said after a few moments of thoughtful silence. "And thanks again for letting me stay at your place. Hope I won't be putting you out for long."

"Putting me out?" Jim grinned as he reached to turn down the radio. "Kid, I'm going to make a fortune off you." His words were followed by a raucous laugh, one that unsettled Johnny's nerves.

For the next couple of minutes he contemplated his choice to get in the car with a total stranger. *Who is this guy, anyway? How do I even know he's an agent? Sure, he says he is, but...* Johnny snuck a peek at the fellow one more time. Could be this Jangles fellow had a few tricks up his sleeve. Maybe he was a scam artist or something. Johnny had read about folks like that. He'd been warned. For a second, fear enveloped him. Just as quickly, it dissipated.

"Listen, kid," Jim said, breaking the silence. "I don't want you to get hung up on what that producer said back there. Don't let his words stop you from becoming what you're meant to be."

"Oh." Johnny paused, realizing just how badly Mr. Conner's words had stung. Could he really shake them off so easily?

"You know what the great Fred Allen once said, son?" Jim asked.

"Fred Allen...the comedian? The one who passed away last year?"

"Yes, may he rest in peace." Jim's voice softened. "He was my favorite. Truly brilliant. Did you ever listen to his radio show?"

"My parents did, from time to time."

"He was a great ad-libber, and those gags he did with Jack Benny were priceless."

"What did he say?" Johnny asked.

"Oh, yes." Jim paused, as if trying to remember. "He said, 'You can take all the sincerity in Hollywood, place it in the navel of a firefly, and still have room enough for three caraway seeds and a producer's heart.'" A hearty laugh filled the car. "Get it?"

"Hmm." Johnny pondered his words. "So, folks aren't sincere in Hollywood? They don't say what they mean and mean what they say?"

"Rarely." Jim changed lanes and exited the freeway.

"So, how do I know I can trust you?" Johnny asked.

"Smart boy, to ask a question like that." Jim kept his focus on the road. After a few seconds of dodging traffic, he answered the question. "The only logical answer is, you can't. But I'm going to ask you to, anyhow." Jim turned and flashed a smile so bright it lifted Johnny's spirits. "We're not all bad, kid. And not all directors are like that guy you met today."

"I'm counting on it."

A few minutes later, Jim pulled up to the front of a large two-story house with a second car in the driveway. "We're home."

"Nice." Johnny couldn't help but stare. The house beat anything he'd ever seen back in Kansas.

"Don't be too impressed, kid," Jim said. "It's mortgaged. Won't be paid off till 1982."

"Wow." Johnny tried to imagine life in 1982, but couldn't think that far ahead. Why, he would be in his mid-forties by then. He'd probably have a wife and a houseful of kids. Maybe they'd live in a place like this. With a mortgage.

Nah. If he made it big in Hollywood, he could pay cash for a house.

Jim led the way to the front door. Johnny followed along on his heels, feeling a bit like a stray pup. He entered the house with his suitcase in hand and looked around, surprised by the home's expansive size. Seconds later, a lovely woman with brunette hair appeared. Her cotton dress and crisp white apron put him in mind of his mother, though this woman was considerably younger. Probably in her mid-thirties.

"Well, there you are." She reached for Jim's jacket. "I was starting to think Toby and I were going to have to have dinner without you."

"Now, would I do that to you, Theresa?" Jim kissed her on the cheek.

She crossed her arms and gave him a stern look.

"Okay, I plead the fifth." He laughed. "But this time I have a good reason. Theresa, meet Hollywood's next teen sensation, Johnny Hartmann."

She flashed a smile and gave Johnny a quick once-over. "Hartmann. Great stage name."

"Oh, it's my real name," he said. "I promise."

"Sure it is." She extended her hand.

He shook it, hoping she could read the gratitude in his expression. "Nice to meet you, Mrs. Jangles. You have a great place here. Reminds me of home."

Jim's wife chuckled. "It's Mrs. Williams, honey. But you can call me Theresa."

"Oh?" He looked back and forth between Jim and his wife.

"Jangles is my professional name," Jim said with a sheepish look. "Adds a lot more splash and color, don't you think? I mean, who's going to sign with an agent named Williams?"

"Uh, *me*?" Johnny laughed.

"True." Jim paused. "And speaking of signing, I've got a form you'll need to sign. Well, both of us need to sign it, actually. Standard stuff. I'll be getting 15 percent of any monies you make off of movie deals and recording projects."

"Fifteen percent?"

"Well, sure, kid. That's standard. Bobby's got the same deal. All the big names do."

"Bobby?" Johnny's curiosity was piqued.

"Surely you've seen him around. Bobby Conrad?"

"B–Bobby Conrad?" Johnny sputtered. "Y–you represent B–Bobby Conrad?"

"Well, sure." Jim shrugged. "I told you I was an agent, kid. I know talent when I see it. Bobby's one of the kids on my team. Now you are, too. Unless you want to play hardball over that 15 percent. Then we might have to talk about starting you off in the minor leagues."

"Oh, no sir." Johnny shook his head.

A youngster appeared next to Jim. His freckled face and closely cropped haircut reminded Johnny of his kid brother.

"This is Toby," Jim said with a smile. "He's part of the team, too. We let him live here year-round, and not just because he's cute. He happens to belong to us."

Johnny laughed.

Toby gave Johnny a curious look. "My dad discovered you?"

"I...I guess you could say that." Johnny shrugged. Right now, he didn't feel "discovered." He just felt like a guy who needed a place to stay and a hot meal. And a shower. A shower sounded mighty good.

Toby nodded. "Bobby stayed at our house for three months after he was discovered. How long are you staying?"

"I have no idea."

"As long as it takes," Jim said. "But if my predictions are right, it won't be long before Johnny will be swimming in the dough."

"Swimming in the dough?" Johnny shook his head, wondering what that would be like. "I...I can't even imagine it."

"Well, sure, kid," Jim said. "Welcome to Hollywood. All things are possible here."

"Hey, that's a scripture," Johnny said. "'All things are possible to him that believeth.' It's one of my favorites."

"Believeth, huh?" Jim's brow wrinkled. "Well, I believe...in you. And I'm going to prove it over the next few weeks by getting you some of the best auditions in town. So, welcome to the family."

"Thank you." Johnny felt his cheeks warm in embarrassment.

Jim's wife gave Johnny a pensive glance. "Looks like it's settled, then. You're the next great thing."

"Well, I…" Johnny wasn't sure how to respond.

"Oh, it's okay." She patted him on the back then reached for his bag. "Jim only brings home the ones he's really sold on, so you must be something else, Johnny."

"Oh, he is," Jim said. "Just wait till you hear him sing, Theresa."

"Mm-hmm. Well, first we eat, then we sing." She dropped Johnny's bag onto the sofa then led the way into the dining room.

Johnny's mouth watered the moment he saw all the food on the table. Meatloaf. Mashed potatoes. Green beans. Homemade rolls. He could almost hear the heavenly choir now. A good home-cooked meal could go a long way in making a guy feel welcome.

"Time for supper, everyone," Theresa said. "I can't keep this meatloaf waiting all night."

As Johnny took his place at the table, he whispered up a prayer of thanks. No way to know if the Emerald City was up ahead or not. But he was willing to make the journey up the yellow brick road, one way or the other.

Chapter Four

THAT'S ENTERTAINMENT

Hollywood Molly here, ready to catch you up on all of the latest break-ups and makeups. Those of you who've been following my column might remember that I predicted the eventual romance of Marlon Brando and film actress Anna Kashfi. The proof is in the photograph. Our camera-man captured an unrehearsed pose of the happy couple coming out of a Hollywood restaurant together, hand in hand. Rumor has it they will marry later this year. We wish them a long and happy future.

Lest you think all the news is good, I must bring you up to speed on the "Are they, or aren't they?" affair between Cary Grant and Sophia Loren, which some speculate has gone on for over a year, since the film-ing of their first movie, The Pride and the Passion. *Supposedly, he has proposed. She has declined. According to my sources—and I know they're trustworthy—Loren is currently singing her swan song to Grant. Readers will remember that Grant is still married to his wife of eight years, Betsy (Drake) Grant. One has to wonder if Drake is singing a divorce ballad at the moment.*

Grant's rumored tryst with Loren is almost as dramatic as the recently publicized breakup of Frank Sinatra and second wife, Ava Gardner. In an ironic twist of fate, their marriage of six years—which started as a highly talked-about affair that ended Frank's first marriage to wife Nancy—has come to an end. Perhaps the lyrics to his recent hit,

"I Get Along Without You Very Well," are tripping across his tongue.

Not every marriage in Hollywood is falling apart, thank goodness. As we reported in a recent issue, actress Elizabeth Taylor has wed film director Michael Todd. This is Taylor's third marriage.

So, there you have it, folks. Breakups and makeups...Hollywood style.

— *Reporting for* Hollywood Heartthrob *magazine, "Star Chasers" columnist, Hollywood Molly*

* * * * *

Johnny's first few days with Jim Jangles and his family passed by at an uncanny rate of speed. All of his concerns faded after that first night. By the end of the first week, he was a member of the family. Or, at least, they made him feel like one. Of course, by then Jim and Theresa had already transformed everything from his hairstyle to his wardrobe. Johnny argued every step of the way, particularly after the couple insisted on purchasing a couple of new Hollywood-friendly outfits for him. He felt a little strange in the new duds. They were too flashy. Uncomfortable, even. Still, Jim and Theresa wouldn't take no for an answer.

In some ways, he felt like that puppet, Howdy Doody—stiff and a little uncomfortable, but strangely popular. These days, it seemed like other people were telling him what to say, what to wear, how to respond. And he'd followed every bit of advice. Why not? Jim Jangles had proven himself trustworthy. And Johnny had never met a nicer family, next to his own.

On Saturday morning Jim greeted him at the breakfast table

with some hopeful news.

"Johnny, I got you an audition for *Arthur Godfrey's Talent Scouts.*"

The spoon slipped out of Johnny's hand into the cereal bowl as his nerves got the best of him. "Really? What do I have to do?"

"It's a vocal audition. Monday morning at ten. I'll get you there. You'll wow them with your voice and your effervescent personality."

Johnny wasn't sure about that last part, but the idea of singing sounded great. "What song?"

"Anything popular." Jim jabbed the butter knife into a jar of preserves and spread the gooey mixture across his toast. "I liked the Elvis tune you did before. You might stick with that. If it ain't broke, don't fix it. That's what I always say."

"Okay." Johnny paused to think about it. "Is that what I'll be singing on the show?"

"No. You'll need to write something new between now and then. Something that will be a signature song for you."

"Ah." Johnny paused to reflect on Jim's words. Writing love songs actually came pretty easy, though he hadn't shared many of them with folks in L.A. just yet. He always figured the day would come...but on national TV? The very thought of it terrified him. And mesmerized him.

"We'll start with television and go from there." Jim gave him a knowing look.

"Go from there? You mean, movies?"

"Sure, movies. We're not gonna rest till we see your name up in lights, kid."

"I see." Johnny pondered that for a moment. "So, which is better—to be in the movies or be on TV?"

"Are you kidding?" Jim looked flabbergasted at the question.

"Actors cut their teeth on television, but if you want to become a star, well, you need to get your face up on the silver screen."

"Hmm. I see. I was kind of hoping being on television would be enough." Johnny pondered that for a moment. Seemed like being on a television show would serve his purposes just fine. All he really wanted, after all, was to sing his songs. Starring in a Hollywood movie would be nice, but it wasn't really at the top of his priority list. Not that he'd turn down a movie script if he felt right about it.

Jim shook his head. "No, being on television isn't enough. You know what the great Fred Allen had to say about that, don't you?"

"Um, no sir, I don't."

"He said, 'Television is a *medium*, because anything *well done* is *rare*.'" Jim let out a laugh that almost caused Johnny to drop his cereal spoon again. "Get it? Medium? Well done? Rare?"

"Yep. Got it." Johnny chuckled. He was finally growing accustomed to Jim's one-liners and wondered how many more of them he had up his sleeve.

Toby's voice rang out, interrupting Johnny's thoughts. "Stick 'em up, pardner!"

Johnny turned to see the youngster dressed in cowboy attire—a hat, fringed vest, boots about ten sizes too large—and holding a metal silver six-shooter.

"Up in the air, I said," Toby repeated, pointing the toy gun his way.

Johnny stifled a chuckle as he lifted his hands. "Am I being arrested?"

"Yep." Toby pulled out a pair of plastic handcuffs. "You're being arrested for disturbin' the peace." He grabbed Johnny's hands and pulled them behind his back, snapping one handcuff around Johnny's left wrist and the other to the back of the kitchen chair.

"Disturbin' the peace?" It took everything Johnny had not to laugh.

"Yep." Toby scowled. "Kept me up all night playing your guitar. That's a federal offense."

"Federal offense, eh?" Jim reached for the newspaper. "Gonna throw him in the slammer, are ya, son?"

"Yep." Toby's brow wrinkled. "Only, I'm not yer son. Name's Earp. Wyatt Earp."

"Ah." Jim gave him a pensive look. "Wyatt Earp, eh?"

"Yep."

Jim put the paper down. "Son, did you by chance steal my latest copy of *Variety*?"

Toby pointed the gun at his father. "What's it to ya, pardner?"

Jim crossed his arms and leaned back in his chair. "Obviously you saw that ABC is holding auditions this week for *The Life and Legend of Wyatt Earp*. They're in search of a boy about your age."

"Yep." Toby tucked his gun into its holster and stared his father down. "So, what's the verdict, pardner?"

Jim sighed and shook his head. "Same as it's been the last ten times you came to me asking to audition for a show. No son of mine is going to be in the television or movie business."

Toby's shoulders slumped a bit and he stomped a boot on the floor. "But, Dad!"

"No, son. We've been through this over and over again. No auditions for you."

"Not fair!" Toby glared at Johnny. "He gets to."

"Son." Jim shook his head.

Theresa entered the room, took one look at Johnny—still cuffed to the chair—and began to scold. "Toby, unfasten those cuffs right now. Johnny needs to eat his breakfast."

"Johnny needs to eat his breakfast." Toby mimicked her words under his breath as he removed the cuffs.

"And take that cowboy hat off before you sit down at my table." His mother extended her hand and Toby yanked off the hat, passing it to her.

"No fair," he muttered as he plopped into the chair next to Johnny.

"No one ever said life was going to be fair, honey." His mother tousled his hair and Toby groaned. She filled a bowl with cereal and placed it in front of him. "Eat your Wheaties, son. It's the breakfast of champions."

"I don't want to be a champion," he groused. "I want to be an actor...like Bobby."

"Eat your Wheaties and maybe you will be an actor someday." Jim reached for the newspaper once again. "Looks like you're off to a good start right now."

The phone rang and Theresa walked into the living room to answer it. "It's for you, Jim," she called out. "Frankie Carmichael."

Jim's face lit up. "Well, I'll be." He headed off to the living room.

Johnny finished up his breakfast, keeping Toby entertained with stories of life in Topeka. Not that life in Topeka was particularly exciting, but as he told one of his childhood tales, Johnny added a bit of theatrical flair to keep the kid hanging on.

About ten minutes later, Jim returned to the kitchen with a broad smile on his face. He glanced at Theresa. "Feel like heading down to Laguna Beach for a Sweet Sal's burger and shake?"

"Really?" Toby squealed. "Sweet Sal's is the best!"

"I had planned to spend the morning working, Jim." Theresa gave her husband a knowing look. "But the temptation of Sweet Sal's is too much. I can be ready to go in forty-five minutes, tops."

"What's Sweet Sal's?" Johnny asked.

They all looked his way, and he suddenly felt like he'd been put on display in a Macy's window.

"Just the best soda shop on the West Coast," Jim said. "Run by an old friend of mine, Frankie Carmichael." His expression shifted to one of concern. "He's been through a rough patch this year and needs my help, so I'm happy to give it."

"What kind of help?" Theresa asked, her brow wrinkling.

"He's asked if I'd be willing to let Bobby do a benefit concert," Jim explained. "So I figure we can head down and have lunch at Sweet Sal's and talk about it. I'm sure Bobby will go along with it, as long as scheduling isn't an issue. He's a good kid." Jim glanced at Toby. "Maybe we can go to the beach after lunch. Would you like that?"

"Neat-o!" Toby hollered. "Two of my favorite things in one day! Cheeseburgers and the beach!"

The youngster's enthusiasm warmed Johnny's heart. However, he felt nearly as excited himself. Two weeks in L.A. and he still hadn't seen the Pacific. Maybe today was the day. If Jim and Theresa included him on their jaunt to Laguna Beach, anyway. He gave Jim a sheepish look, not wanting to ask.

"You're coming with us, Johnny. No arguments. It's high time you met some non-Hollywood types. The Carmichaels are salt of the earth people. And they've got a couple of pretty daughters, to boot." Jim slapped Johnny on the back. "You'll win them over in no time."

Johnny laughed. "With my singing voice or my face?"

"Okay, you got me there," Jim said. "Only, this time I wasn't referring to either. I was thinking you'd win them with your great personality. And the Carmichaels are churchgoers like you, so you have that in common."

Johnny paused to think about how he should respond. Since he'd arrived in Hollywood, he hadn't gone near a church. Strange how far away from God you could feel after just a couple of weeks of distraction. He would do something about that…and quick.

"I'd like to find a church soon," he said at last. "Maybe I could go with you all."

Theresa gave Jim a quick glance then looked Johnny's way. "We're not regular churchgoers. In fact, I haven't been since Toby was a baby." A sad look came over her. "Not sure how it happened. I used to go all the time as a girl. I really enjoyed the hymns. They brought such comfort."

"Well, maybe one day soon we can all—" Johnny never got the chance to finish. Jim interrupted him.

"Enough talk about that. We need to get on the road soon if we're going to stay on schedule."

Less than an hour later, Johnny found himself in the backseat of the family's Chevy Bel Air that Jim proudly called "Tropical Turquoise." Toby talked non-stop at his side. The youngster had removed his boots and fringed vest, but still wore the hat.

As they traveled south on the Coastal Highway, Johnny stared out the window to his right at the beautiful waters of the Pacific. How could anyone question God's existence after witnessing something so majestic? Why, in all of his twenty years, he had never seen anything so glorious. He kept his gaze on the blue waters, not wanting to miss a moment.

Toby, apparently, didn't care much for the view. Or, if he did, it didn't show. He fidgeted with the lock on the door and rolled the window up, then down. Up, then down.

"Son, stop that before I pull this car off the road," Jim's stern voice rang out.

Toby released the window handle and began singing along with the radio at the top of his lungs. "How much is that doggie in the window? The one with the wag-a-lee tail." Before long, they all joined in, singing in joyful chorus. In that moment, with family gathered around him, Johnny almost felt like he was home again.

Until he looked at those amazing blue waters of the Pacific. Then, home seemed a million miles away.

When the song ended, Toby flashed a suspicious grin. "You got a girl back home, Johnny?" he asked.

"No, I don't." Johnny smiled at the youngster, wondering why a nine-year-old would ask such a thing.

"I do," Toby said. "Her name is Patty. She was in my class last year."

"Do you plan to marry her, son?" Jim asked from the driver's seat.

"Maybe." Toby sighed. "But first I have to beat up Mikey Yarborough."

"Beat up Mikey Yarborough?" Johnny asked. "Why?"

"Because." Toby's brow wrinkled as he explained. "Mikey told everyone that Patty is his girlfriend, not mine. So, I'm gonna punch his lights out tomorrow on the playground at the end of our street."

"Tomorrow's Sunday, son," Theresa said. "It wouldn't be appropriate to punch someone's lights out on a Sunday."

"Better wait till Monday, then." Jim's words were followed by a chuckle. "Wouldn't want to offend anyone."

"I guess. But he's got it coming." Toby leaned back against the seat with a sour look on his face.

"All this over a girl?" Johnny asked.

Toby nodded. "Yep."

"You really do like drama, don't you kid?" Johnny tousled the youngster's hair.

A smile lit Toby's face. "Yeah. That's why I want to be a television star."

Jim slowed at a traffic stop. "When he's *grown*, he'll make a great leading man. The kid's quite an actor, as you witnessed this morning. Learned from the best."

"You?" Johnny asked, gazing at Jim's reflection in the rearview mirror.

Jim laughed. "Well, me, sure. And Bobby. And now, you." The traffic began to move forward.

"I want to be a leading man so I can win the girls," Toby said. "Just like Bobby. And Johnny."

"I'm no ladies' man, trust me." Johnny groaned at the thought of it. "I only had one girlfriend back in Topeka, and she broke my heart. She married my best friend six months ago."

"Ouch." Jim's reflection in the rearview mirror showed his displeasure at that news.

"I'm over it," Johnny said. "But it took awhile." Longer than he'd admitted to anyone but himself, but he wouldn't tell Jim that.

"She's going to regret that when you're starring on the silver screen." Theresa glanced back at him, offering a warm smile. "That's all I'm going to say on the matter."

Johnny bit back a response. Katie's marriage to Dean, though painful, was part of his past, not his future. And who was he to tear apart what God had brought together? No, the news had stung, to be sure, but it hadn't devastated him. Not for long, anyway. And in some ways he had Katie to thank for his trip to L.A. Losing that relationship had propelled him in a completely different direction. And now look where he was—cruising down the Coastal Highway toward Laguna Beach with the most beautiful view he'd ever witnessed.

"If you really want to win the girls, you have to sing like Elvis and Bobby," Toby said. "Or play an instrument." He crossed his arms, looking completely defeated. "I wish I could play the piano like Jerry Lee Lewis."

"Son, *no* one plays the piano like Jerry Lee Lewis," his father said.

"He's right," Johnny agreed. "But I'll tell you what, Toby. I'll teach you how to play the guitar, if you like."

"Really?" Toby's eyes lit up. "You will?"

"Sure."

A smile turned up the corners of Toby's lips. "I'll bet Mikey Yarborough can't play the guitar."

"Probably not," Johnny said. "You're sure to win Patty's heart with a song, so why don't you wait a while to punch Mikey's lights out? Sing first. Fight later."

Everyone laughed.

"I think you've just given us the formula for success, Johnny," Theresa said. "Sing first, fight later. I like it." She chuckled.

"Me, too," Jim said. "In fact, I think we'll make that your tagline. Since you're a good boy and all. Your fans need to know you're all about singing, not fighting."

"Sounds good." As Johnny leaned back against the seat, a peaceful feeling came over him. Maybe that was the answer. Sing first. Deal with the problems of life later. Wasn't that how he'd always handled life's challenges in the past? Praise his way through with song then leave the rest to the Lord? It had always worked in Kansas. Probably, the same formula applied in Hollywood.

He began to think through Monday's audition, trying to decide on a song. Sure, he could repeat the Elvis tune, but why not shoot for the stars? Sing one of his own ballads? If they liked it, he might just get to sing it on national TV. But which song? Or, should he come up with something new?

As they passed a sign reading LAGUNA BEACH, Johnny smiled. Maybe this decision was best made after a cheeseburger and shake. A man could think more clearly with a full stomach, after all. And if Frankie Carmichael's daughters were as pretty as Jim had said, Johnny might just find the inspiration to write a brand-new song, one that would knock the socks off those producers at *Arthur Godfrey's Talent Scouts*. Yes, all he needed was a little inspiration.

* * * * *

"They should be here soon, right, Pop?" Debbie stared out the window of the soda shop, her anxiety growing.

Her father looked her way through the opening leading to the kitchen. "He said they would come for lunch, Sunshine. Don't fret."

"And you think he'll let Bobby do the benefit?"

"One question at a time," Debbie's father said. "Let's just have lunch with Jim and see what he has to say. Could be Bobby's too busy."

"Oh, I hope not." Debbie paused to adjust her apron then walked to the register and straightened a stack of menus. If this idea didn't pan out, she didn't have a backup plan. In order for this to work, Bobby had to sweep in and save the day. If he was half the hero he'd played in *First Kiss*, he would do just that. No question about it.

Her father came out into the restaurant with a pitcher of root beer in his hand. He took a look at Debbie and Becky Ann in their red-and-white-striped uniforms and cleared his throat, getting the attention of several patrons seated at the bar.

"Hey, Clifford," he said to the mailman seated on the barstool closest to the register. "Do you know how the Peppermint burned her nose?"

Clifford looked up from his burger with a shrug.

"Bobbing for french fries," Pop said then slapped the counter and howled with laughter. "Get it? Bobbing for french fries?"

The two had a great laugh at Debbie and Becky Ann's expense. Debbie found her father's quirky sense of humor forgivable, especially after all the effort he'd gone to, to get Bobby Conrad here for the concert. Oh, if only they would hear something…soon!

Pop filled Clifford's glass with root beer then made his way to the next customer, then the next. Debbie watched as her mother approached and took the pitcher from him, taking his place so he could rest. Even though her parents had been married for twenty-five years, they still looked at each other in a way that made her smile.

Maybe one day Bobby and I will look at each other that way.

The idea wasn't really far-fetched, not with him coming to do the concert. Debbie found herself lost in her thoughts and almost missed the conversation between her parents and Clifford.

"Did you hear they're thinking about ending the *I Love Lucy* show?" her father asked.

"No!" Debbie's mother gasped. "Who told you that?"

"I read it in a magazine," he said. "Lucille Ball and Desi Arnaz are going to continue doing occasional episodes, but the weekly show will end soon."

"Pop, are you sure?" Debbie could hardly imagine such a thing. Why, *I Love Lucy* was the greatest show in the world.

He nodded. "Yep. Read it in the paper. Not that goofy *Hollywood Heartthrob* magazine, either. A real paper. One with real reporters who know what they're talking about."

"What's happening to this country, I ask you?" Clifford released a breath then shook his head. "No more Lucy."

"Well, at least it's not the unthinkable," Debbie's mother said. "I thought for a minute there you were going to tell me that Lucy and Desi were getting a divorce. I don't think I could handle that."

Pop laughed. "Those two? They'll stay married forever, just like us." He gave her a kiss on the cheek, and she grinned like a schoolgirl.

"You're the sweetest thing, Frankie Carmichael. Don't know what I ever did to deserve you."

Things were just starting to get a little too mushy when the bell above the door rang out. Debbie turned to find a family standing there. Before she could get a good look, her father came out from behind the counter and greeted the group with great enthusiasm.

This had to be Jim Jangles and his family. Oh, how wonderful! They were one step closer to bringing Bobby Conrad to Laguna Beach.

Debbie gave the family members a serious once-over. Mr. Jangles looked like the flashy agent-sort, she supposed. And Mrs. Jangles was quite pretty, with her store-bought dress and cute pillbox hat. The freckle-faced boy seemed distracted by the jukebox near the door. Nothing unusual there. And the handsome young man with the dark hair…

Her gaze landed squarely on the stranger, whose cheeks flushed as their eyes met. Was he Mr. Jangle's son, perhaps? Sure didn't resemble him. His beautiful brown wavy hair held her spellbound for a moment, as did those jade green eyes. They reminded her of a song, though, at the moment, she couldn't remember the lyrics. And his boyish good looks took her breath away, though she guessed him to be close to her own age. Too old to be the Jangles's son, for sure.

His lips curled up in a smile.

Debbie took a few steps toward her father, more curious than anything.

"Everyone, this is my daughter, Debbie." Pop slipped an arm around her shoulders. "She's the one who came up with the idea to host a benefit in the first place."

"It's wonderful to meet you, Mr. and Mrs. Jangles," Debbie said.

"Debbie, nice to meet you." The man extended his hand. "Please, call us Jim and Theresa. This is our boy, Toby." After a few seconds, he gestured to the handsome stranger. "And this is Johnny Hartmann, Hollywood's next teen sensation."

"Oh?" Debbie found herself stumbling over a proper response.

Johnny's face blazed red as he gave her a half nod. "Nice to meet you." He turned to her father, extending his hand. "Nice to meet you, sir. I've heard such wonderful things about Sweet Sal's and your family."

"Thanks, son." Pop shook his hand and smiled. "Well then, if Johnny's going to be the next teen sensation, we'd better notify the teenage girls. And we'll need to add a photo of that handsome face to our wall. Jim, can you send us a headshot of your young superstar?"

"Of course." Jim nodded.

Johnny looked around at the pictures on the wall, clearly

mesmerized. "All these people eat here?"

"Yep." Pop smiled. "It's been fun meeting them, and even more fun when we've got customers from out of state."

"Why is that?" Johnny asked.

"They're star-struck. The out-of-staters are easily impressed, I've discovered."

"You know what the great Fred Allen used to say, don't you, Johnny?" Jim slapped Johnny on the back.

Johnny shook his head. "Um, no sir."

"He always said, 'Hollywood is a place where people from Iowa mistake each other for stars.'" He laughed. "Get it? Out here, everyone looks like a star to everyone else. Well, everyone else who *isn't* from here. Those of us from L.A. are pretty much numb to stardom. We're not easily impressed."

"Unless you happen to be a teenage girl," Debbie's father said, glancing her way. "Then you're terribly impressed with a handful of stars, especially those who look and sing like Bobby Conrad."

Debbie felt a wave of embarrassment wash over her. Not that she was thinking of Bobby right now. No, she suddenly had a thousand questions running through her mind, none of which had anything to do with Bobby Conrad. Instead, they had everything to do with the handsome stranger who'd just caught her eye. Who was this kid? What did Jim mean, the next teen sensation? Was he an up-and-coming star? A singer, maybe?

Hmm. She'd better stay focused. Today was about Bobby, after all.

"Let's have a seat." Pop led the way to the largest booth at the back of the shop. The big round table was plenty big enough for all of them. She happened to land in the spot directly across from Johnny. His beautiful green eyes caught her attention once again, but she pushed all distractions away. *Stay focused, Debbie. Today is one of the most important days of your life.*

Indeed, it was. If Jim liked this fundraiser idea, the whole world would change for the Carmichael family. Bobby would come. The soda shop would be saved, and she…well, she and Bobby could very well end up hitting it off. Riding off into the sunset together, even. Just like the ending of his latest movie.

What a lovely possibility.

Lost in her thoughts, Debbie almost didn't hear her father's words. "Debbie? Debbie? You still with us?"

"Oh." She startled to attention. "Sure. Sorry. Just daydreaming."

"About Bobby Conrad, no doubt," Pop said with a wink. "There seems to be a strange malady going around. Bobby Conrad fever." He chuckled. "I'm praying for a cure."

"Better wait till after the concert," Jim said. "Let's keep the girls hanging on till then."

Debbie felt her cheeks turn warm. Could this possibly get any more embarrassing?

Obviously, it could. At that moment, Becky Ann appeared, dressed in her Peppermints uniform. Her hair—blond once more—was swept back in a tidy ponytail. She took one look at Johnny, and her cheeks turned as pink as strawberry ice cream in the freezer up front.

"Welcome to Sweet Sal's," she crooned. "I'm Becky Ann. Could I take your drink orders?"

Her gaze remained on Johnny as the others ordered. Well, until Jim mentioned something about Bobby. Then, suddenly, Becky Ann could barely string two words together into a sensible sentence.

"See what I mean?" Pop said. "Bobby fever. It's contagious."

Becky Ann's gaze darted to the ticket in her hand, and she quickly scooted toward the kitchen.

"So, let's cut to the chase," Jim said. "When are you looking at doing this fundraiser, and what did you have in mind? If I'm going to fit it into Bobby's schedule, I'll have to do a little shuffling. He's got some big auditions coming up. Really big."

"I was thinking mid- to late-August might work best," Debbie said. "Right before the kids go back to school. It would be a great end-of-summer event for the community, and by then everyone will have seen *First Kiss*, so they'll want to meet Bobby face-to-face."

"So, Bobby croons a handful of tunes, and then what?" Jim asked.

"Well, we can ask for donations," Debbie said. "That's how we'll raise the money for the shop. But there's money to be made for Bobby, too. You could bring along the 45 of his new song and he could sign copies for fans."

"Great idea. I like the way you think. Especially since I get 15 percent of those sales." Jim quirked a brow.

"Yeah, I like the way you think," Toby echoed.

Debbie found her gaze shifting to Johnny Hartmann. Something about his beautiful green eyes captivated her, if only for a second.

"Oh, I have a great idea." Jim's eyes lit up. "Johnny here is a singer, too. He's a new client. Maybe he could sing a tune in the middle of the concert. We could introduce him to Bobby's fans. How does that sound, Johnny?"

"Sure. Sounds fine." He shrugged.

"He'll be singing an original tune." Jim gave him a nod.

"I...I will?" Johnny didn't look convinced. In fact, he didn't look sure of himself at all. Debbie had to wonder if he really had the goods to deliver a song in front of a live audience.

"You don't think Bobby would mind?" she asked. After all, she didn't want anything to upset the real star of the show.

"Why would he?" Jim gave her a curious look. "He was the new kid on the block once."

Becky Ann arrived at the table with the drinks, which she almost spilled all over Jim. He took it in stride, smiling as she handed him his chocolate shake. Poor girl. She couldn't seem to think—or speak—clearly, with her gaze on Johnny.

Jim took a sip of his shake. "Man, this is the best shake I've had in a month of Sundays."

From there, the conversation shifted to the food. Then back to Bobby. Then to the crowd at the beach across the street. As the chatter ping-ponged back and forth, Debbie's gaze kept landing on Johnny. What did it matter if he could sing or not? He was so handsome, the girls were sure to go crazy.

In fact, if he kept looking her way with those gorgeous green eyes, she might just go a little crazy herself.

* * * * *

Johnny kept his thoughts inside his head throughout the meal. Mostly, anyway. He managed to sneak in a sentence or two, but didn't want to interrupt. Besides, Debbie seemed to be pretty good at letting everyone know what she wanted. Not that he found her pushy. Oh no. Her words were excited and laced with love for her father. Johnny knew exactly why she'd chosen to host this benefit…out of concern for him.

And Jim seemed willing to make it work. Hopefully Bobby would like the idea. Johnny couldn't imagine how disappointed Debbie would be if this whole thing fell through.

In the background, *Dream a Little Dream of Me* began to play on the jukebox. Johnny hummed along as Frankie Laine crooned the familiar words. Ironic, since he couldn't seem to shift his gaze from Debbie as she spoke. He tried not to stare at the blond beauty as she carried on with her enthusiastic thoughts about the benefit, but Johnny found it difficult. For a moment, he felt like James Dean in that wonderful scene in *Rebel Without a Cause*, the one where he laid eyes on Natalie Wood for the first time. What was the word that described how he felt? Captivated. Yes, that was it. Captivated.

Debbie continued to share her plan, and Johnny was grateful just to sit and observe. Her Sandra Dee-like appearance held him spellbound, and that red-and-white-striped uniform really took the cake. She looked like something out of a magazine. Maybe it was the ambience—the soda shop, the Pacific across the street, the surfers just off the shore. This whole thing felt just like a scene from a movie he'd seen last summer.

Only one problem. He wasn't the leading man. Not yet, anyway.

Well, maybe one day he would be. In the meantime, he would be content to sit right here in the corner booth of Sweet Sal's Soda Shoppe and enjoy the view.

Chapter Five

IN VOGUE

Appearance is everything in Hollywood. Staying on top of fashion trends is critical to a girl's survival, especially a teen girl. So, what's in vogue this week? Depends on where you're headed.

At the beach: Today's teen girls are finding a variety of options available in bathing-wear. Most popular? The strapless, corseted one-piece suit made of lined cotton or stretch Lastex. While a few of the daring girls have made the switch to a two-piece suit, the one-piece is still the norm. And why not? Most modern varieties are fashionable, flirty, and fun, and that's just what today's teens are looking for. Many of the girls interviewed noted that a trip to the beach was as much a social event as anything. For those who enjoy a dip in the water, stylish rubber bathing caps covered in flower petals and so forth are essential, since modern girls don't care to get their hair wet while swimming.

Everyday wear: Tiny-waisted, full-skirted day dresses are all the rage. These figure-flattering beauties will never go out of style, according to fashion experts like Christian Dior. However, many young women are opting for a strange new look, straight from the runways of Paris—the "sack silhouette" You've seen it around, no doubt. The dress is shaped like a giant almond with sleeves. This reporter has to wonder how a girl could feel comfortable in a dress that tapers to such a narrow hem at the knee.

Hair styles: Today's contemporary girl wears her hair soft and curly. If she must wear it long, then it's most often tied back in a ponytail with a fashionable scarf. For a night out on the town, no amount of work is too much for the picture-perfect female. She undertakes hours of pin curling and rolling, often enduring a sleepless night on uncomfortable rollers. However, most would agree that the end result is worth it.

So, there you have it, girls. If you want to stay on top of fashion trends, stick with me. I won't lead you astray. You can look like a star... if you dress like one.

— Reporting for Hollywood Heartthrob *magazine, "Glamour Girls" columnist, Fashionable Frances*

* * * * *

Debbie looked through her closet for the hundredth time, trying to figure out what to wear. Unlike most girls her age, she didn't have a large wardrobe. After all, she donned the Peppermints uniform five mornings a week. Sometimes six. But with the possibility of Bobby Conrad coming to town, she had to think ahead. What would she wear when they met for the first time? She needed to look just right. After all, a girl only had one chance to make a first impression, and she needed to capture his attention.

Hmm. Maybe a shopping trip was in order. Mom might be willing to take her to Coulter's or May Company. Maybe even JC Penney's. She could use some new skirts and blouses for church, along with some undergarments. Yes, her mother would certainly see the good in this, especially since the new clothes could be worn when news reporters and television cameramen showed up to advertise Bobby's big event.

Soon enough, all of Hollywood would converge on Sweet Sal's, so looking good was a priority.

And speaking of the shop, it could use a little renovating. A bit of paint on the doors. A newer, larger stage, perhaps. Bobby and his band would need more room, for sure. And then there was the issue of putting their best foot forward with the community. Folks in Laguna Beach and beyond needed to see this as a grand event, one not to be missed. That meant a huge amount of promotion—and soon.

On the other hand, they couldn't go overboard, could they? How would they ever afford it? No, they'd better stick to a simple plan. A doable plan. Several thoughts began to percolate.

She turned away from her closet, examining her appearance in the full-length mirror before heading downstairs to the shop. The Peppermints uniform might be cute to others, but she'd grown tired of it. She secretly longed to dress like the other girls her age. Not that she wanted to abandon Mom and Pop. And if supporting them meant wearing the same tiresome dress day after day, so be it.

Debbie ran a brush through her hair then pinned on the tiny white cap. She flashed a smile, realizing how much nicer she looked with a happy expression on her face. Then, with determination setting in, she skipped down the stairs to Sweet Sal's.

As she entered the restaurant, the unmistakable sound of a Four Aces song greeted her. She could hear Becky Ann singing along to "Love Is a Many Splendored Thing" at the top of her lungs. Debbie hoped her sister's enthusiasm wouldn't scare the patrons away.

No, most seemed to be taking the happy-go-lucky teen in stride. In fact, quite a few sang along with her. Debbie smiled, feeling the warmth of family all around her. Oh, how she loved the people of Laguna Beach. And how she depended on them—now, more than ever.

As she reached the cash register, Debbie turned to her father. "Pop, I've been thinking about the fundraiser. Do you think Mr. Kenner at the print shop would be willing to donate some posters about the event?" Before he could respond, she added, "And I've been thinking we might want to touch up the paint on the soda shop. Give the place a fresh face. We've got lots of leftover paint from the last time around, right?"

"Yes, but don't you think you're getting the cart ahead of the horse?" he asked. "I haven't heard back from Jim yet to confirm that Bobby's coming for sure."

"I know, and these have been the longest two days of my life." Debbie plopped onto a barstool and ushered up a dramatic sigh. "Is he ever going to call?"

"Of course," Pop said. "Patience, my dear. It's a virtue, you know."

"One I don't have much of, I'm afraid," she countered. "But I'm trying. I really am."

"As soon as we get the news, I'll ask Brad about the posters. I'm sure he'll agree to do a few. He's a good friend. We'll need to take them around to the various businesses. And I'm sure Nathan at the paper will be happy to run an article without charging us anything. This is a newsworthy story, after all." He paused and for a moment a flicker of something else was evident in his eyes.

"What, Pop?" Debbie asked. "Change of heart?"

"Not really. I guess I'm still struggling with the idea of folks helping our family like this."

"Do you find it embarrassing?" She kept her voice low enough that nearby customers couldn't hear.

"It's not that. It's more…humbling."

"I see." She thought about that for a moment. "Well, you know what the Bible says, Pop. 'Humble yourselves therefore under the mighty hand of God, that He may exalt you in due time.'"

"True." Her father smiled. "Though, I'm not altogether sure I care to be exalted, if that makes sense. I'd rather just…just be Frankie Carmichael, who runs Sweet Sal's. Nothing more and nothing less."

"Well, it's too late for that," Debbie said. "You're Frankie Carmichael: father, husband, friend, and all-around great guy."

"Oh, I am, am I?" He laughed.

"Sure. Everyone loves you." She gave him a kiss on the cheek. "If we took a poll, you'd be elected."

"Elected what?" he asked. "Mayor?"

"No." She giggled. "Nicest person in town."

"Oh." Her father smiled. "Well now, that would be quite an honor. But Laguna Beach is filled with good-hearted people, so I'd have a lot of competition." He pointed to the door. "Here comes one of my chief competitors now."

Debbie glanced over to see their mailman entering the shop.

"Hello, Clifford," Debbie's mom called out. "Have a seat. Rest your dogs."

As the weary fellow eased his ample frame down onto a barstool, Debbie could read the exhaustion in his expression.

"What can I get for you?" she asked.

He didn't bother looking at the menu. "I'll have a couple of poached eggs on toast, no butter."

Debbie hollered back to the kitchen. "Adam & Eve on a raft, scratch the axle grease!"

Her father took a few steps in Clifford's direction and shook his hand. "Good to see you, my friend."

"Good to see you, too. How are things going, Frankie?"

"Oh, pretty good, but I've got a bone to pick with you." Debbie's father took a seat on the barstool next to him, looking more troubled than before.

"What's up?" Clifford asked.

Debbie tried not to eavesdrop but couldn't help herself.

"I hear the post office is thinking about charging a nickel just to mail a letter," her father said, a concerned look on his face. "Is that true?"

"A nickel?" Debbie shook her head. "At those rates, who could afford to write to friends or family?"

Clifford glanced down at his coffee cup, shame all over his face. "Nah. It's not going up to a nickel. Just four cents."

"Still...I just don't know what this country's coming to," Debbie's father muttered. "Our teens are listening to that crazy rock and roll music, parents are allowing their daughters to show up on the beach in those ridiculous two-piece bathing suits, gas prices are rising, and now this. We can't even mail a letter. What next?"

"I guess that pretty much nixes the idea of mailing out postcards to local families about our big event," Debbie said. "We'll just have to hope everyone sees the posters."

"Event?" Clifford looked intrigued. "What's happening?"

"Oh, well..." She paused, not wanting to get the cart before the horse, as her father had already said. "We're thinking about doing a concert at Sweet Sal's. A fundraiser. I'll tell you more about it later."

She headed off to find her mother, who labored over a pot of chili in the kitchen.

"Mom, can we go shopping on Saturday? I need some new things."

Her mother glanced back with a smile. "Oh? What kind of new things?"

"Well, I could use some new skirts and blouses. And shoes, too."

"Any special reason?" her mother asked. "Now that you've graduated, you don't need school clothes. Something else going on?"

She felt her cheeks turn warm. "I just want to make a good impression if Bobby comes."

"Ah, I see." Her mother gestured for Debbie to join her near the stove. "Looking nice is always a good idea, but just remember, honey, it's what's on the inside that counts. You can change the outward appearance—nothing wrong with that—but that's not what God looks at. He sees straight to the heart."

"You think I have heart issues?" Debbie couldn't help but be perplexed.

"Of course not." Mom smiled. "You have the most generous heart of anyone I know." Her mother's eyes filled with tears. "You're so much like your father in that way that it makes me proud."

"Thank you." Debbie gave her mother a kiss on the cheek.

Mom smiled. "I suppose a little shopping trip might be in order. We'll call it an early birthday present. We'll have to be frugal, of course."

"Oh, shopping!" Becky Ann entered the kitchen, squealing with delight over the idea. "When? And where?"

They dove into a lengthy conversation about fashion, and Debbie found herself almost giddy with the possibilities. By the time Bobby arrived, she would look like a million bucks. Maybe two million.

As they wrapped up their conversation, the telephone rang.

Debbie answered it. "Thank you for calling Sweet Sal's, where every day is a sweet day."

"Jim Jangles here," the voice on the other end of the phone rang out. "Could I speak with Frankie, please?"

Debbie's hand trembled so hard, she almost dropped the receiver. "Pop!" she hollered. "Pop, come quick! It's for you!"

* * * * *

Johnny made his way into the audition room with Jim's words still ringing in his ears. "Knock 'em dead, kid."

He wasn't sure he wanted to do that, exactly, but leaving a strong impression was key. That's why he'd chosen to wear one of the new outfits Jim and Theresa had purchased for him. The dark red button-up looked good with his skin tone, or so he'd been told. Felt a little out of character, though. And the newer, hipper hairstyle was interesting, though he still hardly recognized his own reflection in the mirror. Truth be told, Johnny wanted to scrap all of it and wear his jeans and green and blue plaid shirt from home.

A fellow who introduced himself as Mr. Timmons ushered him inside the audition room. "Sorry, Johnny, but we're running short on time. You just start the song, and we'll tell you when to stop, okay?" He glanced at his watch and took a seat.

"Sure."

Mr. Timmons reached for a clipboard, barely looking up. "What are you singing?"

"Oh, it's an original song. I just wrote it a few days ago." Saturday night, to be precise. Less than two hours after leaving Debbie

Carmichael. Something about that blond ponytail…those brown eyes had jarred him. In a good way. He'd gone straight back to Jim's house and composed a ballad inspired by a true beauty, one he wouldn't mind seeing again.

Johnny pulled his guitar out of its case and stood a comfortable distance from the man in the chair. His fingers felt at home against the strings, and as the first few chords were played, he began to relax.

As the first few words of "Dear Debbie" rang out, he closed his eyes. Doing so accomplished two things: First, it served as a nice distraction from Mr. Timmons. Second, playing on the screens of Johnny's inner eyelids were the photos of Debbie he'd captured while writing this song. Her cute smile. Those dimples. Her tall, slender physique. That ponytail, bouncing in a carefree manner as she shared her enthusiastic stories. That red-and-white-striped uniform.

Yes, he could see it all so clearly, and what he saw still inspired him.

Johnny half-expected to be stopped after the first verse, but no one stopped him, so he kept going. The words to the letter he'd composed rang out against a simple, yet deep, melody. Johnny wished Debbie Carmichael could hear the words all the way down in Laguna Beach. Maybe one day he could sing this song to her personally. At the fundraiser, perhaps. If he worked up the courage.

After the chorus, he braved a glance at Mr. Timmons. The fellow had a broad smile on his face. That must be a good sign. Johnny dove into the second verse, the words becoming more real than ever. By the time he reached the end of the song, all jitters were gone, replaced by an uncanny sense of calm.

"You say you wrote that song?" Mr. Timmons looked for a moment like he didn't quite believe it.

"Well, yes," Johnny said. "But I could've done a better job if I'd had more time. I wrote it in less than a day."

"You don't say." Mr. Timmons looked impressed. "Sounds like something the girls would love, but I think the guys will like it, too. I can almost see that soda shop girl now in her red-and-white uniform." He grinned. "She sounds like a pretty young thing."

"Oh, she is, sir." Johnny did his best to hide the smile that threatened to erupt. "I mean, the girl in the song."

"Mm-hmm." The fellow laughed. "You know what, Hartmann? I like you. And I think the folks who watch our show will like you, too."

"Really?"

"Sure. You've got that wholesome boy-next-door look about you. And that song is just the icing on the cake."

"So, does that mean I'm going to be on the show?" Johnny's knees almost buckled beneath him at the very idea of appearing on national television.

Mr. Timmons laughed. "I feel strongly enough about you to make the recommendation to network executives. I'll be in touch with Jim, one way or the other. In the meantime, don't share that song publicly, okay?"

"O–okay." He shrugged. "How come?"

"Because, kid, when teenage girls hear you sing it on *Talent Scouts*, I want it to be the first time anyone hears it. Understand?"

"Sure." Johnny nodded. "I understand. I won't breathe a word."

"We're counting on it." Mr. Timmons paused. "Listen, in case no one else has said it, you have a real gift, Hartmann."

"Really?" Johnny's face grew hot.

"There's something about you that's different, and I don't just mean the boy-next-door thing. You've got a unique voice and a great demeanor. You might wear the Hollywood clothes, but I see a Midwest boy underneath. Am I right?"

"Yes."

"Then do me a favor. When you show up to sing on the air, wear what you'd wear back home. No Hollywood hype. Promise?"

Johnny couldn't help the grin that followed. "Sure thing. Not sure Jim will like the idea, though."

"He will if I recommend it," Mr. Timmons said. "We have enough L.A. guys come through. They're a dime a dozen. With you, we've got something special. Something unique. People like unique. Take Elvis, for instance. Folks love him because he's one of a kind."

Johnny swallowed hard. Had this fellow really just compared him to Elvis?

"A lot of the big names got their start on this show," Mr. Timmons reminded him. "Pat Boone, The Chordettes, Tony Bennett, Rosemary Clooney, Vic Damone, Connie Francis, Patsy Cline, and lots more." He went on naming others. Quite an impressive list.

Johnny swallowed hard. Talk about a lineup.

"Funny, though," Mr. Timmons said. "Did you know that Buddy Holly and Elvis auditioned, but weren't chosen to appear on the broadcast?"

Johnny shook his head, not quite believing it. "Are you serious?"

"Very. Talk about regrets. We've never quite lived that down. So, whenever we see a young star with a lot of potential, we grab him up and put him on the air. We like to consider ourselves door openers for young singers like yourself."

"Door openers." Johnny nodded. "I like that."

For whatever reason, when he spoke the word "door," Johnny saw himself walking through the door at Sweet Sal's Soda Shoppe in Laguna

Beach. Maybe, if he made a name for himself on the *Arthur Godfrey's Talent Scouts* program, a certain young woman with gorgeous brown eyes would meet him on the other side.

Chapter Six

AVENUE OF THE STARS

My, but they do get around. Seems like every time you drive down Sunset Boulevard or cruise past Hollywood's hot spots, movie stars are out in force. Many are itching to be seen by their adoring fans. Others hide under hats and sunglasses, hoping to avoid the pressure. A few of the silver screen's finest have been spotted at the beach. And why not? It's midsummer, after all. Even the stars enjoy riding the waves. Many frequent Malibu, of course, but there are those who prefer the pristine beaches of Orange County to the more northern shores.

Of course, stars have been spotted in other places, as well. The grocery store, the dry cleaners, shoe stores, and the YMCA. You name it. They've been seen there. Rumor has it that a local pastor actually paused mid-sermon to welcome Bobby Conrad to his service last Sunday. This reporter has to wonder if the music director plans to ask him to join the choir. Not a bad idea, really. Maybe Bobby will follow Elvis's lead and record an album of hymns. People young and old would love that.

Speaking of Bobby, sources tell us that he's accepted a fundraising gig in Laguna Beach. No details on the event just yet, but we do know he will be singing. No doubt teen girls in that hip, coastal town are gearing up as we speak. Can you imagine the frenzy at Sweet Sal's Soda Shoppe when he appears in front of locals to croon a few tunes? Talk about stirring up excitement! It's going to be better than the hot fudge sundae special. And I have it on good authority the local media will be there in force. Look for updates soon.

— *Reporting for* Hollywood Heartthrob *magazine, "Man About Town" columnist, Sunset Sam*

* * * * *

On Wednesday morning, Johnny was awakened by the sound of a knock on the bedroom door, followed by Jim's boisterous voice. "Wake up, Johnny. You're going to be on television."

"W–what?" He sat up in the bed and rubbed his eyes.

From the open doorway, Jim laughed. "Well, not this morning, but next month. The folks at *Talent Scouts* loved your audition. And they loved that ballad, too. They definitely want you to sing it on the show next month. You're slotted for Saturday, August tenth."

"So, it's true? It's really happening?" Johnny could barely catch his breath as the truth sank in. "I'm going to be on television?"

"Well, sure, kid. That's what we agents do. We get you singing gigs. And acting gigs. And you give us a nod by paying us 15 percent and moving out of the house into your own place when the money starts rolling in."

"Are you saying I'll earn money from this appearance?" Johnny asked. *And are you hoping I'll move out soon?* For some reason, both of those things seemed a bit unrealistic at the moment. In time, perhaps.

"C'mon downstairs and we'll talk it through," Jim said. "There's a contract you need to sign and a confidentiality clause."

"Confidentiality clause?"

"Yes, they don't want anyone to hear that song you wrote until you're actually on the air. That's standard stuff with these talent shows, by the way."

"I see."

"Meet me downstairs when you're ready and we'll look over the papers together."

As Johnny dressed, he thought about the song he'd written. "Dear Debbie" was certainly a reflection of what he'd been feeling when he met Debbie Carmichael, but would she make the connection if she happened to be watching television on the night the show aired?

Probably not. *Surely she'll think Debbie is a girl from home.*

Girl from home. Hmm. His thoughts shifted to Katie, but he quickly pressed them away. No point in ruining a perfectly good day. Not with so many opportunities on the horizon.

Johnny finished dressing and headed downstairs. He found Jim and Theresa in the living room. She sat at the dining room table, her fingers clicking against typewriter keys. Seemed she'd been spending a lot of time working lately. From what he could figure, she helped Jim with his paperwork. They made quite the team—in marriage and in business.

"So, what are you typing over there, Theresa?" Johnny asked, unable to keep his curiosity in check.

She glanced up, looking a bit startled. "Oh, you know. Work, work, and more work. Jim keeps me busy."

"She's my right-hand gal," Jim said. "Don't think I could keep the agency going without her." He leaned down and kissed her on top of her head.

"Aw, thank you, honey." Theresa's cheeks flushed. "I do my best." She looked at Johnny. "But he does keep me hopping, that's for sure."

Jim took a seat on the couch. "Yes, well, you know what the great Fred Allen once said."

Johnny shrugged and prepared himself. "Um, no sir."

"'An advertising agency is 85 percent confusion and 15 percent commission.'" Jim chuckled. "We've gotta keep at it, working around the clock."

That didn't exactly answer the question about what Theresa was working on, but Johnny didn't mind. How the two of them managed the business was really between, well, the two of them. Still, it seemed a little odd that Jim didn't seem to go to an office or tend to his other clients. Johnny thought about that. Surely he and Bobby weren't the only two. Jim seemed like a bigwig and was certainly well–known among his peers. Probably, he had a host of prodigies in and around the Los Angeles area. Maybe Johnny would meet them someday.

He was just starting to ask about that when Toby came marching in from the kitchen, wearing a Mickey Mouse cap and a milk moustache and singing the Mouseketeers theme song. Theresa stopped her work and watched in silence, shaking her head as her son came tromping across the living room with his hand on his chest.

Toby saluted and his over-the-top voice rang out, albeit slightly off-key. "Hey there! Hi there! Ho there! You're as welcome as can be!"

Johnny joined in and sang, "M-I-C-K-E-Y-M-O-U-S-E!"

"Mouseketeer roll call!" Toby called out. He pointed Johnny's direction.

"Johnny!"

Toby pointed at his mother.

"Theresa!"

He pointed at his dad, who groaned. "Son, you've been reading *Variety* again, haven't you?"

Toby lit back into the song, marching around the room. He came to a halt and turned to his father as he spoke. "Auditions for a new *boy* Mouseketeer are going to be held this coming Friday morning at eleven, Dad."

"Toby, if I've told you once, I've told you a thousand times, no son of mine is going to be on television."

"But Johnny…" Toby pointed in Johnny's direction, stopping mid-sentence. "Aw, never mind." He plopped down in front of the television and tossed the Mickey Mouse ears on the floor.

"Son, Johnny is a grown man," Theresa said. "He's old enough to choose his own career path. You're just a boy."

"So, when I'm grown up, I can be on television?" A spark of hope lit the youngster's face.

"When you're grown up, you can have your own television show," Jim said. "But until then, I've had about enough of this. Just be content to let others have their moment in the spotlight. Johnny's going to be on *Talent Scouts* soon and you can be in the audience clapping for him."

Toby rolled his eyes.

"I still can't believe I'm going to be on national television." Just speaking the words aloud sent a shiver down Johnny's spine. A strange and terrifying shiver, but one laced with possibilities. "I still can't believe it myself, but it's true."

Theresa gave him a motherly smile. "One of these days you'll be a big star and you can invite us to your place in Malibu. Or Beverly Hills, even."

Johnny shook his head, unable to make sense of her words. She began typing once again.

"One thing at a time," Jim said, taking a seat on the couch. "Right now, it's all about exposure. That's what matters. Getting you out there in front of your adoring fans is key."

"You have adoring fans?" Toby gave him an, *I don't believe it* look.

"You've got me, kid," Johnny said. "If they're out there, they must be invisible."

That got a good laugh from everyone.

"Trust me, you will have adoring fans," Jim said. "If I have anything to do with it."

Johnny tried to think of something to say in response, but found himself overwhelmed with the idea of adoring fans and appearing on a live television program.

"I'm going to do everything I can to open a few doors for you, Johnny," Jim said. "That means you'll be singing at talent shows, local radio stations, and so on. Anything and everything to get you in front of people. And, depending on how things go on *Talent Scouts*, I should be able to get you on the *Texaco Variety Hour*. Maybe even *The Ed Sullivan Show*.

"Ed S–Sullivan?" Johnny could hardly get the words out.

"That will take longer, of course," Jim said. "You have to be an established star to make it onto Ed's show. Took Bobby over a year."

"Yeah, and Bobby was really good," Toby said with a knowing look.

"You saying I'm not?" Johnny pretended to look stern but ended up with a grin.

"Nah. I heard you practicing that new song in our room the other day. It's pretty good, I guess. I've heard worse."

"Thanks for the encouragement." Johnny chuckled. He wasn't

sure which made him happier—the fact that Toby had said something nice about his song, or the part where he'd called his bedroom "our" room.

Toby reached to turn on the television, which took a few seconds to warm up. Before long, the theme song to *Flash Gordon* was playing and the youngster had settled down in front of the TV.

Johnny stared at the television, trying to imagine what it must feel like to be on the inside, looking out. Would he be terrified? Surely, but with the Lord on his side, he could get beyond the jitters and just sing.

"I can't believe this is actually happening," he said at last. "Seems like maybe I'm dreaming."

"Oh, it's happening, all right." Jim nodded. "And it's going to keep on happening until you're well-known."

Johnny began to pace the room, his thoughts tumbling madly through his brain. "It's the oddest thing. I've lived my whole life with only a tiny pool of people knowing who I am. And now I have the chance to become known…and it terrifies me."

"That feeling will pass in time," Theresa called out from the typewriter. "Bobby used to get the jitters, too, especially in the first few months."

"Really?" Johnny took a seat on the couch next to Jim.

"Sure," Jim said. "And if it will help you, I'll ask Bobby to stop by for a chat before your appearance on *Talent Scouts*. He can give you some pointers and help calm your nerves."

"He would do that for me?" Johnny still couldn't believe someone as well–known as Bobby Conrad would stop by for a visit.

"Sure. Don't you know that others stepped in and walked him through the process? That's what this is about, kid. Supporting one another." Jim paused a moment. "Well, it's about that…and open doors. Without open doors, none of you kids would make it very far in the industry."

"Yes, well, I just pray the doors that open are the right ones," Johnny said. "Hope I don't make any mistakes along the way. Don't want to make a wrong turn."

"That's why you've got me," Jim said and then smiled. "An agent is really like a…well, a guardian angel. I lead the way and make sure you don't get hurt. And I only push you through the doors that will be most profitable. So stick with me, kid, and I'll take you places." He slapped Johnny on the back.

Johnny thought about his words without saying anything in response. All of that guardian angel stuff might sound good in a movie—or even a song—but in the real world, no one but the Holy Spirit could lead and guide. And certainly no one was looking out for Johnny's interests like the Lord.

Sure, Jim was a great agent. He managed to do all of the things he'd promised and more. But when it came to which doors opened and which doors shut, that was really up to the Lord.

"Hey, speaking of taking you places, I've got to make a run down to Laguna Beach to Sweet Sal's," Jim said. "I'm taking down several head-shots of Bobby, along with some other promo materials, including the 45 of his new song. They're going to put it in that jukebox of theirs to get the teen girls riled up. Want to ride down there with me? I think it would be great exposure for you. I can tell them about your gig on *Talent Scouts*. That ought to bring out the crowds. I'm taking your new head shot, too."

"While you're there, why don't you sing that song you wrote for that Debbie girl," Toby said with a grin.

Johnny's heart gravitated to his throat at the very thought of it. She would likely think he was completely crazy for writing her a love song when he barely knew her.

"He can't do that, son," Jim said. "Confidentiality clause. That song is top secret."

"Top secret?" Toby looked confused.

Johnny nodded. "I, um, well, I promised the guy at the TV show that I wouldn't sing the song anywhere until after I'd sung it on the show. He wants it to be a surprise." *And so do I.*

"Ah." Toby's gaze narrowed. "Guess that makes sense."

Jim flashed a smile. "If it goes over well on *Talent Scouts*, you need to be prepared for a trip to the studio to record it. Then we'll make the rounds to local radio stations. Before you know it, you'll have a Billboard hit on your hands."

Johnny shook his head, unable to absorb any more news. Suddenly, he felt completely overwhelmed.

Oh, well. Nothing a chocolate malt from Sweet Sal's couldn't cure.

Well, a chocolate malt and a smile from a certain pretty Peppermint named Debbie.

* * * * *

Debbie gave herself another glance in the mirror and smiled at the reflection staring back at her. She finished buttoning her new white blouse then tied a soft blue scarf around her neck. As she turned, the petticoat under her full blue skirt made a swishing sound. Oh, how happy she was to be wearing something other than her Peppermint's uniform. And this was the perfect day for it. In just a few minutes, she and the other girls would make the rounds to every business in town to spread the word about the fundraiser.

Exactly ten minutes later, she gathered the group of teen girls around her like chicks hovering around their mother hen. Getting the word out about this fundraiser was critical now that Bobby's appearance had been confirmed. She could hardly believe it. In fact, she'd barely slept since receiving the news.

Bobby Conrad is coming to Sweet Sal's! Saturday, August 17—a day that will go down in the history books!

"Okay, girls, link up. Two of you on a team." She reached to pick up a stack of flyers that the local print shop manager had donated. "I want each pair to take ten of these flyers about the event. Put them up in the most logical places—at the grocery store, the filling station, the playground, the civic center—anyplace you can think of."

"What about the new McDonald's?" Becky Ann asked.

Debbie shook her head. "I don't think so. That's not the best idea. Let's don't cross over into their territory to promote the event. Might give them ideas. They might want to get their hooks into Bobby."

"You don't think he would betray us, do you?" Becky Ann looked horrified at that idea.

"Of course not. Does the manager of McDonald's know Bobby's agent? I think not." She grinned. "Jim is excited about Bobby's gig at Sweet Sal's, and he's doing this because he cares about Pop."

As they opened the door to head out, the music on the jukebox caught her ear. She hummed along with Perry Como as he sang "Hot Diggity." Debbie giggled, feeling younger than her years. All of this chatter about Bobby Conrad had her feeling a little giddy. And talk about being good for the soda shop! Why, this news would propel

Sweet Sal's far above McDonald's or any other competitors who dared rear their heads. Already, folks as far away as L.A. were talking about the event. She wondered if the shop would be able to hold them all.

Well, no problem. Bobby had agreed to do three sets. And she would be there for all three, hanging on his every word and making sure he had everything he needed. She would perform the role of Gal Friday.

The very idea made her want to smile from the inside out. Bobby Conrad. Her dream would soon be a reality. And oh, what a reality!

"You okay, Debbie?" Martha Lou asked as they headed up the road to the hardware store.

"Sure. I'm just happy, that's all."

"That would explain the grin on your face. You haven't stopped smiling all day."

"Neither have you or any of the other girls." Debbie laughed. "I think we're all in agreement that having Bobby here will be the best thing that ever happened to Sweet Sal's."

"Or to me." Martha Lou let out an exaggerated sigh. "I'm going to make sure he notices me."

"Oh?"

"Well, sure. I'm going to offer to sing with him. My mother says I have the best voice in town. He's going to need a backup singer, you know."

"He...he is?" Debbie wasn't so sure about that.

"Well, sure. All of the singers have backups."

"If that's the case, then Jim Jangles will make sure the backup singers are already with him when he comes," Debbie said. "So I wouldn't get my hopes up."

"Hmm." Martha Lou quirked a brow. "Well, if you find out which one is the alto, let me know, and I'll trip her in the ladies' room."

"Martha Lou! Surely you're not serious." Debbie stopped walking and crossed her arms. "Tell me you would not sabotage this event just so you can meet Bobby up close."

Martha Lou sighed. "I guess not. But how else will he notice me?"

"Just be yourself," Becky Ann offered. "Lots of people notice you."

"Take Junior, for instance," Debbie said. "He's had his eye on you for the past year, but you don't seem to realize it."

"I know." Martha Lou smiled. "He's a great guy, but…" She shook her head. "I think I was born for bigger things than a small-town boy. I'm going to marry someone who's rich and famous."

Ginny Anderson rolled her eyes. "You're such a dreamer. And I can't believe you'd overlook a guy as great as Junior."

Debbie paused to think about that for a moment. She could certainly see the draw where her brother was concerned. He would make some girl a great husband someday.

The girls arrived at the hardware store moments later. Debbie approached Bradley Robbins, the owner.

"Mr. Robbins, is it okay to put a copy of this poster in your window?" she asked. "We're doing a benefit at Sweet Sal's as a tribute to my father."

"Your pop, eh?" Mr. Robbins smiled. "Glad he's feeling better, Debbie. He's been on our prayer list at the Baptist church for weeks."

"At the Methodist church, too," a customer said, drawing near. "Frankie Carmichael's a good man, and we're happy that he's on the mend. Gave us quite a scare last spring."

"We were all scared," Debbie admitted. "And I'm so glad he's doing well now. But we want to keep him feeling great, so we're working on a plan that will let him cut back on his hours."

"Good girl." Mr. Robbins nodded. "What can we do to help?"

"Just spread the word that Bobby Conrad is coming to sing at the soda shop on August seventeenth," Debbie said. "Bobby's going to sing, and people can give donations to help the shop. They can buy his records, too."

"That Conrad kid is really making a name for himself," Mr. Robbins said. "I hear he's a Christian, too."

"Yes." Debbie's heart swelled as she thought about it. *I would never be interested in someone who didn't love the Lord.* Not that she could claim a real interest in Bobby Conrad. Right now her feelings were more like those of the other girls—a silly crush. Still, her feelings would probably intensify once she met him face to face. Then and only then could she really consider the possibilities.

Oh, how she prayed there were possibilities. Much as she hated to admit it to others, Debbie longed for someone to love, someone to hold her hand and whisper sweet nothings in her ear. How many times had she prayed the "I'm nearly twenty, Lord!" prayer? Dozens. Still, He hadn't seen fit to bring that certain someone into her life. And now she had to wonder if He'd held back on purpose, knowing Bobby Conrad was on the way.

"Did you ever think about putting a stage outside?" Mr. Robbins asked. "That way you could accommodate more people."

Debbie paused to think about that. "Great idea," she said at last. "I'll tell Pop."

"Let's do more than that," Mr. Robbins said with a twinkle in his eye. "Why don't you let me take care of that for you? I'll approach the different churches in town and we'll pull together. It'll be like an old-fashioned barn raising, only this time we'll build a stage instead."

Tears sprang to Debbie's eyes. "That would be perfect. Thank you so much."

He dove into a lengthy explanation about the various dimensions of the stage and where, exactly, it would go. As he talked, Debbie pondered the possibilities, tickled that they could now accommodate more people. Oh, how she prayed they had a lot of people!

She and the other girls left the hardware store, heading to the bank, then on to the gas station. When they arrived back at Sweet Sal's, Debbie noticed a familiar turquoise Chevy out front.

"Hey, look. It's that Jim Jangles guy," Becky Ann said. A smile lit her face. "Do you think Johnny's with him?"

"Johnny?" Martha Lou gave her a curious look. "Who's that?"

"He's a handsome singer from Kansas," Becky Ann said, her eyes now wide with excitement. "And he's sweet on my sister. You should have seen the way he looked at her. The boy could hardly string two words together any time he looked her way."

Debbie felt her cheeks grow warm as the girls looked her way.

"Is that true, Debbie?" Ginny asked. "Why didn't you tell us?"

"Becky Ann is exaggerating, as always," Debbie said, trying to make light of it. "I don't even think he noticed me, to be honest. He's just a guy who's going to be singing on the day of the fundraiser."

"He is?" Martha Lou looked confused. "I thought Bobby Conrad was singing."

"Bobby is the main act, but Johnny is doing one song," Debbie explained. "According to Jim, he's got a really nice voice." She pondered those words for a moment. No matter how great his voice, the girls would still be clamoring for more of Bobby Conrad. What could she do about that?

Martha didn't look impressed. "Seems like a waste to let some unknown person cut into Bobby's time."

"It's just one song," Becky Ann explained. "And besides, he's so cute that the girls will swoon when he takes the stage, even if he can't sing a note."

"Well, why didn't you say so?" Martha Lou opened the door to the soda shop, all giggles. The minute she clapped eyes on Johnny Hartmann in his jeans and white T-shirt, her mouth flew open.

"Close that garage door, Martha Lou," Becky Ann whispered. "It's open so wide a car could drive inside."

Martha closed her mouth, continuing to stare at Johnny.

Debbie stared, too, realizing once again just how handsome the young man really was. The minute their eyes met, his face flushed, and his gaze shifted to the ground.

"See," Becky Ann whispered. "I told you he was sweet on Debbie. I've never seen a boy blush like that before."

Debbie elbowed her little sister then headed over to Jim. Still, she couldn't help but notice that Becky Ann was right. Johnny did appear to get flustered when she walked in the room...but why?

As he gave her a shy smile, Debbie noticed his beautifully placed dimples. His smile brought them to the forefront, and she found herself enamored by them. How could she have overlooked them before? They were almost as captivating as those beautiful green eyes of his.

Debbie joined Jim and the others at the table, unable to hide the smile on her face. "Hi, everyone. What's up?" She shifted her gaze from Johnny to Jim Jangles.

"We've brought all sorts of things to help you promote the event," Jim said. "Photos, music, you name it."

"Thank you, Jim," Debbie said. "These are really going to help. I can't wait." She paused a moment then snapped her fingers. "Oh, I just had the most wonderful idea."

"What's that?" Her father and Jim spoke in unison.

"Do you ever read *Hollywood Heartthrob* magazine?" She directed the question to the table. Mr. Jangle's gaze darted to her pop, who gave her a "You've got to be kidding" look.

"No, and I hope I never have to."

"Well…" She took a seat at the table, her elbows resting on the edge. "All of the girls read it. It's the most popular gossip magazine around. And they've got all of these different columns. There's a fashion column. And there's a great column on music trends that a guy named Hepcat Harry writes."

Johnny snickered at that one. "Hepcat Harry? Obviously a contrived name."

"Oh, all of the names are made up," she said. "Cinema Cindy does the movie reviews and shares all of the gossip on who's starring in what movie. Then there's Sunset Sam. He's the one who talks about celebrities out on the town. That sort of thing."

Johnny looked confused. "We don't get this magazine in Topeka, so I'm clueless. What does it have to do with the event?"

Her excitement grew as she laid out the plan. "Well, I was thinking that Cinema Cindy would be a great person to invite to our event. She's always writing about Bobby Conrad. The teen girls love her column. And I know she would do a great write-up for us."

"Ah." Johnny nodded. "That might work. So, when are you going to contact her?"

"Hmm…" Debbie pondered the question. "She doesn't know me

from Adam. But she probably knows all about…" Her gaze shifted to Jim Jangles, who looked a bit flustered.

"M–me?" Jim asked. "You think I know Cinema Cindy?"

"I'm just saying that she would probably know you because you're Bobby's agent. So, would you do it, Jim? Would you contact her and ask her to come? I just know she'll write a great article."

"You were hoping I would contact her?" Jim looked unsure of himself for a change. "Let her know about the event so she could be here?"

"Exactly!" Debbie clasped her hands together. "Oh, Jim, would you really do that for us?"

He shrugged. "Well, I suppose I could issue an invitation. Who knows if she'll show or not. I'm sure she's up to her eyeballs in stars and starlets. I wouldn't get my hopes up."

Debbie sighed.

"Still, if she does come, it will be great press for Bobby." Jim slung his arm over Johnny's shoulder. "And for Johnny, too. Oh, I can't wait till you hear his new song, 'Dear Debbie.' Sorry, but we can't say any more than that."

Johnny's cheeks flamed redder than Bobby's convertible, and his gaze shifted to the plate glass window.

"'Dear Debbie'?" Debbie turned to face him. "Wow. That's an interesting coincidence."

"Yeah, some coincidence," Becky Ann said with a smile. "I told you he was sweet on you, Debbie."

An awkward silence filled the room. For a moment, anyway, Junior added the new 45 to the jukebox and Bobby Conrad's theme song from *First Kiss* began to play. Becky Ann began to sing along in her usual boisterous way. Before long, she had everyone chuckling.

"What?" she asked. "You think I'm too loud? I was hoping to sing backup for Bobby."

"Backup, as in 'back of the room'?" Junior asked then laughed.

Becky Ann slugged him on the arm. "I'm going to get you for that, Junior."

"Keep on practicing, Becky Ann," Pop chuckled. "In the meantime, why don't you girls take these photos Jim brought and start putting them up around town next to the posters Mr. Kenner donated."

"Johnny, why don't you help the girls with that while I hang out with Frankie and talk business." Jim turned his attention back to his soda.

Johnny shrugged. "Sure. Sounds good."

Jim waved his hand. "Great. You kids scoot on out of here and start drumming up some interest in this fundraiser while we talk."

Debbie tried not to sigh aloud, but found it difficult. She might be turning twenty next month, but adults still saw her as a kid. What would it take to prove she was a young woman, not a starry-eyed teen?

Johnny rose and gave her a winning smile. "Where are you headed next?"

"I guess we could go to the grocery store and the library. But it makes sense to put posters up at the beach before we head that way."

"Are you going to tack them onto a sand castle?" he asked. "So they can get washed out to sea?"

She laughed. "I was thinking we'd put them up on the bulletin board by the restrooms, but that sand castle idea might work."

"Sand castles." Jim grunted. "Kid, you have a lot to learn."

This time Johnny's rosy cheeks caught Debbie's attention for a longer period of time. He really was a handsome guy. And down-to-earth, too. She enjoyed his sense of humor and his boy-next-door personality.

Snap out of it, Debbie. She shook her head, determined to stay focused. These next few weeks were all about putting Sweet Sal's on the map. About paying off the mortgage. Only one way to accomplish that... by remembering that Bobby Conrad was on his way to save the day.

Suddenly, she felt like telling everyone she knew about the big event.

"C'mon girls," she said, waving at Becky Ann, Martha Lou, and Ginny. "We've got more posters to hang. And look!" She held up a photo of Bobby. "Now we've got pictures, too!"

Martha Lou squealed and ran to the photo, pressing her lips against it.

"Look what you've done," Debbie groaned. "You've got pink lipstick on his cheek."

"Oh, if only!" Martha Lou giggled, and for a moment looked like she might swoon. "Can you imagine?"

This got a laugh out of everyone.

"Besides, that's not pink lipstick," Martha Lou added. "It's Rose Petal Blush."

The girls headed toward the door. Debbie looked back at Johnny with a smile. "You coming with us?"

"Sure. I've never been to the beach before."

"You mean Laguna Beach?" she asked.

"No." He shook his head. "Any beach."

"Never been to the beach?" All the girls stopped in their tracks.

"Nope. I saw it the last time we drove down, but we never actually got to go there because the meeting lasted so long. This will be my first time."

"Where did you say you're from, again?" Becky Ann asked.

"Topeka, Kansas."

"Kansas," the girls echoed.

"There aren't any beaches in Kansas?" Becky Ann asked.

Johnny laughed. "Well, if you could call a grassy mound by the creek a beach, then yes. But nothing like what you've got here."

"Well, c'mon, then!" Martha Lou took him by the arm as she headed for the door. "We've got a lot of sightseeing to do!"

Chapter Seven

LOVE LETTERS IN THE SAND

It's mid-summer in Southern California, and romances are blossoming at every turn. Wedding bells pealed across the skies throughout the month of June, and now we're headed into more romantic unions in July. Couples are winning us over with their doe-eyed looks everywhere we turn. Desi loves Lucy. Ozzie loves Harriet. Pat loves Shirley. And Timmy loves Lassie.

Maybe that last one doesn't count.

Still, you get the point. Love is in the air, and here at Hollywood Heartthrob, *we're always ready to give you the scoop on who's dating who. Readers are anxious to see if rumors are true. For example, we've heard that Connie Francis and Bobby Darin are fighting an uphill battle with their courtship. Her strict Italian father is not a fan of young Darin. Will they or won't they end up married? Only time will tell.*

Another hot topic among teens: Is Bobby Conrad really dating Brenda Valentine, his love interest in First Kiss? *If so, the hearts of many a girl will be broken. This reporter interviewed a gaggle of teens outside Grauman's Chinese Theatre just this afternoon, and over three-quarters of the girls admitted they would cry if they heard that Bobby was, indeed, dating Brenda. One said she would burn her journal, and another stated that she would jump off of the Empire State Building. We take no responsibility for that last one. Or any of the others, for that matter.*

This reporter tends to believe the would-be romance is staged. Why else would Conrad and Valentine suddenly be seen together so close to the release of their new movie and in the hottest spots in town? Clearly contrived. On the other hand, Brenda is a beautiful girl. A true Italian beauty. Perhaps she has won the teen heartthrob over with her gorgeous looks. Based on her singing abilities in the movie, one would have to conclude she has not won him with her voice.

— Reporting for Hollywood Heartthrob *magazine, "Star Chasers"*
   columnist, Hollywood Molly.

* * * * *

Johnny left the soda shop arm-in-arm with a girl he'd never met until today. Martha Lou. She seemed nice enough, in an over-the-top sort of way. Still, he wished she'd release her hold on his arm so he could focus on the only girl in the group he really wanted to spend time with. Debbie.

As Martha tugged him along toward the highway, Johnny pondered Jim's words back at the soda shop: *"Kid, you have a lot to learn."* No doubt about that. Right now, he felt like a fish out of water. And his dreams—no matter how substantial—felt about as solid as that sand castle he'd referred to moments ago. Chasing after fame was a bit like praying a strong wave wouldn't come along and sweep the sand castle out to sea.

He was thankful when one of the other girls called Martha Lou's name, and she released her grip on his arm, skipping ahead. Johnny walked in silence behind the quartet of giddy females, trying not to think how much they reminded him of Katie and all the other girls back home in Topeka.

To distract himself, Johnny looked across the highway at the white sands and the brilliant waters of the Pacific, almost as blue as the skirt Debbie wore today. Almost. The sun felt warm on his skin, and the breeze off the water felt glorious. For a moment he almost forgot about the creek back home. About all of the hours he and Katie had spent there with their friends.

Stop it, Johnny. You'll never move forward if you keep hanging out in the past.

After a couple of minutes of pensive thoughts, he stepped into place beside Debbie. Something she'd said earlier raised a few questions in his mind.

"So, do you really read that *Hollywood Heartthrob* magazine you were talking about back there?" he asked.

"Well, I, um…" Her cheeks turned the prettiest shade of pink, completely distracting him. Johnny tripped over a crack in the sidewalk and the girls ahead of him cackled like the hens outside his bedroom window back home.

"Watch where you're going, Gene Kelly!" Martha Lou hollered out. "You'll never be a star if you fall down and bust your nose."

Johnny groaned and turned his attention back to Debbie as they continued walking together. "So, you were telling me about that magazine."

"Well, um, I used to read it…when I was a teen." She took on a more serious expression. "I'm turning twenty next Saturday."

"It's almost your birthday?" he asked. "What are you doing to celebrate?"

"Hadn't really thought about it," she said. "If you'd asked me that a few years ago, I would have said a roller skating party or maybe some sort of party at the beach. But we've been so busy with the shop and getting ready for the fundraiser, I guess we'll just do the usual thing. Mom will bake a cake, and Pop will embarrass me by singing in front of everyone who happens to be in the shop at the time."

Johnny laughed. "Sounds like something my dad would do. Only, in his case he would sing in front of the entire congregation."

"Congregation?" She looked puzzled.

"He's a minister."

"Oh, that's interesting, Johnny. I had no idea you were a preacher's kid."

He nodded. "Yes. But despite what you've heard about us, we're not all bad."

She laughed. "I never thought that, anyway. I guess it must be hard to have the pressure of appearing perfect in front of the congregation, though."

"Well, in our house we were all free to be ourselves," he said. "My parents are just regular people. They weren't hard on us. Really loving, in fact."

"It sounds like your father is a lot like mine," she said with a smile. "Especially if he embarrassed you in front of the whole congregation. Don't get me wrong. I've gotten used to Pop's antics. I'd miss it if he didn't sing. Besides, it's one of the many things he's known for, and everyone in Laguna Beach loves him for it."

Johnny paused to think about her words before responding. "He seems like a great guy, Debbie," he said, finally. "It's obvious he has your best interest at heart, as well as the interest of your whole family. My dad's always been the same. He puts himself last."

"You're describing my father, all right," Debbie said. "He always thinks of others first."

"That's a great trait," Johnny said. "I sometimes feel like I'm never going to be as good as my dad. Gotta wonder if I'm too focused on myself."

She stopped walking and turned to him, giving him a smile so sweet, it almost melted him right there on the sidewalk. "But you're young, Johnny. When you're—how old are you?"

"Twenty."

"When you're twenty, you're supposed to dream. I think God has placed those dreams in your heart. So don't be afraid you're self-centered. You don't come across like that at all." She grinned. "Trust me, I've seen a lot of people who really are self-focused. I would tell you if I thought you were one of them."

Johnny reached for her hand and gave it a squeeze. "Thank you so much for saying that. I really needed to hear it. I don't want to be like the prodigal son we read about in Sunday School."

She shook her head. "You don't strike me as a prodigal at all. You're just on a journey to see what adventures God has for you, that's all."

"I think my dad hoped I'd go to Bible school. Maybe even enter the ministry like he did. I don't know." He sighed.

"You are your own person, Johnny. I'm sure he realizes that."

He gazed into her eyes, lost in his thoughts. Her words brought such comfort. Well, until Becky Ann turned back their way and let out an ear-piercing whistle.

"See, I knew you were sweet on my sister, Johnny!" she called out. "You don't waste any time, do you?" She waved the photos and posters and hollered, "C'mon, you two. We've got work to do!"

Johnny let go of Debbie's hand, suddenly overcome with embarrassment. He turned and began to walk in step with her again. "Sorry about that."

"Johnny, don't ever be sorry for sharing your heart with someone." Debbie rolled her eyes. "And about my sister…well, just ignore her. She's a silly little pest, and she knows it. Before long, she'll be twenty like me and realize that making plans for the future is far more important than giggling over boys."

Johnny reflected on her words. Planning for the future was, indeed, at the top of his list right now. And if he had anything to say about it, Debbie Carmichael would walk alongside him as he journeyed toward that yet-unseen place. Right now, however, that place appeared to be the beach. He squinted as the sun reflected off the water. After a few moments of silence, Debbie turned his way.

"What are you thinking?"

He smiled. "I'm thinking that's a lot of water."

She laughed. "Might as well enjoy it. Take your shoes off, Johnny. Walking on the beach is no fun with shoes on. You can't get your feet wet that way."

"I guess you're right. I still haven't been in the water."

"Are you scared of it?"

"Scared?" He shrugged. "Hadn't thought of that. I guess I am a little intimidated. The waves are stronger here than I imagined." He glanced out at the water once more, pursing his lips as he watched the waves pound against the sandy shore.

"You'll get used to it in no time."

Debbie flashed a smile as bright as the sun overhead, and Johnny decided right then and there that he could get used to a lot of things. Spending time with her, for instance. Yes, spending the afternoon with this Laguna Beach beauty was turning out to be a very good idea, even if it meant tromping through the waves to put a smile on her face. He sat down and took off his shoes, stretching his feet.

"Roll up your jeans a little or they'll get wet." Debbie gave him a pensive look as she pulled off her saddle shoes and socks. "And if you're going to be hanging out with us, you'll really need to invest in some shorts or a bathing suit."

"I guess." He squinted against the glare. "I didn't come to California to swim. I came to…" He paused, unsure of how to finish.

"Become a star?" she asked.

He shrugged. "Yes. I guess. I hate putting it like that, though. I really just came to see what folks thought about my music, not turn into some kind of superstar."

A hint of a smile crossed her lips. "Well, today, just be Johnny Hartmann from Kansas, walking on the beach."

"With the prettiest girl in Laguna."

Had he really said those words aloud?

Looked like he had. She stared at him, those cocoa-brown eyes widening. Her look of surprise eased into a gradual smile, and before long she took off walking again.

Clutching his shoes in his hand, Johnny rose and joined her.

He walked alongside her, listening to the crash of waves. Oh, how he longed to reach for her hand once more. To lace his fingers through hers. To tell her how beautiful she looked with the sun shining down on that golden hair. How he wanted to tell her that the color of her eyes reminded him of the chocolate bar Toby had shared with him yesterday. Instead, he found himself tongue-tied, unable to say a word. Every now and again she gave him a questioning look, as if to ask, "Are you still here?" He could only smile in response.

Finally they approached the water's edge. Johnny closed his eyes and breathed in the salty air, overcome by both the smell and the feel of the mist across his cheeks. And the sound! The overwhelming sense of God's majesty rushed over him as he tuned in to the sound of the waves pounding the shoreline and the cliffs nearby. Truly, he had never heard anything so powerful. The words to "How Great Thou Art" came to mind at once, and he almost found himself humming the melody as he opened his eyes and focused on the vastness of the mighty Pacific. Instead, he whispered a prayer, thanking the Lord for this amazing opportunity.

After a few moments of silence, he turned to Debbie. "This is unbelievable."

"What?"

"The water. The beach. All of it."

As she turned to face him, Debbie gave him a shy smile—his first ray of hope. Johnny's heart began to thump against his ribs. Just a few feet away, the waves continued to race against the shoreline. In the distance, the chatter from the other girls rang out. Johnny was thankful for the noise, in part because he couldn't seem to speak a word. Debbie wasn't saying anything, either. Instead, the two stood, near breathless, facing each other. He sensed a certain wonder in the air and imagined the spell would be broken should either one speak. He fought the temptation to reach for her hand once again.

Finally, Johnny could fight the temptation no longer. He slipped his fingers through hers, not uttering a word. She didn't seem to mind. After a few seconds, she gave a little squeeze and then released her hold.

"Better go ahead and face your fears," she said, pointing to the water. "Get your feet wet, Johnny."

"Oh, I'm not afraid to get my feet wet. I'm just…" He stopped as the cool water swept over his feet. "Yikes!"

She laughed. "Takes a little getting used to. The Pacific is pretty chilly."

"You can say that again."

She gazed directly into his eyes, teasing him with a sly smile. "The Pacific is pretty chilly."

A ripple of laughter followed as she kicked up the icy water to soak his legs. Debbie then took off running, looking very much like a child at play. He enjoyed watching her almost as much as he enjoyed the feel of the sand between his toes. Clearly, she felt at home here. Maybe he would, too. In time. He could certainly get used to spending time with her. No doubt about that.

Before long he'd caught up with her, and they made a game out of splashing the cold water. He didn't mind. No, with Debbie, everything felt right. Natural. He would brave the cold waters of the Pacific, just to be near her.

Did she feel the same?

The hint of laughter in her eyes felt inviting, but he couldn't be sure. Maybe she was this way with everyone. It would take time to know if she might give him a second look.

Or not. Debbie glanced his way, smiling as she watched him plop down in the wet sand nearby.

"What are you doing?" she asked.

"Building a sand castle."

Her smile disappeared at once. "But we don't have time for that. We have to put up posters, remember? Besides, I don't want to get my new skirt all dirty."

"You're going to tell a guy from a land-locked state that he can't build a sand castle on his one and only trip to the ocean?" Johnny flashed his best pretend pout. "You would do that?"

"Well, when you put it like that, no."

She grinned and called for her sister. Becky Ann came running with the posters and photos in hand.

"What is it, Debbie?" her sister asked.

"Could you girls put up the posters? Johnny wants to build a sand castle."

"Um, okay." Becky Ann laughed and the wind caught the posters, causing one to fly away. She called out, "I guess so!" as she ran after it.

Seconds later, she caught up with the poster. Then she and the other girls took off toward the restroom area.

"Don't worry about us!" Martha Lou called back, waving her arms. "We'll put these up. You two lovebirds go on and play in the sand. Build a house together."

Johnny shook his head. "They're determined to play matchmaker, aren't they?"

"Yes." Debbie settled down next to him, her blue skirt a beautiful contrast against the white sand. "Silly girls. It's what they do. When they aren't writing love letters to Elvis."

"Love letters?" He smiled. "They really do that?"

"Oh yes. My sister is the president of the Laguna Beach chapter of Elvis's fan club. Well, she used to be, anyway. Lately, she's been in love with Bobby. She found the information about his fan club in the back of *Hollywood Heartthrob* magazine and joined immediately."

"Wow." He paused. "Sounds like all the girls are in love with Bobby. He must really be something."

"You haven't met him in person?" She looked stunned. "I figured you two knew each other since you both work with Jim."

"No. I haven't met him. Not yet, anyway. Have you?"

"No." A smile turned up the edges of her mouth. "But I will… soon. And so will you."

"So, it's just his image they're in love with?" Johnny asked. "Not the real person?"

"I guess." Debbie looked startled at that question. "He's really handsome and he sings like an angel."

"That's what they say."

"Oh, it's true." She sighed. "Did you see him on *The Ed Sullivan Show* a couple of weeks ago? And have you seen his movie, *First Kiss*?"

"No," Johnny said. "Haven't had time."

"Oh, you have to see it. It's playing at the Royal, just down the street."

"Is that an invitation?"

He squinted to get a better look at Debbie in the sunlight. A smile crept across her face.

"Well, I, um…"

He laughed. "I was just kidding. One of these days I'll see the movie. But first let's get past this fundraiser." He dared himself to say the next words. "Just promise me this."

"What?" She squinted, her sun-kissed nose now wrinkled.

"If I haven't seen it by the time the concert is behind us, you'll go with me."

She shrugged. "Sure. I could see it again." A smile lit her face. "And again. And again."

Johnny groaned and continued working on the sand castle, hoping her Bobby-a-thon would soon end. "Let's get to work on this thing."

"It's easier if you have a shovel and a bucket," she explained. "But you're doing pretty well."

Before long, the two of them had put together a decent-looking structure, though not exactly castle-like. Johnny sat back and looked at it, thinking about the earlier discussion in the soda shop about how one giant wave could wash a sand castle—or a fella's dreams—out to sea.

No point in fretting over that right now. Not with such a pretty girl sitting beside him.

Unfortunately, the only thing on her mind…was Bobby. On and on she went, singing the star's praises.

"The girls are going to come out in droves once the word gets out that Bobby's coming." She giggled. "It's going to be the best thing that's ever happened to Laguna Beach."

"Ah."

She paused and gave him a pensive look. "You don't think it's true that he's dating Brenda Valentine, do you?"

"Guess I never thought about it."

"It's all the girls are talking about this week." She sighed. "But I'm sure he's not. Sounds like something Jim staged. A good career move, but nothing more."

Johnny shrugged. "No idea." A silence as wide as the ocean grew up between them as they worked.

Finally Debbie paused and gazed into his eyes. "Oh, I'm sorry, Johnny. I'll bet you're getting sick of hearing about Bobby."

He didn't respond for a moment. After all, he didn't want to appear rude. "There's plenty of time to talk about him later on, I guess."

"True." She went back to work on the sand castle. As she did, their hands crossed. Johnny took advantage of the moment and allowed his fingers to trace hers. She looked up at him with a shy smile, and for a second they lingered, hands touching.

Overhead, a seagull shrieked, shattering the moment. Johnny went back to work as if it had never happened, hoping the thumping in his heart wouldn't give away his emotions.

Her lingering smile seemed brighter than the overhead sun. Johnny gazed into her eyes, wondering just what he'd ever done to deserve a day like this—a wonderful, perfect day.

* * * * *

Debbie's gaze lingered on Johnny far longer than it should. Still, she couldn't help herself. Neither of them could deny the sparks that appeared to be flying. And when he'd held her hand, she could hardly breathe. How could one focus on a fundraiser with such a handsome young man distracting her? Oh, but what a lovely distraction.

"A penny for your thoughts."

She looked up as he spoke, embarrassed to be caught thinking of him.

"Oh, I was just…"

Thankfully, she didn't have to answer. The other girls rushed their way, posters in hand, and plopped down in the sand next to them. "Hey, you two! Great sand castle, but we'd better hurry if we're going to the library and the grocery store. No lollygagging."

"Or ogling," Martha Lou said, waggling her thinly plucked brows at Johnny.

Debbie shook her head, embarrassed at the girls' outburst. Surely someone as kind as Johnny didn't need this sort of teasing from a group of silly teens he barely knew. This had to be awkward for him. It certainly felt awkward for her.

"Let's race back to the highway," Becky Ann said.

"Oh, not me." Ginny shook her head. "I always come in last place. I have weak ankles."

Becky Ann didn't appear to be listening. "Ready, set, go!" She took off running, but no one followed. The sure-footed teen didn't seem to notice. Instead, she blazed toward the highway, her feet leaving prints in the sand.

"That's my sister." Debbie sighed. "Always leading the way, but never really paying attention to what's ahead of her or who she's leaving in the dust."

Johnny laughed. "At least she's got gumption. You've got to give it to her."

They brushed the sand from their feet and slipped on their shoes. Then Johnny rose, extending his hand. Debbie took it, but didn't stand right away. Why rush? If she sat here a moment longer, the reality of what she was feeling might just kick in. Wasn't it just an hour ago her thoughts were on Bobby Conrad? Her potential relationship with Hollywood's heartthrob? She chided herself for being so fickle and forced herself to think about the fundraiser.

After a couple of moments deep in thought, Debbie allowed him to pull her up. Once she stood in front of him, they remained close. Face-to-face, in fact. She could feel his breath warm against her cheek. Neither said a word for a moment, but she didn't mind. The silence felt right. Comfortable. She marveled at how comfortable.

Lord, what are You doing here? Or am I just imagining this?

She heard the other girls let out a couple of squeals as they headed toward the highway. Debbie took this as a cue to brush the sand from her skirt.

Martha Lou turned back and hollered, "C'mon, you two. Let's go!"

"I think she's got a little crush on you." Debbie gave Johnny a playful wink.

"W–what?" Johnny's cheeks turned red. He glanced Martha Lou's way then shook his head.

"You didn't notice?" Debbie smiled, wondering how he could have missed it. Was he completely blind to the silliness of teen girls? Maybe.

He looked stunned, and not in a good way. "She's only, what... sixteen?" Johnny stammered.

"Seventeen," Debbie said. "But sometimes she thinks she's twenty-one."

"No thanks." He laughed. "If I wanted a girl..." He paused and stared into her eyes, not finishing the sentence.

Debbie felt her breath catch in her throat. If he wanted a girl... what?

Unfortunately, she never had the chance to find out. Johnny hollered, "We're coming!" then reached for her hand. Together they took off running across the sand toward the highway.

Chapter Eight

STAR QUALITY

Hollywood has become known as a Mecca for younger would-be stars. Drive by Pink's Hot Dog Stand on La Brea, and who do you see? The young ones. Cruise by Mel's Diner on Sunset and who's chomping away on burgers and fries? Starry-eyed kids in their teens and twenties with visions of grandeur, ready to believe the impossible about their potential careers on the big screen or on television.

Sure, these youthful amateurs are just as likely to be working at Mel's to pay the rent before they strike oil (sign that first big contract), but they don't seem to mind. Kids these days are willing to work hard to become "overnight" successes. They're ready to pay their dues, no matter how high, just like the stars of yesteryear. They're prepared to claw their way to the top as long as they can see their name up in lights once they get there, and they're looking for open doors every step of the way.

What happens to the ones who don't make it, in spite of their clawing? The ones who face slammed doors at every turn? The ones who've spent their last dollar on the bus ride from Bozeman or the train trip from Tucson, only to face rejection after rejection? Many stick around, unwilling to let go of the dream. Others fall in love with California's sunny shores and take on more sensible jobs, like shoe salesman or dental assistant. (And why not? Californians will always need shoes and root canals.) Some head back to places like Omaha,

Birmingham, and St. Louis, hoping to put the memories of Holly-wood behind them.

Even those who succeed face obstacles. Of course, it's been said that obstacles make us stronger. If that's the case, then the stars of tomorrow must be made of steel.

— *Reporting for* Hollywood Heartthrob *magazine, "Man About Town" columnist, Sunset Sam*

* * * * *

Late Saturday night Johnny sat in the living room watching television with Jim and his family. He'd always enjoyed *Talent Scouts,* but watching it with Toby at his side only made it more entertaining. The kid knew enough about music—and musicians—to keep up a running commentary on every guest. Maybe one day Toby would be an agent, too. Or a star. One could never tell about these things.

"Just think, Johnny," Toby said as he shifted his attention away from the television show. "Pretty soon that's going to be *you* up there. You'll be singing on national television in front of millions and billions of people." The youngster's eyes widened and his voice became more exaggerated. "Cameras will zoom in close, and you'll have to open your mouth and sing in front of everyone...in...the...world."

A shiver ran down Johnny's spine as he thought about it, and for a moment he felt a little nauseous, trying to imagine what folks in Michigan, Texas, North Carolina, and the like would think. Would they boo him back home to Kansas?

"Don't let him make you nervous, Johnny," Theresa said from her spot at the typewriter. "You'll do fine. It's not as nerve-wracking as he's making it sound, anyway."

Easy for her to say. Had she ever been on national television?

He was thankful when Jim's voice interrupted his reverie. "Theresa's right, Johnny. It's no more nerve-wracking than the audition process, and you've already made it through that. Besides, *Talent Scouts* is just a door to get you onto *American Bandstand*. From there, we'll be talking movies, studio recordings, and a lot more. One open door leads to another, son. You'll just keep walking through them, one after the other." Jim went off on a tangent, talking about the many doors that were about to open and all the possibilities that lay ahead. His rousing speech served to encourage Johnny, but it didn't squelch his nerves. Singing in front of millions of Americans was bound to be nerve-wracking.

"It's no fair that everyone else gets to be on television but me," Toby huffed. "You made Bobby a star, and now you're gonna make him a star." He pointed to Johnny, who shrugged.

"That's my job, son," Jim said. He rose and took a few steps in the youngster's direction. "If I didn't do my job—and do it well— our lives would be a lot different. So, yes, I turn people into stars. Or at least point them in the direction of people who can turn them into stars."

Toby muttered something under his breath.

Jim took another step in his direction. "You know what the great Fred Allen once said, don't you, son?"

Toby sighed. "No. But I have a feelin' you're gonna tell me."

Jim nodded. "You bet I am. Fred Allen said, 'A telescope will magnify a star a thousand times, but a good press agent can do even better.'" He slapped his knee and laughed. "Get it? A good press agent can magnify you." His expression sobered. "That's my job. I magnify people. Make sure others know who they are. And in doing so, I earn a living for our family. Put food on the table. Give young hotshots like Johnny here a chance at the big time."

Johnny felt compelled to offer a quick, "And I'm grateful," at the end of Jim's passionate speech.

"I know you are, son." Jim turned his way. "And this television gig is only the beginning. I'm going to get you into the movies, too. How would you feel starring with the likes of Kim Novak or Doris Day? Not a bad gig, eh?"

"I can think of worse."

Toby groaned and turned back to the television. "Still say it's not fair."

As they went back to watching the show together, Johnny paused to think about Jim's words. Seemed like he'd been talking about open doors for a while now. To Johnny's ears, it rang out like a song on the radio, playing loud and clear.

Sure, Johnny had been looking for open doors. What up-and-coming actor wasn't? Without opportunities, how could he be expected to move forward? Still, Jim continued to overlook something that had been obvious to Johnny from the beginning: the only true door opener was the Lord. Not that every opportunity was heaven-sent. Just because a door opened didn't mean you should walk through it. Only God could whisper to the heart which ones were the right ones. And who would want to walk through the wrong one, anyway? To do so would mean stepping off the correct path. Right?

He turned his attention back to the show, watching as a young man about his age entered the stage with a guitar in hand. He sounded a little shaky. And the song wasn't great, either.

Johnny sighed, praying things would go better when it was his turn. He also whispered up a prayer for the guy with the guitar. Looked like he was going to need it.

Unfortunately, things didn't end well for him. He was pretty much booed off the stage once he opened his mouth to sing.

"If I went on that show, the Clap-o-Meter would go crazy!" Toby jumped up and began to play an imaginary guitar as he sang the lyrics to Little Richard's catchy song, "Tutti Fruitti." Toby's boisterous, "A-wop bop a-loo bop, a-wop bam boom," rang out across the living room.

About one *bop a-loo bop* into the second chorus, Jim cleared his throat. Loudly. "Son, have you been reading *Variety* again?"

"Yeah, Dad." Toby dropped his invisible guitar and gave his father a pleading look. "Did you know that *Talent Scouts* is doing a special night for child stars at the end of August? A back-to-school special. I thought maybe I could—"

He never got to finish. Jim shook his head. "I've told you, son…"

"I know, I know." The youngster sighed and a look of defeat settled on his face. "No son of yours is ever going to be on television."

"Until you're grown up, anyway." Jim gave him a sympathetic look. "Maybe your old dad can help open a few doors for you when the time comes."

"Really?" Toby flashed a smile. "That'd be great, Dad." He settled back down on the floor, watching the rest of the show in silence.

Johnny tried to pay attention but was distracted by the ongoing exchange between father and son. Though he never mentioned it, Johnny often wondered what his father thought about his decision to come to L.A. To sing. To get into the movie business. Was his dad back in Topeka tonight, wondering about his son's career choices?

Sometimes Johnny had to wonder himself. The words, "How did I get here?" often played through his mind, especially when he thought about standing on that stage at *Talent Scouts,* singing in front of millions of people.

Long after Johnny went to bed that night, Jim's words lingered in his mind: "One open door leads to another, son. You'll just keep walking through them, one after the other." He tossed and turned, images of doors front and center in his mind. The door to his house back in Topeka. The door to the church he'd grown up attending. The door to Sweet Sal's Soda Shoppe. The door to Jim's car. In a crazy montage, they rolled by, one door after another, wooing Johnny to sleep.

Just as exhaustion settled in, an old scripture came to mind, one his dad had preached on a couple of months back. He couldn't place it at first, so he slipped out of bed.

"You okay, Johnny?" Toby's voice was sleepy from the upper bunk.

"Yes, sorry to wake you."

"Worried about being on TV in front of millions and billions of people?" The youngster's groggy voice made his words almost indistinguishable.

"No. Just need to take care of something. Go back to sleep, kid."

"Okay." Toby yawned and rolled back over.

Johnny reached into his duffle bag, fishing around for his worn Bible. He eventually located it. He tiptoed out into the hallway, making his way to the bathroom. Once inside, he flipped on the light then closed the door, so as not to disturb anyone else. He took a seat on the edge of the bathtub, flipping through the pages of the Bible until he finally landed on the verse in question. John 10:9. "I am the door: by me if any man enter in, he shall be saved, and shall go in and out, and find pasture."

Johnny pondered the familiar verse. Really, when it came right down to it, *that* was the only door that mattered. He thought again of Jim and Theresa, how they lived life without really knowing the Lord. Unless they walked through the door—unless they came to know Christ—none of the accomplishments of this world would matter in the least.

A somber feeling passed over Johnny, and he read the verse again in an attempt to ease his concerns. For the first time since arriving in Los Angeles, something rather startling occurred to him. Maybe he'd been sent here, not just to pray for open doors for himself, but to help open them for others. Maybe the Lord wanted him to share the message of his faith with people like Jim and Theresa in such a way that they would want to walk through the only door that mattered…into a relationship with Christ.

Wow. Now, that put a whole new spin on things.

He spent the next few minutes looking for the word "door" in the Bible. After reading over many verses, he found one that caught his eye. "I know thy works: behold, I have set before thee an open door, and no man can shut it: for thou hast a little strength, and hast kept my word, and hast not denied my name."

The words from Revelation jumped out at him. If God opened a door, no man could shut it. In order for that to be true, however, Johnny would have to keep God's Word. And keeping God's Word meant finding a church. Getting back in the habit of worshiping with others.

Seated there, on the edge of the tub, Johnny turned the bathroom into a prayer closet. He spent several minutes asking the Lord to guide him. "I don't want to get ahead of You," he said aloud. "Just show me what to do, and I'll do it. Show me where to go, and I'll go there."

"Johnny?" Theresa's voice startled him to attention.

He opened the door a crack and peeked out. "Did I wake you up?"

"No." She gestured to the bathroom, and he suddenly felt embarrassed for having taken possession of the room for so long. Still, who would have known she'd need it in the middle of the night?

"Sorry." He pulled the door open and stepped into the hall.

Theresa looked at the Bible in his hand then back up at him. "You really are a good kid, aren't you?"

"If the words in this book are true, then none of us is really good. We're all in need of God's forgiveness."

Her eyes grew misty. "Well, you're an impressive kid, Johnny Hartmann. That's all I've got to say about it." She paused to give him a motherly smile then stepped inside the bathroom and shut the door.

Johnny made his way back into the bedroom, exhaustion leading the way. By the time he settled into the bottom bunk, his eyes felt weighted. As he drifted off to sleep, his thoughts shifted to the time he'd spent at the water's edge with Debbie Carmichael. That sand castle they'd built together had surely been swept out to sea within hours of its building. Would his time in Los Angeles disappear as quickly, or was he here to stay?

Moments later he drifted off to sleep, with visions of the mighty Pacific front and center in his mind.

The following morning Johnny awoke feeling a little homesick. He lay in bed, thinking about what his parents were doing right now, back in Topeka. Of course, it was later there. They were probably already in church. His father was probably leading the congregation in a prayer right about now, or maybe they were singing "When the Roll Is Called Up Yonder," one of his mother's favorite hymns.

A light rap on the bedroom door startled Johnny from his reverie. Jim popped his head inside and whispered, "Johnny, I hope you don't mind, but I've taken the liberty of arranging an appointment for you this morning."

"An appointment?" *On Sunday?*

"Sorry for the inconvenience," Jim said. "You'll need to get up and put on those new clothes. Be ready to leave in forty-five minutes."

Johnny groaned inwardly, wondering what sort of business Jim had arranged on a day like today. He went through the motions, showering, shaving, dressing, and combing his hair the way he'd been taught. Still, the reflection in the mirror didn't lie. Johnny wanted to return to the old days...and the old ways. Back home in Topeka, he'd never think of working on a Sunday. Or looking like something he wasn't.

At nine o'clock sharp, the front doorbell rang. Johnny made his way to the living room, watching as Theresa opened the door. What he saw on the other side—or, rather, *who* he saw on the other side—caught him totally off-guard. Bobby Conrad.

"Hello, Williams family!" Bobby's happy-go-lucky voice rang out across the house. "Hope you've got a pot of coffee brewing. And some of those wonderful cinnamon rolls I love."

Theresa nodded and gave him a warm hug. "Good to see you again, Bobby. Glad you could come home."

Jim gave him a pat on the back and offered up a warm smile. "Thanks for stopping by, Bobby. I know you don't like to talk business on Sundays."

"This is a little different." Bobby turned to face Johnny, who suddenly felt insecure and a little out of place. "You must be Johnny."

"I—I am." He extended his hand and Bobby shook it. "Good to meet you."

"Nice to finally meet you, too."

Johnny had just started to respond when Toby's voice rang out from down the hallway.

"Bobby!" Toby came tearing into the living room, still in his pajamas. "You're here."

"I'm here, but not for long." Bobby tousled Toby's hair. "How you doing, little brother?"

"Fine." Toby shrugged. "Dad still won't let me audition for any parts."

"Nothing new there," Bobby said. "Your day will come. Remember all those talks we had about it?"

"Yeah." The youngster's smile faded for a moment then returned. "I didn't beat up Mikey Yarborough, even though he stole my girlfriend."

"Oh?" Bobby grinned. "You went a different route?"

"Sing now, fight later. That's my new motto." Toby nodded. "Johnny came up with it."

I like it." Bobby gave him a warm smile. "Sounds like your new discovery is a smart guy, Jim. Can't wait to hear him sing." He gave Toby a pretend punch on the arm. "Sing now, fight later. I like it."

"Johnny would never fight with anyone, anyhow," Toby added. "He's too nice for that."

"Even if someone stole his girlfriend?" Bobby grinned.

Johnny fought the urge to say something. Instead, he just

shrugged. "Singing your way through any situation is great medicine. That's the way I look at it, anyway. Music always helps me relax and put things in perspective."

"That's what it does for our fans, too," Bobby said. "If it's good music."

"Oh, his songs are good," Jim said.

Toby waggled his brows. "You should hear the one he wrote about this really pretty girl in Laguna Beach."

"Pretty girl?" Bobby quirked a brow. "Anyone I know?"

The strangest sensation swept over Johnny—a possessive feeling. He didn't want Bobby Conrad to know just how pretty Debbie Carmichael was. He would see soon enough, anyway.

"Someone you're going to get to know," Jim said. "She's the daughter of that friend of mine who owns the soda shop in Laguna Beach. Pretty little thing with blond hair and a great smile."

Bobby looked at Johnny. "Oh yes. I've heard about her. Did you meet her?"

Johnny hesitated, finally managing, "Oh, well, yes."

"She as pretty as they say?"

Any potential words stuck in Johnny's throat. If he shared too much information, Bobby might be interested in Debbie. And who could compete with Bobby Conrad?

Strange, the twinge of jealousy that passed over him as he pondered the Hollywood heartthrob getting to know Debbie. He was glad he didn't have long to think about it.

Bobby glanced at the wall clock then looked Johnny's way. "Doesn't look like I'm going to have time for that cup of coffee after all. You ready to go?"

"Go?" He didn't know quite how to respond. "Go where?"

"To church, of course. Jim told me you wanted to come with me this morning."

Johnny turned to look at Jim, who gave him a slight grin.

"Go on, kid. Have a good time with Bobby. How I ever ended up with two choir boys as clients I'll never know."

Bobby laughed and slapped Jim on the back. "Don't worry about us, Jim. We might not be the rebels you were hoping for, but we're going to make you proud in the end."

"You've already made me proud." Jim wrapped him in a bear hug then opened his arms to usher Johnny into his embrace. Before long, Toby had weaseled his way in, too. "You might as well come over here, Theresa," Jim said. "These boys of ours aren't going to let go until we're all in on this."

She chuckled then joined the circle.

"Say, why don't you guys come with us to church," Bobby said when the hug ended. "We don't mind waiting, and I know you'd love it."

For a moment, Johnny saw a hopeful glint in Theresa's eye.

"Don't really have time today, boys." Jim loosened his grip on them and took a step back. "Papa's got a lot of work to do if we want to keep this family fed and dressed."

"Well, if you ever change your mind…" Bobby smiled.

"Maybe." Theresa gave them both a quick hug before heading off to the kitchen.

Johnny followed Bobby outside to his car. He let out a whistle when he saw the gorgeous red convertible.

"Wow. Never been in a car like this before."

Bobby laughed. "Neither had I, until I bought it. Climb on in."

Johnny half-expected to see Bobby hop over the side of the car, but he opened the door and got in the usual way. Johnny followed suit. Minutes later, they roared down the freeway, the wind whipping through Johnny's hair.

"Want me to put the top up?" Bobby called out.

Johnny shook his head. He wouldn't miss this experience for anything.

After a few minutes they turned off on a side road and things seemed quieter.

"Okay, one question right off the bat." Bobby glanced his way.

"Sure. Ask me anything."

"Where did Jim find you?"

"At an open audition for a movie. What about you?"

"Same thing. I was pretty down that day."

"Same here," Johnny said.

Bobby chuckled. "Did he feed you that line about Horace Hinkley?"

"Yes," Johnny said. "Why?"

"I've been by the service station he told me about and they've never heard of a Horace Hinkley. I think Jim made him up."

Both of the guys laughed then Bobby took the opportunity to open up and share his heart about working in the industry. Johnny listened as his new friend expressed his thoughts on Hollywood, on fame and fortune. He found himself mesmerized by Bobby's stories, particularly the ones about all the auditions he had to go through just to get his first break.

"Don't let all the glamour and fame get to you," Bobby said. "It's hard, but it is possible to keep your head on your shoulders. And if what I heard about you is true…"

"What have you heard about me?" Johnny asked as Bobby turned the car off the road into the church's parking lot. He couldn't help but wonder what Jim had said.

"You're a good guy. From Kansas. Son of a preacher." Bobby pulled the car into a parking space and turned to him with a concerned look on his face.

"Yes." Johnny nodded. "Guilty as charged."

"I'll tell you the truth," Bobby said. "When I got my first big singing gig, I let it go to my head. Almost forgot where I'd come from."

"Sorry to ask, but where *do* you come from?"

Bobby smiled. "Most folks assume I was born and raised in L.A., but I'm from a little town in Wyoming. When we talked about cattle calls, we meant the real deal. The kind with long horns." He pushed a button and the top of the car rose to cover them. Johnny looked on in awe. So did a couple of folks who happened to be passing by.

"How did you end up here?" Johnny asked, once the top was safely in place.

"Oh, same as you, I suppose," Bobby said. "People started telling me I could sing and act when I was a kid. And when I graduated from high school, I went to our local college, but it just wasn't right for me, so I took a job at a local store as a clerk. That wasn't a good fit, either. I just wanted to perform. It's all I ever wanted to do."

"I hear you," Johnny said. "I feel like I'm doing what I was born to do when I'm on that stage singing. There's something pretty amazing about it. Not sure I can explain it."

"Good thing is, you don't have to. I get it," Bobby said. "I'm probably one of the few who really understands. That's why I said to hang on to who you really are on the inside. And not just for the sake of the girls who want to believe you're the boy-next-door. Do it so that you stay strong from the inside out."

"Great advice."

"Ready for church?" Bobby smiled, and reached to open the driver's side door.

"Am I ever." Johnny swung his door open, ready to face whatever this day might bring his way.

* * * * *

Debbie entered the front door of Grace church and was immediately swarmed by teen girls.

"Debbie, is it really true?" a preteen girl named Julie asked. "Bobby Conrad is coming to Sweet Sal's?"

"Yes, he's coming." She clasped her hands together at her chest, suddenly feeling woozy. "I still can't believe it. We're going to meet him...in person."

"It's too wonderful to be true!" Cassie Jenkins said, her cheeks turning pink.

"I'm going to ask him to sign my record sleeve then tack it to my bedroom wall and keep it there forever," Martha Lou added.

"I'm going to propose to him the minute he finishes singing the theme song from *First Kiss*," Becky Ann said. "I hope he says yes."

Debbie shook her head. "You're too young to get married, Becky Ann." *But I'm not.*

"Can you even imagine what it would be like to be Mrs. Bobby Conrad?" Martha Lou reached for a church bulletin and began to fan herself. "To be his...forever?"

For a moment, Debbie allowed her thoughts to go there. What would it be like, to live in a mansion in Malibu with one of Hollywood's golden boys? Different from her life in Laguna Beach, to be sure. The strangest feeling of sadness came over her as she thought about leaving her family. Hmm. She'd never pondered that complication before.

Becky Ann released a lingering sigh. "Bobby hung the moon."

"Actually, *God* hung the moon," Debbie's father said as he passed by. "And this is the Lord's Day, girls. Can't we just take a sabbatical from talking about Bobby for once?"

"I guess so, Pop." Becky Ann didn't look convinced.

Debbie grinned and whispered her response in the direction of the girls. "Talk to me after church, okay? I'll give you all the details."

Her mother drew near, Bible in hand. "What did I miss, girls?"

"Oh, we're just talking about…" Debbie paused, afraid her mother might not be happy with the response.

"Let me guess. Bobby. Again."

She nodded. "But it's just to promote the event, Mom. I promise."

"Good, because I would hate to think you were swooning in church." Her mother gave her a warm smile, filled with understanding. "Now, finish up with your friends and come inside. Pop is waiting on us."

As Debbie walked through the double doors leading to the sanctuary, Mildred Hamilton, one of the congregation's older members, greeted her. "Good morning, Debbie. I understand you've been a busy little bee, getting ready for this fundraiser concert."

"Yes." She grinned.

Mildred leaned down, whispering in Debbie's ear as she handed her a church bulletin. "I have a little crush on Bobby Conrad myself.

Do you think he has an older brother?" She gave Debbie a wink, and her thinly plucked brows arched.

"I, well…" Debbie wasn't sure how to respond. She stifled a smile then stepped through the door into the sanctuary, bulletin in hand. Once inside, she found Becky Ann, Martha Lou, and Ginny Anderson engaged in deep conversation. They weren't talking about the upcoming service, or the lesson they'd just heard in Sunday school. No, the only real topic holding anyone's interest today…was Bobby Conrad.

Debbie suddenly wondered if any of the girls would pay a bit of attention to this morning's service. Hopefully they could all get past their infatuation long enough to listen to the sermon. One glance at the bulletin and Debbie took note of today's sermon title—*The Ten Commandments, Week Two: An Idol-Free Life*—along with a scripture from Exodus, chapter 20. Ouch. She suddenly felt a little warm. Surely she and the other girls hadn't made Bobby into an idol. Had they?

The organ began to play, and the familiar strains of "Is Your All on the Altar?" pealed out across the sanctuary. She made her way to the seventh pew on the left, the one where her family had taken up residence several years ago and never budged from since.

Debbie scooted into the place next to her mother and turned to smile at Junior, who took the space on the other side of Pop. Now, if only her sister would leave the tight-knit circle of teen girls to join the family. Becky Ann eventually made her way up the center aisle. She scooted into the space to Debbie's right.

"Martha Lou just announced that she's going on a hunger strike if Bobby doesn't choose her to sing backup. She's not eating another bite until he invites her up on the stage."

Debbie groaned, though the sound of her displeasure was buried underneath the ever-loudening organ. "What if he never changes his mind? What if he just doesn't like the idea?"

Debbie's thoughts became very animated at this point, listing all the reasons why Bobby should keep everything just the way it was before this crazy day ever started.

Oh well. Tomorrow is another day.

Right now…well, right now she'd better stay focused on worship.

Chapter Nine

BLOCKBUSTER

You heard it here first, folks. Cinema Cindy's got the scoop on upcoming movies and their stars. For some time now, Paramount Studios has hinted at the fact that they're thinking of recreating an age-old classic. Just this morning they issued a press release stating that the musical extravaganza will move forward. Ready for this, girls? Heartthrob Bobby Conrad has been chosen to play the role of Romeo in a musical remake of Shakespeare's classic Romeo and Juliet. *The movie's title?* Oh, My Romeo!

While some might find the musical remake a bit of a stretch from the original, others will flock to the theaters to see Bobby take on the role of the star-crossed lover. Fans will be particularly delighted to learn the new movie will have a beach theme and will be filmed primarily in Huntington Beach. So, grab your suntan lotion and head to the sunny shores, friends. Maybe you'll be cast as an extra in this one.

As for who will play the lucky Juliet, a variety of females are under consideration, including Sandra Dee, Natalie Wood, and Brenda Valentine. If you want my opinion—and I know you do—any one of those girls would be lucky to play opposite Bobby Conrad.

Can you imagine the balcony scene? Talk about romance at its finest! Bobby—as Romeo—strumming his guitar and singing a gentle ballad to the winsome Juliet as she pines away from her beachfront balcony, Pacific waves crashing against the shoreline in the background. The mind reels with the possibilities.

Filming for the movie will begin soon. Rumor has it, Conrad will have to cancel a few scheduled events to make it work, but the payoff with fans will be worth it. So, practice up on your surfing skills, Bobby. We'll see you at the beach with fair Juliet. In the meantime, "Good Night, Good night! Parting is such sweet sorrow, that I shall say good night till it be morrow."

— *Reporting for* Hollywood Heartthrob *magazine, "On the Big Screen" columnist, Cinema Cindy*

* * * * *

On the morning of her birthday, Debbie found her mother leaning over the counter in the kitchen at Sweet Sal's, tears pouring down her face.

"Mom, what's wrong? What happened? Is it Pop?" Debbie's heart raced. Her father had been gone for a couple of hours to a city council meeting. Had something happened to him while he was there?

Debbie's mother looked up and smiled. "Oh, I'm so sorry, honey. I was just cutting these onions." She pointed to a mound of thick iridescent slices. "They always make me cry."

A wave of relief washed over Debbie. "Well, you scared me. I thought maybe something happened."

"No." Her mother smiled through the tears. "All is well, honey. And just for the record, you need to stop fretting so much. For one thing, you're far too young to give your time over to worry. For another thing, you need to let go of the reins and give those worries to the Lord. He's big enough to handle them." She sniffled.

Debbie paused for a moment. "I know you're right. It's just tough to let go sometimes. And it's hard, too, because we don't know what's going to happen next. We can't see what's coming around the bend with Pop, and that scares me."

Her mother's eyes filled with tears once more, only this time it couldn't be blamed on the onions. "Honey, that's why the Lord tells us to take one day at a time and to cherish the moments we have with people. We don't know what's coming, but we have today. So we might as well take advantage of today and live it to the fullest."

Debbie sucked in a deep breath. She wanted to counter with something, but nothing sounded just right. Finally she whispered, "I know, Mom. It's just scary, not knowing if he's going to be okay. I wish we could know for sure what tomorrow holds."

"Yes it is." Her mother nodded. "Just wait till you have teens. Then you'll see how hard it really is to trust God with the future!"

Debbie reached over and gave her mother a warm embrace. "Aw, Mom."

Her mother's eyes grew misty. "You are twenty today, honey. Twenty." She shook her head.

Debbie chuckled. "I know. It's hard for me to believe, too. Are you sad that your kids are growing up?"

"Not sad, really. Just, aware. Very aware. And when I think about your sister learning to drive..." She shuddered. "Well, let's just say that I'm having to trust the Lord more than you know. Trusting the Lord to grow your children into the men and women they were born to be isn't always easy."

Debbie found herself surprised at how quickly the tears came.

For a moment she thought it was her emotions kicking in. Then she realized she'd leaned right over the mound of sliced onion.

"Let me put these into a container." Her mother went to work, filling a large plastic bin with the slices. After covering it and placing it in the refrigerator, she walked to the sink and scrubbed her hands. A few seconds later, she joined Debbie at the front counter.

"Did you see that The Palace is playing that new Deborah Kerr movie?" her mother asked with a slight twinkle in her eye.

"Oh, you mean the one with Cary Grant? *An Affair to Remember*?" Debbie must've spoken the words a little too loud. A customer turned to give her an inquisitive look. She quickly explained, "It's a movie."

The woman nodded and went back to eating her chicken sandwich. Junior approached with a pitcher of water in his hand. He refilled the glasses of several customers at the counter then joined Debbie and their mother.

"Daydreaming about Cary Grant again, Mom?" Junior asked with a wink.

A flicker of a smile lit her face for a moment. Debbie's mother chuckled. "You've got to admit, he is very handsome. When the Lord handed out looks, he gave Cary a double portion."

Debbie laughed.

Her mother's expression shifted. "But if you want the truth, I'm interested in that movie for another reason. I hear there's some great footage of the Empire State Building in the film and that intrigues me. I'd like to see it someday. In person, I mean. Not in a movie."

"You and Pop should go," Debbie said. "And maybe you can, after this fundraiser. If anyone deserves a vacation, you two do." Her heart twisted as she spoke those words. Except for a couple of drives down the coast to San Diego, she couldn't remember her parents ever taking a real vacation. Well, that would change as soon as they paid off the soda shop.

Yes, the more she thought about it, the more she liked the idea. She and Junior and Becky Ann would plan something special for their parents just as soon as this concert was behind them. Perhaps a twenty-fifth anniversary gift. Yes, that would be perfect.

Her mother shrugged. "Right now I'd settle for an evening at The Palace with your father. Cary's new movie looks like something we would both enjoy."

"I saw the preview the night we went to see *First Kiss*," Debbie said. "It looks really good. You and Pop should go."

"I agree," Junior said, drawing near. "You've been working too hard, Mom."

Debbie added, "I don't want you to make yourself sick."

"Someone has to bear the load." Her mother glanced through the opening into the kitchen. "Pop is still recovering and I need to do what I can."

"I'm just afraid you're going to wear yourself out," Debbie said.

Junior squared his shoulders. "We can do more. We're perfectly capable."

"You kids already work too hard. Sometimes I feel like we're robbing you of your childhood by making you work like you do, but I can't figure out another way to keep the shop going."

Debbie shook her head. "I'm not a child, Mom. I'm twenty now."

"How could I forget?" Her mother smiled. "I was there the day you were born, remember?"

Debbie chuckled. "Well, I don't remember firsthand, but I've certainly heard the stories."

"Mom, you know you can count on me." Junior seemed to grow taller as he said the words. He stood ramrod straight, creases settling between his brows. "One of these days I'll take over all of the cooking so you and Pop can get out of the kitchen for good."

"You're a good cook, son." She gave him a warm smile. "No one flips a better burger."

"I learned from the best." He reached over and gave her a hug.

In the background the familiar refrain of "The Legend of Davy Crockett" played on the jukebox.

Debbie rang up a group of boys at the register then walked to the booth at the back of the restaurant where they had been sitting. She wondered how three teenage boys could possibly have consumed so much food. Between them, they'd ordered five burgers, two hot dogs, two orders of onion rings, two large orders of french fries, two malts, one soda, and a hot fudge sundae with whipped cream on top. On top of all that, they'd neglected to leave a tip. Not even a teensy-tiny one.

Happy birthday to me.

Debbie sighed as she cleaned up the mess they'd left behind. Some days this job hardly seemed worth it. Countless hours serving people…and for what? Most days they didn't even so much as say thank you for the service or the good food. A few even grumbled that McDonald's was cheaper.

Well, all of that was bound to change once Bobby showed up. Debbie's spirits lifted at once. Why, she would clean a thousand messy booths if she could just meet Bobby Conrad in person.

Debbie took a seat at the booth under the guise of wiping the table. Her thoughts, however, were on the teen heartthrob's upcoming appearance. She tried to imagine what it would be like the first time they met. She would wear a new pink skirt and white blouse, with a pink scarf around her hair. No, on second thought, perhaps she'd better not wear the usual ponytail. Ponytails were for girls. She wanted to look like a woman.

This might take a bit of work. Coming up with just the right hairstyle was key. And so was the choice in lipstick. Blushing Rose or Pollyanna Pink? She'd better try out both, just to make sure. After all, she only had one chance to make a first impression and wanted it to be a good one.

Debbie closed her eyes, picturing Bobby's reaction the first time their eyes met. Would he look at her with hope in his expression, sure he'd met his perfect match? Would she be able to control her enthusiasm, so that she wouldn't come across like Martha Lou and the others?

She might have to work on that last part. After all, she wanted him to see her as a woman, not a girl.

Oh, but whenever she thought about Bobby, she felt like a schoolgirl all over again. Her heart fluttered, her eyes closed, and she felt warm and tingly all over.

Kind of like she'd felt last Saturday at the beach.

With Johnny.

She smiled as she remembered what fun she and Johnny had shared. Building a sand castle together. Chasing each other in the waves. Splashing him until he laughed so hard he could barely breathe.

Hmm.

As much as she hated to admit it—what with Bobby coming and all—Debbie felt herself drawn to the handsome young man from Topeka with the gorgeous hair and beautiful jade green eyes. His soothing voice. His even-keeled temperament. His boyish charm. Why, even his faith came ringing through…very unusual in someone headed for stardom.

Was he headed for stardom? Would Johnny Hartmann one day

be as famous as Bobby Conrad? The idea washed over her like a gentle wave then settled far away, on the evening tide. Nah. He was just Johnny Hartmann from Topeka. A regular guy. She rather liked him that way.

Becky Ann walked up with a smile on her face. "You must be daydreaming."

Debbie shook off her ponderings and focused on her sister. "Oh? What makes you say that?"

"I haven't seen a smile like that since you got the news that Bobby would be coming." She giggled. "Did I catch you thinking about him?"

"Actually, no." Debbie fought the urge to say more. She couldn't even explain what she was feeling to herself, let alone someone else.

"Did you hear the news?" Becky Ann took a seat across from Debbie. "Bobby just signed to do a new movie."

"Of course I heard. It was the headline story in the *Laguna Beach Times* this morning. The mayor is beside himself. He thinks this will help bring more people to the concert. I hope he's right."

"I just love *Romeo and Juliet*. It's going to make a great musical. Can you even imagine playing opposite Bobby?" Becky Ann clutched her hands to her chest and looked upward. "Oh, Romeo, Romeo… wherefore art thou, Romeo?"

Debbie laughed. "You've got that part memorized. No doubt about it. Are you thinking about trying out for Juliet? I hear they're looking for just the right girl."

"Oh!" Martha Lou sidled up next to them. "I wonder if they're having open auditions."

"Only if your name is Natalie Wood or Brenda Valentine." Debbie shrugged. "But don't worry, Martha Lou. You're still going to meet Bobby in person. Soon."

"I know." A radiant smile overtook Martha Lou's face. "I've already picked out the dress I'm going to wear the day of the concert. And your father told me I can help, so I'll be close to Bobby."

"Help?" Debbie bit her tongue, careful not to speak her mind. With Martha Lou chattering Bobby's ear off, he was liable to turn and run.

"Sure. I'll do whatever he needs. If he doesn't like my singing voice, then I'll be his personal assistant. They're always near the actor. And if he doesn't like me as an assistant…" Martha Lou's words faded once more. "Anyway, I'll keep working at it. Hopefully he'll fall in love with me." Her cheeks turned red. "Well, maybe not love, but serious *like*. It takes some time for love to grow."

Debbie thought about the winsome look in Junior's eye whenever he saw Martha Lou enter the shop. Clearly, his affections were not noticed on the other side. Despite his best intentions, the distracted teen seemed to overlook him at every turn. Nothing he could do would ever change that…unless Martha Lou happened to come to her senses. Then his puppy-dog expressions wouldn't have been in vain.

Deep in thought, Debbie barely noticed the ringing of the phone. She snapped to attention as her mother's voice rang out. "Debbie, phone call for you."

"For me? At the shop?" That rarely happened.

As she drew near, her mother whispered, "It's a man's voice. Maybe a reporter or something."

Her heart skipped a beat. Maybe someone from *Hollywood Heartthrob*, agreeing to come to the event. Cinema Cindy, perhaps? Or maybe Hepcat Harry? Oh, she could hardly wait to find out! She tentatively reached for the phone and greeted the person on the other end with a shaky "Hello?"

"Debbie, is that you?"

She recognized the voice on the other end of the line at once. "Johnny." For some reason, the word stuck in her throat. She couldn't seem to add anything to it. She felt a smile tug the edges of her lips upward and did her best not to let her embarrassment show to those nearby. From the other end of the line, she heard the familiar strains of the *Kukla, Fran, and Ollie* theme song. "What are you watching?"

"Oh, I, um…nothing. It's Toby. It's his favorite."

"No, it's not my favorite!" Toby's voice rang out from the background. "*Lassie* is my favorite. You made me watch this dumb show, Johnny. Admit it."

Debbie laughed. "So, you're a fan of puppets?"

He sighed. "Maybe a little. But Toby's got me hooked on *The Mickey Mouse Club* now, too. You should hear his impression of Annette."

"Oh, we all watch that," she admitted. "And we love Annette." After a pause, she asked the obvious question. "Have you been to Disneyland yet?"

"No, but I'd love to. Maybe we could go together sometime. We could take Toby."

"Mm-hmm." She fought to hide the smile. Was Johnny asking her out on a date? If so, would she go? After a few seconds, his words brought her back to reality.

"I called because it's your birthday," Johnny said.

Debbie couldn't help but smile. "I can't believe you remembered."

"Of course. How could I forget the birthday of the first person who ever introduced me to the Pacific? And sand castles?"

She chuckled. "Happy to be of service."

"So, did your father embarrass you in front of the customers like you said he would?"

"First thing this morning." She groaned. "Sang at the top of his lungs. The mayor was here to talk about the fundraiser. Then they left together for a meeting. Everyone is so excited about Bobby coming."

"Oh, speaking of which, something interesting happened last Sunday," he said. "I went to church with Bobby."

"You...you what?" She nearly dropped the phone. "You and Bobby...in church?"

"Yes." Excitement laced Johnny's words. "And we had a chance to talk about a lot of things."

"Like what?" she asked, trying not to let her excitement show too much.

"Well, our faith, for one thing. Bobby was really straightforward about where he stands with the Lord and that impressed me. I know you and your family are believers, so I thought you might find that interesting."

"Very. I'm so glad he's the real deal." Debbie lost herself in another daydream. What would it be like to sit in the pew next to Bobby Conrad? To hear his amazing voice as he sang from the hymnal? What would it feel like to walk arm in arm from the church building with him? Maybe one day she would know. In the meantime, she'd better pay attention.

Johnny kept talking, his tone growing more serious. "We had a great conversation about being in the world, but not of the world. Really helped me put things in perspective." A long pause followed. "Anyway, I wanted to call you and tell you all of this, but there's something else you need to know, too."

"What's that?"

"Well, he's got this big movie deal coming up. That *Romeo and Juliet* thing."

"Yes, I read about it."

"He's a little concerned about his schedule. In fact, he asked if I would pray about that."

"His...his schedule?" At once, a lump rose in her throat. Debbie took a seat on the barstool and leaned an elbow on the counter. "You don't think he would cancel the fundraiser, do you?"

Another lengthy pause followed. "I don't know. I just know that he's feeling a little overwhelmed and asked me to pray. So I have been."

Tears welled up in Debbie's eyes as she contemplated the situation. "Oh, Johnny, I don't know what I'd do if he couldn't come. It would ruin everything."

His tone changed once again, his words now more upbeat. "I'm sure God has a plan, Debbie. So don't give up. I probably shouldn't have mentioned it anyway. It's Jim's place to talk about Bobby's career moves, not mine. I'm just speculating."

A wave of relief washed over her. "Jim is good friends with my father. He would have said something by now if the plan for the fundraiser had changed."

"I'm sure you're right. Anyway, I just called because..." Johnny's voice drifted off.

"Because...?" She echoed. For a second, her thoughts shifted from Bobby to the handsome boy from Topeka on the other end of the line.

"Well, I...I wanted to say 'happy birthday,' but mostly..."

"Mostly what?" Her curiosity was piqued, to be sure.

"Mostly, I just wanted to hear your voice." He paused and she felt a curious tingle wriggle its way up her spine. "I had a great time with you last Saturday. I've been thinking about the beach all week. And...and you."

She couldn't stop the smile that followed, and all the more as she found herself caught up in the memory of the time they'd spent together at the water's edge. "I had fun, too, Johnny. Next time you come down, maybe we can go again. I know the best spot by the cliffs. It's a private little pocket of sand, completely hidden away from everyone and everything. Perfect for a picnic." A wonderful idea came to mind. "Since you and Bobby are friends now, maybe you could ask him to join us."

"Sure. I'll do that."

Debbie thought she heard a hint of a sigh in Johnny's voice and changed the subject. "Anyway, I'm so glad you told me about his schedule. I'll be praying. Thanks for letting me know."

As they ended the call, she thought about what a great guy Johnny was. And he certainly seemed interested in seeing her again. She smiled, wondering why he continued to put up with her when she couldn't seem to see past Bobby Conrad. Debbie's thoughts drifted back to that day on the beach once again, and she could almost feel Johnny's hand in hers as they raced along the water's edge.

Maybe a picnic would be a nice idea, once this concert was behind them. Until then...she had work to do.

* * * * *

Johnny hung up the phone feeling defeated. He had called Debbie to cheer her up with birthday wishes, and instead he'd worried her with the news about Bobby's schedule.

What did it matter, anyway? Debbie Carmichael only had

eyes—and ears—for one person right now. And that person's name wasn't Johnny Hartmann. It was Bobby Conrad.

"Everything okay, Johnny?"

He turned as Jim came in the room. "Yes. I mean, I guess."

"Not the most convincing line I've heard. You'd better hone your acting skills if you want to get a job in this town. What's really up?"

He sighed. "Jim, how do you get a girl to notice you if she's only got eyes for someone else?"

"Ah." Jim gave him a fatherly look. "I see. This is about Frankie's daughter, then."

Johnny sighed. "Yes sir."

"Let me tell you something I learned early on, son," Jim said, slipping an arm over his shoulder. "If something's meant to happen, it's going to happen."

Johnny gazed at him, curiosity growing. Pretty interesting stuff, coming from a man who didn't claim a belief in the Lord.

"So, I shouldn't try to win her?"

"You're already winning her, Johnny. Don't spend much time fretting over the competition."

"Even if that competition is Bobby Conrad?"

"Ah." Jim grew silent. "I see your problem." He slapped him on the back. "Well, look on the bright side, son. Pretty soon you'll be as famous as Bobby and you'll have a whole gaggle of beauties fawning over you. What will it matter if one little blond slipped away?"

Thanks a lot. So even Jim didn't think he stood a chance with Bobby in the picture. A guy might as well give up early on rather than keep fighting, only to lose the war in the end.

Oh, but every time Johnny thought about Debbie's hand in his, he felt carefree, happy. When he remembered the sight of her long blond hair as she ran along the edge of the water, his breath caught in his throat. Did she have any idea what she'd done to him?

Obviously not. Debbie Carmichael wasn't the sort to toy with a guy's emotions. From what he could tell, anyway.

Johnny chided himself. *How could you give your heart to someone so quickly? Didn't you come to Los Angeles to pursue your dreams?* Yes, he had. And staying focused on the goal was key to achieving success. Falling for a girl—especially the wrong girl—would distract him, possibly keep him from thinking clearly.

"You sure you're okay, kid?" Jim gave him a curious look.

Johnny startled to attention. "Yes sir. I've just made a decision, that's all."

"Oh?"

"Yes." He nodded. "I'm going to focus on my career first and my love life second." *After the Lord, of course.*

"Well, I should hope so." Jim slapped him on the back again, this time nearly knocking the breath out of him. "So, get upstairs and practice that song. You've got a big show coming up, remember?"

"How could I forget?" The usual ripple of fear wriggled its way down his spine, and he found himself shaking in his boots. On August 10, just one week from tonight, he would stand in front of America and sing a song he'd written for a girl who couldn't see beyond Bobby Conrad to know that he existed.

Johnny headed upstairs, deep in thought. As much as he wanted to focus on his career, his thoughts kept gravitating back to Debbie.

Shake it off, Johnny.

He entered Toby's room and found the youngster on the bottom bunk playing some sort of game. Johnny stared down at him.

"What are you doing, Toby?"

The youngster shook a cup in his hand then dumped out five dice. "Playing Yahtzee."

"Yahtzee?" Johnny took a seat across from him. "What's that?"

"A new game. Don't you ever get out, Hartmann?"

"Guess not. But I love board games. We used to play them all the time back home. So, how is this game played?"

"Well, look here." Toby pointed at a piece of paper. "I need to get as many ones as I can. And as many twos. Like that."

"So, it's the luck of the roll, basically."

"Yeah. Kind of like becoming a star in Hollywood." Toby gave him a quick glance then turned his attention back to the game again, pointing to the bottom of the paper. "Anyway, down here, I need to get a straight, a three of a kind, a four of a kind, and a Yahtzee."

"What's a Yahtzee?"

"It's where all five dice are exactly the same number."

"What are the odds of that?" Johnny asked.

Toby rolled his eyes. "About the same as my dad letting me audition for a television show."

"What's that one?" Johnny pointed to a spot near the bottom of the paper.

"Oh, that one's called *chance*. It's for when you don't get a good roll."

"Hmm." Johnny paused to think about it. "Sounds like playing this game is exactly like trying to start a career in Hollywood." *Or winning the heart of a certain girl who only has eyes for someone else.*

As he took the cup in his hand and shook the dice, Johnny's thoughts remained fixed on Debbie. He willed himself to think about something else. Anything else. When he tipped the cup over, the five dice fell out.

"A straight!" Toby stared at him with wonder in his eyes. "One, two, three, four, five. How did you do that, Johnny?"

"No idea." Johnny shrugged.

Toby's carefree expression shifted as he stared at Johnny. "Some guys have all the luck, I guess."

Johnny's heart went out to him. "Just hang on, kiddo. One of these days you'll get to follow your heart. You just have a little growing up to do first."

"I guess."

For some reason, the words "follow your heart" forced Johnny's thoughts back to Debbie. He did his best to shake them, but couldn't seem to. The lyrics and melody to that song he'd written about her ran through his mind, forcing all of his attentions to her.

In that moment, he realized what he must do to empty his mind—and heart—of Debbie Carmichael. He'd rename the song. Sure, why not. "Dear Donna" would work, too. Or "Dear Darla." Who said the name had to be Debbie?

A sigh followed as he filled in the number on the Yahtzee form. Passing the cup back to Toby, he realized the truth. If he changed the name, he'd never be able to muster up the right emotion to croon the song as it was meant to be sung.

It was "Dear Debbie"…or it was nothing at all.

Chapter Ten

HEARTBREAK HOTEL

It's official, folks. The nationally syndicated American Bandstand *will be airing today, Monday, August 5. Dick Clark, of Philadelphia fame, will host the show, which will run daily, Monday through Friday. Parents, you might want to vacate the premises while the show is on. Chances are pretty good the volume is about to go up! Clark plans to feature songs by Jerry Lee Lewis, Billy Williams, the Chordettes, and many more. Talk about energy! I predict this will be a show viewers will talk about for years to come. Decades, even.*

The format of the show will be much the same as the local Philadelphia version. Music, dancing, and interviews. Clark will quiz the teens, asking their opinions of the songs being played. How they will respond…well, that's anyone's guess. No doubt, with lots of enthusiasm, if I know today's teens. Likely, they view musicians in a different light than their parents do.

Speaking of musicians…it sounds like this new show will be a real door opener for established singers and newcomers, alike. One can't help but wonder if Clark will play the songs from Bobby Conrad's upcoming film, Oh, My Romeo! *Probably. And why not? With a voice like Bobby's, the teenage girls are sure to swoon.*

Hey, speaking of swooning, rumor has it, there's a new singer in town with a voice that's wooing the women, a kid out of Kansas named

Hartmann. Johnny Hartmann. We hear he's going to be debuting on next Saturday night's Talent Scouts. *Who knows, maybe he'll end up on* American Bandstand, *too. If our sources can be believed, Bobby Conrad plans to take young Hartmann under his wing and show him the ropes. Not a bad mentor, I'd say. Lucky kid, this Hartmann. Of course, Bobby Conrad doesn't have much time these days for socializing. Filming for his new movie begins shortly and it will be "Bye-Bye Bobby!" for six weeks. Sorry girls...but don't fret. He'll be back on the scene. Eventually.*

— *Reporting for* Hollywood Heartthrob *magazine, "Jukebox Jive" columnist, Hepcat Harry*

* * * * *

On Monday afternoon, just after the televised debut of *American Bandstand*, Debbie's father asked to speak with her downstairs in the soda shop. She left Becky Ann and the others upstairs, laughing and talking about the new show. Looked like they had plenty to talk about.

Debbie practically skipped down the stairs. When she reached the restaurant, the familiar refrain of Johnny Ray's song "Cry" sang out from the jukebox. Funny. The lyrics didn't match her mood at all.

She found her father in the kitchen, flipping burgers. When he saw her, a smile lit his face. "Let me finish this, Sunshine. Then we'll talk."

"Sure." She reached for a glass and filled it with ice and soda from the dispenser then took a seat on one of the barstools.

Minutes later, Pop joined her. "So, how was the show?"

"Amazing." She lit into a discussion about how all the girls had fallen head-over-heels for Dick Clark, and before long, a grin spread across her father's face.

"Well, I'm glad you enjoyed it, even if it means there's another heartthrob I'm going to have to hear about."

Debbie chuckled. "You've got that right. Martha Lou has already written him a letter. But seriously, thanks for giving us the afternoon off, Pop. Glad Junior was willing to work extra-hard to make it possible."

"Your brother's a good guy," her father said.

Debbie nodded. An awkward pause rose up between them, and a niggling feeling of fear kicked in as Pop's smile shifted to something... well, something else. She couldn't really make it out. After a few seconds, Debbie couldn't stand it anymore. "Is everything okay?" she asked.

"I don't know how to tell you this, Sunshine." Wrinkles formed in Pop's brow. "You've worked so hard, and all."

Fear trickled over her as she tried to anticipate what he might say. "Tell me...what?"

He gave her what could only be described as a sympathetic look. "Honey, I got a call from Jim Jangles last night."

Debbie felt her stomach begin to churn.

"Bobby's not going to be able to do the fundraiser after all," Pop explained. "His new movie is going to begin filming the week of the seventeenth and he's got to be there."

"W–what?" Debbie shook her head, praying she was dreaming. For a minute, the room appeared to be spinning. Perhaps she was having one of those out-of-body experiences she'd heard about in those science fiction movies that had become so popular.

She closed her eyes and shook her head, hoping the room would stand aright again once her eyes popped open. She opened them and stared into the concerned face of her father.

"You okay, honey?" he asked. "Taking the news kind of hard, I see."

Debbie shook her head. "Start over, Pop. Please."

He repeated the story, adding details about Bobby's upcoming schedule conflicts. Debbie listened, but none of this was sinking in. Surely there had to be some mistake.

"I'm so sorry about all of this, Debbie," her father said. "But Bobby just isn't going to make it."

So, Johnny had been right all along. She'd doubted his speculations, but they'd been accurate. "No. That can't be right. You've misunderstood Jim, Pop. He was probably just saying that Bobby would be late or something. He wouldn't cancel. Not at this late date."

"It's true, honey." Her father reached over and gave her a hug. "I've been dreading telling you, to be honest. I knew it would crush you."

"Crush me?" Debbie slid off the barstool and paced the soda shop. "It's devastating, Pop. Jim Jangles gave his word that Bobby would be here. He promised." She tried to force back the tears as she pleaded her case. "Can't we hold him to that? Didn't you two sign something? A contract? Something? Anything?"

"Of course not. We're friends. Why would we let a piece of paper come between friends? And how can I hold it against him that his client has a great opportunity to do something big? Something he's been hoping and praying for? This can't be helped, honey."

The song on the jukebox came to an end, and seconds later, "Teenage Crush" kicked in, Tommy Sand's familiar voice now filling the soda shop, providing an ironic backdrop.

"Are you sure? Are you absolutely, positively sure?" Hopefully, if she argued long enough, she could convince him otherwise. Jim Jangles had given his word. Bobby was coming. Everyone in Laguna Beach knew about it. Her mother's bridge club. Pop's golfing buddies.

Junior's basketball team. And every teen within a hundred miles. In fact, the cheerleaders from Laguna Beach High were planning to make an appearance in uniform to cheer Bobby on. Why, even the mayor and city council members had agreed to support the endeavor, officially naming August 17 *Bobby Conrad Day.*

"Sunshine, it's true. Jim was very apologetic. He said this movie is a once-in-a-lifetime thing for Bobby, and they just can't pass it up. And remember, we weren't paying him to come. He was doing it out of the goodness of his heart."

Debbie swallowed hard at those words. In the furthest reaches of her imagination she couldn't picture Bobby Conrad doing something to hurt others. Surely he didn't make this decision. If he had any idea just how badly the soda shop needed to pay off that mortgage, he would be here in a heartbeat.

Heartbeat. She blinked away tears, thinking about her father's heart condition. If they canceled the concert, the mortgage wouldn't get paid off. If the mortgage didn't get paid off, Pop would have to go on working when he should be resting. And Mom would be exhausted all the time. She snapped back to attention as her father continued speaking.

"This movie deal is the biggest thing that's happened in Bobby's career, according to Jim."

"I'm sure it is," she countered, "but this fundraiser is the biggest thing to happen to Sweet Sal's." She wanted to add, "and to the girls of Laguna Beach," but didn't.

"Sorry, honey," her father said. "We did our best. That's all anyone can ask of us, right?"

She shook her head, unwilling to give up. "Pop, we're only talking one Saturday here. And Bobby committed to be here. Maybe they won't be filming on that particular Saturday."

"I'm afraid so," he said. "And to make things even more interesting, they'll be filming in Huntington Beach."

"Well, that's perfect, then." A new possibility took hold. "He can spend the day with us then film afterwards. Or vice-versa." Her determination increased with each breath. Debbie stood and began to pace the room again. "We can make this work, Pop. We'll schedule the concert to work with the filming of the movie."

"It's too much to expect," her father said. "I know you've got to be disappointed, but we can't expect him to be two places at once."

She shook her head. "I'm not the only one who's going to be disappointed. We've already put posters all over town. People are going to show up that day expecting Bobby Conrad. And we've got nothing to give them."

"Well, of course we do." Her father's face brightened. "We've got the best possible alternative, actually. Did I leave out that part?"

"What do you mean?" She took a seat on the barstool, suddenly hopeful.

"I can't believe I didn't say this earlier to put your mind at ease. Jim suggested we use Johnny Hartmann in Bobby's place. He said the kid's got a great singing voice and has some wonderful original tunes."

"Johnny Hartmann?" She thought of that moment on the beach when Johnny had taken her hand. In that moment, she felt the same spark, the same hopeful possibilities rise to the surface. Just as quickly, they faded. As much as she might like Johnny—and she did—the girls of Laguna Beach were counting on someone else. They would boo him off the stage. Debbie sighed. "He's a great guy, but no one even knows who he is. Why would people want to see him?"

"He's going to be on *Talent Scouts* this coming Saturday," her father said. "Jim seems to think he'll do really well. It will be a door opener for him. Then, if Johnny follows on the heels of that performance with a great concert here, it will help boost his career."

"But that's not what this is about," she said. "We're supposed to be bringing in someone famous. Someone with a recognizable name. Even if Johnny does really, really well, he still won't be a household name. He's not a star, like Bobby is. Maybe he never will be." She regretted those last words but couldn't take them back now.

Debbie drew in a deep breath, trying to gather her wits. How could she make her father understand that without Bobby, this would never work? In the middle of her ponderings, her mother walked up.

"What have I missed?" her mother asked. "You two are about as cheerful as a funeral procession."

Debbie filled her in with a three-word explanation: "Bobby can't come" and then added, "He can't sing at the fundraiser, I mean."

Her mother's mouth rounded into an O.

"This is just the most tragic thing that's ever happened to me." Debbie shook her head, suddenly overcome with emotion. Tears filled her eyes and she swiped them away.

Her father shook his head. "You've never been the drama queen in this family, Debbie. Let's leave that role to Becky Ann. Have a little faith. This is all going to work out."

"Work out?" Debbie sighed as she contemplated her options. Really, there were none. Not without Bobby. If he didn't show, the outcry from the girls in the community would be awful.

"What are you thinking, Debbie?" her mother asked.

She looked up. "I'm thinking about that movie *Roman Holiday*. Do you remember it?"

Her mother shrugged. "Of course. Who could forget it?"

"Remember how Audrey Hepburn's character—Princess Ann—ran away from her life, just for a night?"

"Sure." Her mother nodded. "Are you saying that you want to run away?"

Debbie sighed. "They're going to lynch me."

"Who?" Her mother asked. "Who's going to lynch you?"

"The teen girls of Laguna Beach and all of the neighboring cities. Perhaps every girl in Orange County."

"C'mon now, honey," her father said. "They're not going to lynch you."

Debbie felt her heart rise to her throat. "Yes, they are. I promised them Bobby Conrad. Everyone in town thinks he's coming. We've done this big build-up, and now…" She groaned. "Now they're getting a substitute no one's even heard of."

"Substitute?" Her mother looked confused.

"Johnny Hartmann," Pop explained.

"Oh!" Mom clasped her hands together and smiled. "Wonderful idea! Just the ticket."

"But no one's heard of him, Mom." Debbie shook her head. "Honestly, I don't know what we're going to do."

"For one thing, you need to stop fretting," her mother said. "The show will go on, honey. You know that. Johnny will do a great job. Besides, a handful of girls will recognize his name. He got a little write-up in *Hollywood Heartthrob* this week."

"You read *Hollywood Heartthrob*?" Pop looked stunned at this news.

Debbie's mom blushed. "Well, I, um…if I happen to see it lying around. It's research."

"Research?" He didn't look convinced.

"Well, sure." She nodded. "I've got to stay on top of who's popular and who's not, so we know which photos to keep on the walls."

"I see."

She gave him a little wink.

He laughed and kissed her on the forehead. "Don't be embarrassed, honey. I think it's cute."

Debbie interjected her thoughts. "That's just it, Mom. The kids who come in the shop *know* who's in and who's out. They know what they want. . .and they *want* Bobby. I promised them Bobby. Now I'm going to look like a liar."

"Folks who know you will know better," her mother said. "And sure, the kids are bound to be disappointed, but we'll still have the event. People will still come."

"I was counting on a large crowd," Debbie argued. "Bobby was such a great draw. But Johnny…" She shook her head.

"I wouldn't be so quick to judge," her mother said. "He's going to be on *Talent Scouts*, remember."

"This coming Saturday night," her father repeated.

"Yes. And I'm sure he'll be really good, too. But that won't fix anything. There's not enough time in one week to turn him into a star. It's impossible."

"He just needs a chance, Debbie. We all have to start somewhere," her father said. "That show could be his springboard, and I can't help but think the concert here at Sweet Sal's will help launch his career."

"But this wasn't about launching anyone's career," Debbie said again. "It was about saving the soda shop."

"It's a good thing we can't see into the future. I'm not sure we'd want to know what's out there. But we can trust God with it...one day at a time."

"But, the posters..."

"Jim Jangles offered to cover the cost of having them remade," Pop explained. "He feels really bad about what's happened." Her father paused. "But on the other hand, he's really excited that Johnny is singing. I wish you could have heard him on the phone."

"I guess."

The song on the jukebox switched again. Pat Boone's silky voice rang out, the words to "Ain't That a Shame" hovering overhead. Debbie's mom excused herself to wait on some customers, but Debbie could tell Pop wasn't done with the conversation yet.

He took a seat and she could read the exhaustion in his eyes. "Honey, you watch the show *Father Knows Best*, right?"

"Sure." She nodded.

"It's a great television show, but the concept is even better."

"What do you mean?"

"Father Knows Best." He paused. "Here's the truth, plain and simple. Your Father—the one who created you and knows everything about you—really does know best. So don't get upset if it looks like things aren't going to work out according to your plan. Could be He has a plan of his own. He knows best, Debbie. So you can trust Him."

"I can trust Him." Drawing in a deep breath, she repeated the words, this time as a whisper. "I can trust Him."

"And there's one more thing." He reached to squeeze her hand.

"Something I've been wanting to talk to all of you girls about. Something has been troubling me lately."

"What do you mean, Pop? Something we've done?" Debbie looked at her father with that little-girl-caught-with-her-hand-in-the-cookie-jar feeling.

The expression in his eyes spoke concern, but his words were loving. "Well, let me ask you something. I hear you girls using the word 'heartthrob' all the time."

Debbie shrugged. "Sure."

"What, exactly, is your definition of a heartthrob?"

She paused to think before responding. "Someone—or something—that you pine after, I guess."

"The object of one's affections?"

"I guess you could say that." Debbie nodded.

"Right. And most heartthrobs have a following, wouldn't you say?"

"Sure." She couldn't figure out where Pop was going with this.

"I just want to challenge you to think about this, Sunshine, and it's not an accusation of any kind. Just pray about it. You know the Ten Commandments. You've had them memorized since you were a kid."

"Of course, Pop." She gazed at him, still wondering where this was going.

"You know the one about not having idols."

A sinking feeling came over her. "Y–yes sir."

"Pastor David preached on this very thing last week, in fact."

"Y–yes."

Pop's brow wrinkled in concern. "Just think about it, Debbie. That's all. Seems to me that every rising star out of Hollywood is an idol, of sorts. Someone who's revered and touted as the latest, greatest thing. Someone the people clamor after…follow after."

She released a breath as a wave of guilt passed over her. "I suppose."

"It's fine to be drawn to someone because of his or her talent," he said. "And I guess it's only natural that we're captivated by things of beauty."

"Bobby Conrad *is* a thing of beauty, for sure." Debbie sighed. "No doubt about that."

A group of teens entered and waited to be seated, but Becky Ann came bounding down the stairs at that same moment and took charge, leading them to a booth.

Pop continued talking, seemingly oblivious to the tears forming in Debbie's eyes. "Yes, but I would challenge you to pray about how much time and attention you give to people of fame. Are you idolizing them?"

"Pop, I…well, I did give all of this some thought during that sermon, but I'm not sure having Bobby come do a fundraiser is really idolizing him. You know?"

"I'm not trying to make you feel guilty, honey. I'm really not. We've all done it to one extent or another. But before you go chasing after the most popular or most famous, check your heart, okay? Make sure the only one you're chasing after—and I truly mean this—is the One who created that person with all of the talent and ability."

She paused before whispering, "I understand."

Her father rose and gave her a hug. After taking a couple of steps toward the kitchen he turned back to face her. "Oh, and one more thing I forgot to mention, honey. Even the least talented, least lovely person is precious to God. The very ones whose photographs will never end up hanging on our wall. And, interestingly enough, those are the ones that Jesus sought out to pray for. To care for. He wasn't interested in chasing after the latest, greatest thing. He went to the ones who felt they were the least."

Debbie felt the sting of tears. Had she really been fawning over Bobby Conrad because of his looks? His talent? Shame washed over her. Pop was right. God didn't play favorites with His kids. Did it really break His heart to think that she and the other girls did? "It's easy to get caught up in all of the star-gazing," she said at last. "But you're right, Pop. We've been chasing after the wrong thing. At least…I have."

Debbie pondered her father's words as she waited on customers that afternoon. Looking at all of the autographed photos on the walls, she felt a little queasy. How many times—and in how many ways—had she elevated people to star-like status because they were famous? She had never thought about that before the pastor's sermon. Now she couldn't help but wonder if putting folks on a pedestal broke the Lord's heart. If He saw everyone in the same light—talented or not, popular or not—shouldn't she do the same?

A lingering sigh escaped as Debbie considered that question. It looked like God had a little work to do in her heart. And surely He had an answer to the mortgage problem. Maybe, just maybe, that answer didn't include Bobby Conrad.

Even if he was the greatest thing since sliced bread.

* * * * *

Late Monday night, Johnny paced the living room, trying to formulate words. "But, Jim…" He couldn't seem to finish the sentence.

"That's your fourth 'But Jim.'" Jim flashed a comforting smile. "Cat got your tongue, kid?"

Johnny shook his head. "No sir. I'm just stunned. You really want me to take Bobby's place at the fundraiser?"

"Sure, it's the only logical move."

"No one knows who I am."

"Yet." Jim's expression spoke of confidence. "But that's because you haven't won *Talent Scouts* yet. Once that's behind you, every girl in California will be clamoring to see you."

Funny. He didn't want every girl in California. He only wanted one girl, and she seemed to look right through him.

On the other hand, maybe she would change her tune once she heard him sing. Maybe that would do the trick.

Jim continued talking about his plan of action, how he hoped to make Johnny a star before the fundraiser. A staged appearance at Grauman's Chinese Theatre tomorrow afternoon. Photo ops for reporters immediately following. An impromptu singing gig at a local restaurant on Wednesday evening.

Johnny released a slow sigh, wondering how in the world he'd wandered so far from Topeka. In Kansas, everything was logical. Made sense. In Hollywood, the earth beneath his feet seemed to be moving at every turn. He could hardly stand for falling. His thoughts reverted to that line in *The Wizard of Oz*: "There's no place like home."

A sane person would turn and run. He wouldn't risk everything to look like a fool in front of millions of people. He wouldn't lay it all out there for the world—and Debbie Carmichael—to see.

On the other hand, he'd never been accused of being sane. No, he'd always been a little different. And if there was ever a place where "different" was okay, it was Hollywood, California.

Chapter Eleven

A STAR IS BORN

Hollywood Molly here, ready for a little Hollywood Kiss 'n' Tell. I've got the scoop on who's smooching who, and who's saying 'Sayonara.' Puckered lips and swan songs...I specialize in both. The breakups and make-ups have been delicious this week, but we've also learned that sometimes rumors are just that...rumors.

My confidential source tells me that Bobby Conrad is definitely not involved with Brenda Valentine, even though she has just been named as his co-star in the upcoming Shakespeare musical. She might be the Juliet to his Romeo, but that's just onscreen, folks. In the real world, she's dating a waiter from Mel's, and Bobby remains unattached. No doubt, teen girls across America will faint dead away at this revelation. As speculated by this reporter in a previous column, the staged appearances by Conrad and Valentine were just that...staged. Probably to get folks hyped about their upcoming movie.

If you want to know Bobby's real first love, you might have to take a seat next to him in the church pew to get the answer. When asked this simple question, his response was rather startling—something about loving the Lord with all of his heart, soul, mind, and strength. Turns out the Almighty gets top billing. Pretty stiff competition, girls.

Speaking of competition, this reporter is looking forward to the debut of Bobby's new sidekick, Johnny Hartmann, on Talent Scouts *this* coming Saturday night. His agent, Jim Jangles—of West Coast Talent— sent this reporter a headshot of Johnny. Yummy doesn't begin to describe it. Girls are sure to fill the studio audience at this weekend's show, and the Clap-o-Meter will reflect their enthusiasm. We can only hope this hunk-of-handsomeness can sing.

On the other hand, who cares? If he's as cute in person as he is in that headshot, we can always turn down the volume and just stare at him.

— Reporting for Hollywood Heartthrob magazine, "Star Chasers" columnist, Hollywood Molly

* * * * *

On Wednesday morning, Debbie stayed in bed extra long. She wrestled with the sheets and tried to pray about the benefit situation. In the two days since Pop had given her the news, she hadn't told a soul. She'd been operating under the assumption that something would change. But Monday had rolled to Tuesday, and now Wednesday, and still no change. Bobby Conrad would not be singing at Sweet Sal's on August 17…and there was nothing she could do about it.

Oh, she'd already stormed heaven's gates, pleading with the Almighty. He'd remained strangely silent, even after Debbie's heart-breaking pleas. And her reminder that this was all for Pop didn't seem to sway the Lord, either. Looked like He had something else up His sleeve here, and she'd better jump back into gear, getting ready for whatever it happened to be.

After showering and getting dressed, Debbie put on her bravest smile and headed downstairs to face Laguna Beach's teens head-on. Today she would tell them. And they would all get through this…somehow.

As she entered the soda shop, Debbie saw her brother at the juke-box. He turned and grinned as "Why Do Fools Fall in Love?" came on.

"Oh, hey." He blushed. "I, um, well, this song came on by accident."

Sure it did.

She gave him a hug, realizing he must be thinking of Martha Lou… who was probably thinking of Bobby Conrad. Or Johnny. Or Dick Clark. Debbie sighed. "In case I haven't said it lately, I think you're the greatest brother ever."

"Oh?" He gave her a suspicious look. "What's up? You need to borrow money?"

"No, goofy." She slugged him in the arm. "Just trying to be nice." After a pause, she added, "And one of these days, Martha Lou's going to see what's been in front of her all along. She just has to get the stardust out of her eyes."

Junior shrugged. "If you say so."

"Hey, speaking of Martha…" Debbie paused as she heard Martha Lou's voice ring out from the counter. "I need to talk to her. And the others. Pray for me, Junior. It's time to let them know."

"About Bobby?" he asked.

"I've put it off long enough. Today's the day." She drew in a deep breath, and—like David facing the mighty Goliath—took slow, calculated steps across the soda shop to do business with the giant. Well, the giant that was Laguna Beach's teen girls.

"Debbie, where are the posters with Bobby's picture?" Martha Lou asked as she drew near. "I wanted to take some up to the ballpark, but I can't find any."

"There's a reason for that." Debbie pulled Martha Lou aside. "We need to talk." She explained in detail the news she'd received on

Monday. As the story took its inevitable turn for the worse, Martha Lou paled. She looked for a moment like she might cry.

"I'm sorry," the tearful teen said at last. "My ears must be playing tricks on me. I thought I heard you say Bobby Conrad isn't coming after all."

"What? Bobby's not coming?" Cassie Jenkins approached, eyes wide. "Of course he is. We told everyone."

The jingling of the bell above the door alerted Debbie to the fact that someone had entered the shop. She turned and sighed as she saw Ginny Anderson standing there with her parents. Before she knew what had hit her, Debbie saw Martha Lou approach Ginny to share the awful news.

"What's this?" Ginny's father turned to face Debbie. "The fund-raiser has fallen through?" His brow wrinkled.

"Oh, no, Mr. Anderson," she said. "Not at all. We've run into a little glitch with our entertainment, but it's all worked out. We've got an up-and-coming star performing. A boy that's going to knock everyone's socks off." *I hope.* "The girls are going to love him." *I pray.*

The dour-faced banker didn't look convinced. He muttered something under his breath about the mortgage then asked to be seated. Debbie took care of him as quickly as possible, hoping to put his mind at ease. Oh, if only she could put her own mind at ease, then convincing others wouldn't be such a challenge.

The voices of several teen girls rose to a dangerous level as they discussed—a little too loudly—Bobby's absence from the concert. On and on they went, each one growing a bit more frustrated than the last. Debbie did her best to keep working…to ignore them, but they were making it difficult.

Martha Lou and a couple of the other girls left abruptly. Though she knew they were off to share the bad news with others, Debbie still breathed a sigh of relief. By lunchtime, half the girls in Laguna Beach would know that Johnny was coming in Bobby's place.

Oh, well. Just fewer people she'd have to tell herself.

Debbie headed to the cash register where she found her mother counting out change for Clifford. While she waited, Ginny Anderson came up to the counter. She pulled Debbie aside.

"Debbie, I'm so sorry this happened. I want you to know that I feel really bad for you." She paused, her gaze shifting to the ground. "I know I always make fun of the girls for being so gaga over Bobby, but I also know how much you were depending on him coming. This has to be hard."

"It is." Debbie fought back tears. "Harder than you know." She leaned over to whisper the next words. "I was counting on this fund-raiser to bring in enough money to actually pay off the mortgage. I'm so worried about Pop."

"I'm so sorry." Ginny's eyes reflected genuine concern. "And I'm sorry about my dad. I don't know why he is the way he is."

"He's running a business," Debbie said. "You can't blame a person for wanting his business to succeed. If all of his customers stopped paying, the bank would go under."

"The bank's not going under." Ginny rolled her eyes then shot a glance in her father's direction. "Are you kidding me? It's doing great. He could extend a little mercy. Wouldn't hurt more than a pinch. But he's just stubborn. He likes things the way he likes them." She sighed.

Debbie rested her hand on Ginny's arm. "I'm sure God has an answer for this problem. He's a big God."

"Still…" Tears welled up in Ginny's eyes. "I wish my dad was different. It's so hard living with someone who treats people so…" Her words drifted off.

Debbie shrugged, unable to relate to Ginny's situation. After all, her pop had never been anything but kind and gracious—to everyone.

"I wish my dad would come to church with Mom and me," Ginny added. "I've been praying about that for years, but he's not interested. I think he would be a completely different person if he, well, if he came to know the Lord like we know Him. It's so much easier to extend mercy once you've received it."

"Kind of like you're doing now?" Debbie asked.

Ginny gave her an inquisitive look. "What do you mean?"

"You're going out of your way to console me on a day when I've let you—and all of the others—down. You're such a good friend."

"No, you're the one who's a good friend, Debbie. You keep me in the circle, even though I'm a little different from the younger girls."

"Different?"

"Well, not quite as giddy. And a little on the quiet side."

"Trust me, with all the chatter from the others, I could use a little quiet every now and again." Debbie grinned. "And I think they get a little silly sometimes."

"True." Ginny nodded. "They're dreamers, all right. You would think Bobby Conrad was going to sweep in here on a white horse and carry them off into the sunset." She giggled. "Can you imagine?"

Ouch.

Ginny headed back to the table to eat with her parents. When "First Kiss" came on the jukebox, she shot a glance at Debbie, who shrugged.

No point in getting worked up about things. No, she'd better release her problems into the Lord's capable hands.

That's exactly what she determined to do all morning long. Long after Ginny left, Debbie contemplated her words: *It's not like Bobby Conrad was going to sweep in here on a white horse and carry them off into the sunset.*

As much as she hated to admit it, Debbie had been just as giddy as Becky Ann and Martha Lou over Bobby's arrival. Oh, she hadn't let it show to others, but in her heart she really had been hoping he would sweep in on his white horse and save the day.

Even as the words flitted through her mind, she was reminded of her chat with Pop. The one about idols. What would he say in response to all of this? Surely he would remind her that the only one worthy to be worshiped was the Lord. Only He could fix this situation.

For the first time all day, Debbie actually felt a glimmer of hope. Still, she needed to get alone for a while to think. She needed time and space to pray. After that, maybe she could put together some sort of plan.

About ten minutes after twelve, she approached her mother at one of the booths. "Can I take my lunch break, Mom?"

"Sure, honey. Going upstairs?"

Debbie shook her head. "I'm tempted to go up and take a nap, but I need a little away time."

Mom gave her a curious look. "Away?"

"The cliffs." She gestured toward the ocean. "I like to go to the pocket beach just beyond the cliffs. It's private. I, well, I pray better when I'm there."

Her mother smiled. "You are your mother's daughter, that's for sure. I know just the spot you're talking about. Spent a lot of time there when I was your age."

Debbie smiled. "Do you think you can do without me for an hour?"

"I feel sure we can handle that. Let me fix you a sandwich to take with you. Ham and cheese?"

"Mm-hmm." Debbie nodded, but didn't really have food on her mind. She wanted to get out of here—away from the crowd of teens who'd spent the morning peppering her with questions about the concert. Getting away—alone—would do the trick.

Minutes later, with a wrapped sandwich in hand, she headed outside. No sooner had she crossed the street and stepped onto the sand than she found her tensions begin to release. She could breathe again. Think clearly. Yes, away from the crowd, she could finally gather her thoughts. Deal with her doubts and fears. And maybe, once gathered, she could wrap them in a tight little bundle—and toss them out to sea.

* * * * *

Johnny entered the soda shop, pausing at the door to drink in the aroma. "What is that wonderful smell?"

From the opening into the kitchen, Mr. Carmichael's happy-go-lucky voice rang out. "Burgers?"

"Mm-hmm." Johnny drew in a deep breath. "And onion rings. And…" He paused, trying to place it. "Bacon?"

"You've got it." Mr. Carmichael smiled. "Just plated a bacon cheese-burger. Good nose, kid."

"Thanks. Smells great."

Debbie's mom stepped up to the counter and hit the little silver bell to let Junior know he had an order up. Johnny gave her a nod. "How are you?" he asked.

"Fine and dandy. What brings you down this way?"

"Jim sent me with new posters." Johnny held up one with a large photo of him posing with his guitar.

Mrs. Carmichael let out a whistle. "Well, look at that. You really are a pro, aren't you?"

He felt a wave of embarrassment wash over him. "Don't know that I'd say that, exactly. But I'm making headway."

"No kidding. Say, isn't this the week that you're going to be on *Talent Scouts*?"

"Yes, this coming Saturday night. Jim's been running me ragged all week, doing promo gigs." He couldn't seem to get anything else out past the sudden lump in his throat. He forced a smile and spoke around the lump. "I...I'm excited."

"A little nervous, too, I'd guess," she said.

He nodded. "Very."

"My knees would be knocking, for sure. But then again, I'm not a singer. I hear you're really good. Jim sure sings your praises." She chuckled. "Sings your praises. That's funny. I don't think Jim Jangles sings a note."

"No, he doesn't," Johnny concurred. "And as for all of those praises he's been sharing...well, he's probably exaggerating. He is my agent, after all."

"I hope he's not too far off-base," she said with a sympathetic look. "Because the girls of Laguna Beach are going to come out in force to hear you sing on the seventeenth."

He tried not to let his embarrassment show. A new song began to play on the jukebox, and Johnny paused as the familiar introduction to Vic Damone's song, "On the Street Where You Live," came on. It reminded him of Debbie. Looking around, he tried to figure out why he hadn't seen her yet. Was she sick, perhaps?

Becky Ann approached with a handful of menus. "Hey, Johnny. What's up?"

"Just came to deliver some new posters."

She sighed. "Yeah, we just found out this morning that Bobby's not coming. The girls are all devastated."

"Sorry about that," he said. "But I'm going to give it my best shot. If I make it through this *Talent Scouts* thing."

"Oh, I forgot about that," Becky Ann said. "Are you nervous?"

A wave of nausea hit him. "Mm-hmm. Let's don't talk about it."

"Don't talk about it?" Becky Ann laughed. "Are you kidding? Of course we're going to talk about it." A look of excitement came over her. "Oh, I have the best idea. Why don't we go to the taping of the show? We could be part of the studio audience."

"Really?" Mrs. Carmichael looked intrigued by this idea. "Oh, I think that would be a lot of fun. The audience decides who wins, right?"

Becky Ann clasped her hands together at her chest. "Oh, then we should bring everyone we know. If Johnny wins, then the people really will want to come to the fundraiser to hear him sing."

"First he has to win." Mrs. Carmichael gave him a pat on the back. "But I have a feeling he's a shoo-in."

All of this flattery was really starting to get to Johnny. He was more than ready to change the subject. "Where's Debbie?" he asked, looking around.

"She's in a mood." Becky Ann rolled her eyes.

"A mood?" He wasn't sure what to make of that comment.

"Yes, she's upset because Bobby can't come." Becky Ann sighed. "We're all upset."

"Ah. I see." He paused a moment. "Do you mind if I ask where she is?"

"Same place you'll find her every time she gets upset. Walking at the beach."

"Any particular spot?"

"Beyond the cliffs at the pocket beach. When you cross the highway, walk out to the edge of the water and go left. That's south. You won't have to go very far to find the cliffs. She likes to hide away in there and talk to God when she's upset."

"Sounds like a scripture," Johnny said.

"Oh?" Becky Ann looked confused.

"You know that one, about God hiding us away in the cleft of the rock," Johnny said. "I think it's from Psalms. It's a scripture about getting away from things. Finding a quiet place to get alone with the Lord."

"Well, that's what she's doing," Becky Ann said. "Only, let me warn you, she's not in a good mood. I'm afraid if you go there…" She paused.

"What?"

"She's really upset about not getting to meet Bobby."

"Ah. Guess I'll take my chances." As Johnny left the restaurant, the afternoon sunlight beamed down, warming him from the outside in. He squinted, looking toward the beach. Somewhere over there Debbie had hidden herself away from the crowds. Would she mind if he interrupted her private time? Would she send him packing because his name wasn't Bobby Conrad?

He approached Coastal Highway and ran across the road. What was it Becky Ann had said, again? Ah yes. Turn left. South. Keep walking until he got to the cliffs.

When he reached the beach, Johnny pulled off his shoes and wriggled his toes in the warm white grains of sand. He was reminded of that day when he'd stopped to build a sand castle. No doubt, it had been carried away by the waves by now. Just like any hopes of winning Debbie's heart.

Was that what he'd been trying to do?

Instead of walking, Johnny picked up speed and began to run. His heart raced nearly as fast as his feet. What would he say when he finally saw Debbie? Surely she realized he felt drawn to her. He'd sensed the same feelings from her, as well. Or had he just imagined it? Was she just treating him nicely because of his ties to Jim Jangles—and to Bobby Conrad?

Johnny slowed his stride as the idea settled in. He hated to admit it, but how could he deny the possibility?

Up ahead Johnny saw the outline of the cliffs against the backdrop of the blue sky. He kept walking until they were in full view. From here, waves pounding the cliffs sent off a spray more than a dozen feet high. And the ocean had an unfamiliar sense of foreboding.

He looked around but didn't see Debbie.

"Hmm." She must be on the side facing the water.

Johnny glanced down at his bare feet, trying to figure out how to maneuver the rocky cliffs. Looked like the shoes were going to have to go back on. After putting them on, he took his first slippery step, then his second. About halfway to his destination, he slipped, nearly falling into the water below. Johnny breathed a prayer and asked God to help him make it to Debbie, safe and sound.

Rounding the cliff, he finally saw her. She sat alone on a private sandy beach, secluded from everyone and everything. Here, the pounding of the waves subsided. They lapped the sand in a quieter way. No more the roar of the water. No more spray. In this peaceful place, the water seemed more friend than foe.

Would Debbie seem more friend than foe? Only one way to know.

"Debbie." He called out her name as he moved in her direction. She looked up, her red-rimmed eyes widening in surprise as she saw him.

"Johnny? What are you doing here?"

He drew nearer, stopping as he realized she'd been crying.

"I…well, I was worried about you."

Silence greeted him. She stood, brushing sand from her skirt. "I…I'm fine. Really."

"No you're not." He reached for her hand. Thankfully, she didn't pull away. He gazed into her eyes. "This thing about Bobby has really upset you."

"I just…" She stopped. "I feel like a fool, if you want the truth. I made such a big deal out of this. And we promised so many people that he would be here. I got everyone's hopes up, and now they've been dashed."

"It's a big problem," Johnny whispered. "But we serve a big God."

Debbie gazed out at the ocean. "Whenever I come here, it's so easy to see just how big He is. How big His plans are. No wonder He doesn't ask me for my opinion about things."

"He cares what you think, though," Johnny said. "He really does. And what hurts you, hurts Him."

She released another sigh. "I hardly think the Lord is in heaven right now thinking about a rock-and-roll concert at a soda shop in Laguna Beach. He's got far more important things to take care of. Like the Cold War, for instance."

"True, but He does care what happens to Sweet Sal's, Debbie. He wants to see your dad healed and whole and able to rest. So, maybe He is in heaven right now thinking about a rock-and-roll concert at a soda shop in Laguna Beach. And surely He's got this all figured out, even the parts we can't see yet. You know?"

He gazed into her eyes.

She glanced down at their hands. In that moment, he almost let go. Almost released his hold on her.

Oh, but he didn't want to release his hold on her. Why would he have braved the cliffs only to let go of her hand?

No, if he risked his life, he might as well risk his heart.

* * * * *

Debbie glanced down at her hand, still gently cradled in Johnny's. Talk about a perfect fit. But maybe he just felt sorry for her. He'd seen her tears.

His gorgeous eyes gazed into hers, startling her with their tenderness. And with the wind blowing in his hair like that, he looked like he was ready for a close-up shot. She suddenly forgot what they'd been talking about.

The breeze off the water caught a loose piece of Debbie's hair and whipped it across her face. Before she could push it away, she felt the touch of Johnny's hand against her cheek. With the tip of his finger, he brushed the loose strands out of her eyes.

After a few seconds, she stopped trying to make sense of her thoughts and simply gazed at him. His hand never moved from her cheek. As Johnny narrowed the gap between them, Debbie's heart began to dance in anticipation. She realized she actually enjoyed being this close to him. More than she cared to admit. She could read the sweetness in his eyes and suddenly felt like a fool for going on and on about Bobby.

Johnny's breath grew warm against her face, though he didn't say a word. He didn't have to. Unspoken messages traveled back and forth between them. The waves crashed off in the distance, the perfect backdrop for this unexpected but lovely moment. Debbie closed her eyes as Johnny traced her cheek with his index finger. Her heart now pounded in her ears, and she could barely think straight.

What had started as a tear-filled afternoon had magically transformed into a scene from a movie, one she happened to be living out...for real.

For a moment, they stood in silence. Then she dared to open her eyes. When she did, she could clearly read the message Johnny was sending with his smile. Debbie gently reached up to rest her hand against his, and before she knew it, he'd swept her into his arms. Her heart pounded in steady beats, and her eyes fluttered closed once more.

Debbie melted like a chocolate bar in the sun as Johnny's lips met hers. His kiss was intense, yet gentle at the same time—if such a thing were possible. It certainly topped every kiss she'd ever witnessed on the silver screen. She was lost in the wonder of the moment, enjoying its sweetness.

After a few seconds, Johnny leaned away and gave her a shy smile. Debbie wanted to say something, but nothing sounded right. Instead, she slipped an arm around his waist and pulled him into a cozy embrace.

They stood in silence for a few seconds, watching the waves crash against the shore. And in that moment, Debbie suddenly understood the lyrics to Elvis's beautiful song, "Love Me Tender," firsthand. In her twenty years of living, she'd never known the tenderness of such a beautiful moment…until now.

Debbie rested in Johnny's comforting embrace. Her mind began to reel at all that had happened. Already she could see God's hand at work in this situation. And with that revelation fresh in her mind, she was suddenly struck by the most amazing idea. One that would truly save the day for everyone involved, including Johnny.

"Johnny! I have a wonderful idea."

"Oh?" He gave her another gentle kiss on the cheek.

She took his hand and began to walk along the water's edge as the idea rooted itself. "Let's call Joe Davies at the *Laguna Beach Times* to see if he'll write an article about you. Maybe he can play up your appearance on *Talent Scouts* this weekend. That might work."

"It might."

She found herself distracted by his beautiful green eyes but finally managed to get a few more words in. "Oh, and tell me what you think about this idea." Her voice grew more animated as she explained. "*Talents Scouts* is open to the public, right?"

"Right." He nodded. "From what I understand, anyway. You might need tickets, but I'm sure Jim could get them for you."

"I wonder if he could get lots of them," she said, the plan still percolating. "Lots and lots of them."

Johnny gave her a curious look.

"Maybe if I put together a group of girls to sit in the audience, we can all cheer you on. Make a really big deal out of your performance. We'll clap so loud that the Clap-o-Meter will go off and you'll win the whole thing. No one else will stand a chance. We'll outsmart them by bringing a lot of fans."

"You're saying we should rig the show by filling the audience with people who've been told to clap for me whether they think I'm worth clapping for or not?" His expression reflected his displeasure at that idea.

At once, Debbie realized just how awful her words had sounded. Shame washed over her. "Johnny, I'm sorry. I didn't mean it like that. I'm not saying we're going to have to do anything special. I just want to be there to support you."

He didn't look convinced. "So, you think the only way I could win is to fill the audience with people who are there to support me."

"Oh, I, well…" She paused as she attempted to figure out how she could redeem this. "I'm not saying that, really."

She went on and on, listing all the things they could do to sway people. Funny, the more she talked, the more she wished she could just close her mouth and put an end to this nonsense. Why was she making things so hard on him? Johnny was a great guy. He didn't deserve her condescension. Still, the more she tried to explain things, the deeper the hole she dug. By the time she finished, the pained expression on his face told her all she needed to know. She'd hurt him. And she didn't know how to undo it.

* * * * *

Johnny drew in a deep breath and stared into Debbie's eyes. Her words had stung, whether she meant them to or not.

"I'm going to do my best, Debbie," he reiterated. "Whether the audience likes me or not. Whether they vote me off the show or not."

"I–I know." She gave him a sheepish look. "I guess I'm just so worked up about this fundraiser because it's so critical for my family." She paused and her eyes filled with tears. "Johnny, my dad almost died last spring. We almost lost him. And I won't rest until I've figured out a way to help him through this."

"He's a grown man, Debbie," Johnny argued. "He knows what's best."

"He thinks that working hard is what's best," she said. "The doctor wouldn't agree with that. I think he needs to take it easy, but that can't happen if this event isn't successful. How will we ever get caught up on the mortgage?"

"Who said it won't be successful?"

The expression on her face wasn't easy to read. Did she really think this whole thing would crater because of Bobby's absence? Was that why she felt she had to fill the audience at *Talent Scouts* with people to cheer him on? So that he wouldn't let everyone down?

Obviously so.

Well, he would prove her wrong. Johnny gave her a hopeful smile. "I'm going to be there, Debbie. I'll sing every song I know, if it will help."

"Oh, I'm sure you'll be great," she said. A sigh rose up between them.

"What?" he asked.

"There's no way to say this without hurting your feelings."

"I'm not as popular as Bobby, so you think people won't come to see me?"

She sighed again. "Y–yes."

"Well, instead of worrying about that, let's just put together the best show we can. I'll do my best. You do your best. That's all God requires of us, right?"

"I suppose." Her lengthy pause worried him. What was she thinking? "I'm…I'm never going to get to meet Bobby," she said at last.

"Ah." He paused. "Is that what you're really upset about?"

"Well, it's all of the other stuff, too," she said. "But I can't help saying that I was looking forward to meeting him."

"What *is* it about Bobby Conrad?" Johnny asked.

"Well, he's handsome, of course. And you've heard his voice. But there's more to it than that," she said. "He's a great guy. You know how you can tell by looking at some people that they're the real deal?"

He nodded.

"Well, Bobby Conrad is the real deal. He's not just a big star or a famous singer. He's a good person. And I wanted to get the chance to see that for myself."

Johnny wanted to ask her if she'd secretly longed for something more, but didn't dare. Had she been pining away for Bobby, hoping he would take an interest in her?

Would Bobby be interested in her?

The very idea set the hairs on the back of Johnny's neck straight up in the air. He couldn't bear the idea of Debbie and Bobby as a couple. Then again, why wouldn't she choose Bobby over him? Bobby was popular. Famous. Girls fawned over him. No one even knew who Johnny Hartmann was. And unless Debbie somehow rigged this weekend's appearance on *Talent Scouts*, maybe they never would.

Slow down, Johnny. Don't get ahead of yourself.

He released a couple of slow breaths, willing himself to think more clearly. If he wanted to win Debbie—and he did—it couldn't be done through jealousy. No, this was one battle that could only be won through prayer.

Why, then, did he suddenly feel like punching Bobby Conrad's lights out? Bobby didn't even know Debbie Carmichael. Johnny suddenly hoped he never would.

Drawing in a deep breath, he forced his thoughts to Toby's new motto: "Sing now. Fight later." Perhaps that was the only way to deal with this one.

Hmm. Looked like he had a lot of singing to do.

Chapter Twelve

LIGHTS, CAMERA, ACTION!

What makes a fella handsome? Is it his smile? His eyes? His tall, suave physique? Sure, good-looking guys have a certain built-in advantage, but these days, nearly every boy can catch the eye of a pretty girl. All he has to do is dress the part.

So, you want to look like a heartthrob, guys? Listen up. Let's take note of what modern teen boys are wearing. Grab your pen and a piece of paper. We're going to cover a few fashion do's and don'ts.

These days, kids are more fashion conscious than ever before. Perhaps that's because so many of them are now shopping for themselves. And clothing manufacturers are playing along, giving them just what they want.

So, what do they want?

Of course, the conservative look is still in, especially among the high school and college set. The Ivy League preppy boys wear everything from casual suits to cardigan sweaters with trousers. And while the athletes are turning up in letterman jackets, their counterparts—the "bad boys"—are shocking adults with their jeans and leather jackets. We can thank James Dean for this new look. This reporter has to admit that the new trend toward rolling up the sleeves to show off the male bicep has its benefits. The girls aren't complaining.

Of course, many boys lean toward a fashion compromise. They wear a button-up shirt—often in plaid or check—over slacks. The open collar

189

*suggests a more relaxed look, and that certainly jibes with today's gen-
eration. Relaxed. Now that's what modern teens were born to be. (Hey,
we've all got to aspire to something.)*

— *Reporting for* Hollywood Heartthrob *magazine, "Glamour Girls"
columnist, Fashionable Frances*

* * * * *

On the afternoon of Saturday, August 10, Johnny buttoned up his
plaid shirt and double-checked his appearance in the mirror over the
dresser. He ran a comb through his hair, styling it the same way he'd
done before moving to California. Strange, staring at his reflection,
he couldn't help but think about how much he looked like Johnny
Hartmann from Topeka, Kansas. Gone were any remnants of Jim and
Theresa's Hollywood makeover. Not that he missed his trendy duds.
His old clothes suited him just fine. He could breathe better. Think
more clearly.

Johnny put the comb down and reached for his guitar, strumming
a few chords. He somehow made it through "Dear Debbie" a couple of
times before his nerves got the best of him. When they did, he rose and
paced around Toby's bedroom, his heart nearly thumping out of his
chest. Johnny thought of all the things that could go wrong at this evening's show. Just as quickly, he pushed away any worries and concerns
and ushered up a prayer, leaving it in the Lord's hands.

A rap on the door interrupted his solitude. Johnny looked up as
Jim stuck his head inside.

"Hey, kid."

"Hi, Jim. Just…" He paused. "You know. Getting ready."

"Just got a call from Frankie Carmichael. They're bringing a handful of teen girls to the show, so you'll be among friends. Thought that might put your mind at ease."

Johnny forced a smile, but his thoughts immediately went back to the conversation he'd had with Debbie on the beach. So she'd gone through with it. The girls were all coming, after all. Did she really think so little of his talent when she hadn't even heard him sing?

"You okay?" Jim's brow wrinkled as he looked Johnny's way.

"Yeah." Johnny shrugged.

"Nerves, eh? I expected that. Deep breath, kid. You'll do great."

I'm glad someone thinks so.

Johnny took another look at his reflection in the mirror. His smile had faded, replaced by a look of concern. Really, only one thing could make him feel better about all this. He needed to talk to someone from home. He needed his dad.

Johnny followed Jim out into the living room. Toby sat in front of the television wearing an Indian costume.

"Son, it's time to get dressed for the show."

"Aw, Pop. Are you sure I can't audition for *Tonto's Revenge*? I'd be great on the warpath."

"No doubt about that, but son, if I've told you once, I've told you a thousand times…"

"I know, I know." Toby rose and brushed past Johnny on his way to his room. "But I still say it's not fair. Johnny gets to be on television."

And he's a nervous wreck about it, too.

After Toby disappeared into the hallway, Johnny gave Jim a weak smile. "Can I ask a favor?"

"Sure." Jim glanced at his watch. "What do you need?"

"I was wondering if I could use your phone to make a long-distance call before we leave."

Jim gave him a concerned look. "Everything okay?"

"Yes sir. I, well, I just need to talk to my dad."

A look of understanding settled into Jim's expression. "Gotcha. Well, don't stay on too long."

"I won't. And I'll pay you back for the call, I promise. I just need to talk to my dad."

Jim laughed. "Pay me back, eh? Don't worry, Johnny. Just go out there and knock 'em dead tonight. That's all I'm asking."

"I'll do my best, sir."

"What's with all of this 'sir' business? It's just me...Jim." Jim gave Johnny a fatherly slap on the back then glanced toward the hallway. "I'd better go see what's holding Theresa up. We don't want to be late."

As soon as Jim left the room, Johnny walked over to the telephone and dialed the operator. When she came on the line, he gave her the familiar number.

From the moment he heard his dad's friendly "hello" Johnny could hardly catch his breath. He found himself transported all the way back to Topeka. Oh, if only he could forget about *Arthur Godfrey's Talent Scouts* and just spend the evening hanging out with his family. He would trade it all in a heartbeat.

"Dad, this is Johnny." The words came through a bit choppy, what with the catch in his throat.

"Johnny. Son." Just two words, but they spoke everything. "Mom and I have been talking about you all day. She got your letter about the television show tonight. We've got half of Topeka coming over to watch it with us."

"Really?" Johnny's heart swelled with excitement at the picture that painted in his mind.

"Well, sure. Your mom made one of her special 7-Up cakes, and she's going to stir up a batch of that punch you like so well. You know... the one with the sherbet in it."

"Mm." Sounded good.

An awkward pause followed. Johnny worked up the courage to say what needed to be said.

"Dad, can I ask a question?"

"Sure, Johnny."

"Do you...do you think I'm a prodigal?"

"A prodigal?" His father sounded stunned. "Why would you ask that?"

"Because I'm out here in Hollywood, chasing my dream. I've left home to go off to a distant place, like that guy in the Bible story."

A pause from the other end made Johnny a little nervous. His father responded at last. "Son, let me ask you a question, but don't answer right away. Think about it."

"O-okay."

"Have you left your first love?"

"My first love? What do you mean?"

"Think about it. From the time you were a youngster, you've been in church. You were always the one telling others about your faith. You made a commitment to the Lord when you were nine. Your mother and I always knew God had special plans for you because you were so passionate—about life, about your faith, about everything."

"Sometimes I feel like that fire is fading," he admitted.

"Well, let me ask you a question, son. Has it faded because you've been putting other things first? If so, then I might be able to help you answer that prodigal question."

"Maybe." He sighed.

"That's all I meant when I asked the question about your first love, Johnny. God wants first place in your heart. He doesn't mind if you chase after your dreams. He put them in your heart. He just doesn't want them to take first place above Him. Does that make sense?"

A wave of hope washed over Johnny as he responded. "It makes perfect sense, Dad. And it helps set things straight in my mind."

"Nothing wrong with being a dream-chaser, son. That doesn't make you a prodigal. The only thing that makes you a prodigal is walking away from your first love. Letting the things of the world take precedence. If you can strike a balance between your relationship with the Lord and those dreams you're chasing, I think you'll be just fine."

Johnny clutched the phone a bit tighter.

"And by the way, Johnny, in case I haven't said it lately...I'm proud of you."

Relief crashed over Johnny like ocean waves. "Dad, I always thought you were disappointed that I didn't go to Bible college and enter the ministry like you."

"Son, we all have our own path to follow." A brief pause followed. "And who knows...you may preach a better sermon in a movie you're in than I preach from the pulpit. I believe such a thing is possible. God is sovereign. He can use any means He chooses to touch the hearts of people. So don't discount the fact that He can use a movie or a song to touch others."

"Never really thought about it like that," Johnny said.

"Well, give it some thought. And pray about it. Maybe one of God's primary purposes in sending you to California is to share His love with people. Could be you'll meet someone tonight at this event. Or tomorrow. Or the next day."

"California is filled with people, Dad." Johnny chuckled. "You've never seen so many people. And you should see what they wear out here. It's…well, it's different."

"I can imagine."

Johnny heard his mother's voice in the background. Seconds later, she was on the line, chattering a hundred miles an hour, sharing her excitement about tonight's event. Johnny hardly got a chance to toss in a word or two. Clearly, she was thrilled that her boy was going to be on national television.

A few moments later Jim and Theresa entered the room. As Johnny glanced at them—Jim in his gray flannel suit and Theresa in her beautiful blue evening dress—he thought about his mom and dad once again. If they were here—in California—they would be going to the studio with him. Oh, but how wonderful he felt, knowing they were enjoying every moment of this, even if their celebration was taking place halfway across the country.

Jim pointed at his watch, and Johnny realized he'd better end the call.

"Mom, I've got to run," he spoke into the phone. "Thanks for praying for me."

She responded with, "Sing your heart out, son."

Her words resonated with Johnny long after they ended the call. He pondered them as he climbed into the back seat of Jim's car. He mulled them over all the way to the studio. Once there, however, he shifted gears. He began to rehearse the "Dear Debbie" lyrics in his head, one line after another. The words felt jumbled in his brain. Was the part about her beautiful brown eyes in the first verse or the second? Suddenly, he couldn't remember. Maybe he really would fall flat on his face and let everyone down. Then what? Would they cancel the fundraiser altogether, convinced it would be a flop?

Deep breath, Johnny.

As they walked from the parking lot to the studio building, Jim gave him a little pep talk. "Tonight's just the beginning of your life, Johnny-boy." He slapped an arm around Johnny's shoulder. "From here on out, it's the movie biz for you."

"Sounds like you've done this a few times." Johnny gave him a nervous smile.

"Oh, a few. But you're my first prodigy since Bobby."

"I've been meaning to ask you about that, Jim. I haven't met any of the other actors or actresses you represent. And I've never been to your office."

"Sure you have. You sleep there every night." Jim paused. "See, here's the thing, kid. I only take on the ones that really jump out at me, and I stick with 'em till they've signed a contract that will ensure they're well on their way. Then I pick up a new one and start all over."

"Are you saying I'm the only person you're representing right now?" Johnny could hardly believe it.

"Well, you're the one I'm focusing on. Let's just leave it at that."

"Wow. So, you're more of a mentor, then."

"Guess you could say that. I like the personal approach. Tried it the other way, early on in my career. Had a big agency with a nice office and all that. But I've found that I can't really give a gal—or a guy—my all when I'm distracted. This works for me."

Johnny pondered that a moment. "So you won't be taking on any more clients until I've got a movie deal?"

"Probably not." Jim shrugged. "I've got my existing ones, of course. Including Bobby and a few others. And I'll stick with you after the producers and network execs come knocking on your door, just like I've stuck with them. But soon you'll be living in your own place. And folks will be coming to you. I won't be drumming up gigs for you. Just making sure you get the best possible contracts. See how that works?"

"Wow." Johnny could hardly imagine such a thing but took Jim's word for it.

When they arrived inside the studio, Jim led the way to the director. Some quick instructions were given, and then Theresa and Toby headed off to find their seats in the studio audience. Jim took Johnny to some place called the green room. Strange, since it wasn't even green.

"Johnny, you'll wait in here," Jim explained. "About five minutes before you're scheduled to go on, someone will come and get you."

Johnny tried to speak, but fear seemed to have locked his jaw shut. He gave a lame nod then settled onto the sofa, guitar in hand. His thoughts shifted to Debbie. He wondered what she was doing right now. Settling into her seat in the audience with a host of friends around her? Praying he wouldn't flop?

Jim patted him on the shoulder. "Your whole life is going to change tonight, Johnny. This is the night you go from being a kid from Topeka to a star...someone folks clamor to see."

Johnny shook his head. "Seems impossible." He had to wonder what that would feel like—folks clamoring to see him.

"Well, you know what the great Fred Allen said, don't you, son?" Jim crossed his arms.

"No." *But I'm sure you're gonna tell me.* Johnny stifled a chuckle as he realized just how much he sounded like Toby.

"Fred always said, 'A celebrity is a person who works hard all his life to become well-known then wears dark glasses to avoid being recognized.'" Jim grinned. "I told you I'd turn you into a star. Guess I should've told you that stardom comes with a price tag attached."

Johnny didn't have much time to think about that or he might've turned and run.

Jim disappeared with a wave and a hearty, "Break a leg, kid."

"I thought that was a theater term," a guy with red hair said as he entered the room. "Strange." He took one look at Johnny and gave a sympathetic nod. "I feel your pain. Feeling a little green around the gills myself. Name's Mark Stevens."

Johnny shook his hand then glanced toward the door as a young woman with long hair and a bright smile entered the room. She looked anything but nervous.

"We're gonna take this crowd by storm!" she said, lifting her guitar in the air. "At least I am. Can't speak for you two." After a chuckle, she introduced herself as Katie Brennan. Strange, but as Johnny heard her name, he thought about his old girlfriend back home. Katie. He wondered if she and Dean were going to be watching the show.

Thinking about Katie pressed his thoughts along to something else—or someone else—entirely.

Debbie.

The memory of their kiss came rushing back. It swept over him like an ocean wave, washing away any traces of hurt feelings. When he closed his eyes, he could see it all so clearly—her long, blond hair. Her freckled nose. Those gorgeous brown eyes.

Instantly, the words to "Dear Debbie" came rushing back, clear as a bell. As long as he kept his eyes shut. Well, no problem. When he got on stage, he probably wouldn't have the courage to open them, anyway, especially with Debbie in the audience. Knowing she would be there caused an additional fluttering of butterfly-like sensations to take over his stomach. What would she and her friends think of the song? Did it even matter?

The stage director appeared minutes later, ushering Mark to the stage. Katie continued to talk non-stop, which served to relax Johnny a bit. At least he didn't have to think with so much chatter going on.

Only when the stage director came to fetch Katie did Johnny find himself alone in the room with nothing but his thoughts—and nerves—to keep him company. He started thinking again about Debbie. Wondered where she was sitting.

Johnny didn't have long to think about it. The stage director appeared in the doorway.

"Hartmann, you ready?"

Johnny swallowed hard and clutched his guitar. Then, whispering up a prayer, he followed the man to the backstage area.

"Hope you do better than that first kid," the stage director said then chuckled. "He had a rough go of it."

"Oh?" Johnny didn't ask for more details.

"That gal Katie gave you a run for your money, though. She's a pistol. I think she'll really go places. You should've heard the applause."

Gee, thanks for the confidence booster.

Johnny followed along behind the director, to the stage.

"Okay, kid. We're on a commercial break right now, so you can go ahead and take your spot on the stage. See that microphone there?" He pointed to the mike stand and Johnny nodded. "Well, go on. What are you waiting for?"

Um...for the earth to open up and swallow me whole? For a host of heavenly angels to carry me off so that I don't have to face this—the most terrifying moment of my life?

On the television monitor to his right, Johnny could see a commercial playing. As he took a few tentative steps toward center stage, the show's director approached.

"As soon as we're back on the air, you'll be introduced," the fellow in the black suit said. "But don't worry too much about the questions you're asked. The kids really just want to know if you can sing, that's all."

Yeah, they all do.

"So, when the lenses zoom in and you're feeling like you're surrounded by lights and cameras, just relax and play along. Nothing's going to harm you in any way, I promise."

"O-okay."

As he settled into his position on the tiny stage, Johnny heard a shrill whistle. He turned in its direction, realizing it had come from the studio audience. Toby.

The words, "Knock 'em dead, Johnny!" rang out.

Johnny squinted, trying to make him out. With the stage lights glaring, seeing anyone in the audience was tough. As one of the bigger lights shifted, however, he finally caught a glimpse of the one thing— or rather, one person—he'd hoped to see. The only one who could truly settle his nerves.

Debbie.

She gave a little wave then pointed to Becky Ann, Martha Lou, and several others. A thumbs-up followed from Becky Ann. Johnny swallowed hard. Looked like the gang was all here. Better give 'em what they'd come for.

Suddenly the room came alive. The lights grew brighter. The sounds magnified.

The director gave some final instructions, and the cameras zoomed in close. Johnny clutched his guitar, suddenly thankful for something to hold on to. Beads of sweat popped out on his upper lip and he brushed them away with the back of his hand. He somehow made it through the question and answer section, though the whole thing unnerved him.

Finally, the moment came. Johnny stood alone, center stage, strumming the first chords of "Dear Debbie." He closed his eyes once again and saw her—not in the audience—but standing with her bare feet in the Pacific, waves dancing in majestic, God-breathed rhythm. He saw the beauty in her smile. Remembered the sweetness of her kiss. Felt the gentleness of her embrace.

Truly, that was all he needed. The song that followed flowed like oil. Holy, blessed oil.

* * * * *

Debbie rested against the seat, happy that Johnny was finally getting his turn at bat. She whispered up a prayer that he would make it through.

"Be sure to clap extra loud when Johnny's done," she whispered to Becky Ann. "Pass it down. We'll set off that Clap-o-Meter, if it's the last thing we do."

Her sister giggled and passed the message along to Martha Lou, Ginny, Cassie, and the others.

Debbie glanced up at the stage, smiling as she reflected on Johnny's simple wardrobe—jeans and a button-up plaid shirt in great shades of green and blue. So much for the trendy Hollywood duds. He could toss those, anyway. She much preferred him this way.

Johnny's song started and Debbie found herself caught up in the gentle melody coming from his guitar. *Wow. He can really play.*

And then he opened his mouth to sing.

What happened next was dizzying. Debbie shook her head, trying to make sense of it. Johnny Hartmann wasn't just good—he was spectacular. And the words to his song—"Dear Debbie"—were clearly meant for her. She drank in every syllable, marveling at the beauty and tenderness of the lyrics.

Becky Ann turned her way, eyes wide, and mouthed the word, "Wow!"

Debbie nodded then turned back toward the stage. She was overwhelmed with embarrassment. After all, she'd made such a big deal about bringing along all of her friends to ensure Johnny's win. How wrong she'd been. Johnny certainly didn't need any help from them. Judging from the audience's response, he would've done just fine on his own.

The idea intrigued and terrified her. For, while she wanted him to do well, she suddenly realized she didn't want to share him with every other teenage girl in America.

Hmm. Nothing she could do about that now. Looked like cheering him on was really the only option. And so she did just that.

* * * * *

When Johnny struck the final chord on his guitar, he was half-relieved that the song had come to an end and half-disappointed. The whole experience had been overwhelming, but not in a bad way. In an "I-can't-believe-I-actually-got-to-do-this" sort of way.

It's over. And I lived through it.

Overhead, the stage lights dimmed slightly. The roar of applause from audience members sounded muffled to his ears as the emcee pointed to the Clap-o-Meter. Suddenly the sounds were clear as a bell. And loud. Deafeningly loud. The crowd cheered and shouted, and the applause—well, it floored him.

Must've floored the emcee, too. He looked at Johnny wide-eyed. "We haven't seen this kind of crowd reaction in months. Congratulations."

Johnny stood, dumbfounded, unable to move. Or breathe. Only when he was announced the winner did he dare draw a real breath. Even then, he couldn't think clearly—not with the crowd's enthusiastic response.

Perhaps he would never think clearly again.

Chapter Thirteen

THE SHOW MUST GO ON

Hold your horses, fellas! We had a live one on Arthur Godfrey's Talent Scouts *last Saturday night. In his first televised appearance, Johnny Hartmann, the clean-cut kid from Topeka, knocked the bobby socks off every girl who happened to be watching. He also won over the audience with his mellow, self-penned ballad, "Dear Debbie." Not bad for a newcomer. Rumor has it he'll be asked to return. In fact, prospects are looking good for a gig on* The Ed Sullivan Show *and perhaps even an eventual movie deal. Talk about a quick rise to stardom! And with famed agent Jim Jangles leading the way, the crooner's career is bound to follow in the footsteps of Bobby Conrad, Jangles's former prodigy.*

Our sources also tell me that Johnny will soon be performing at a fundraising event in Laguna Beach. Likely the girls of Orange County are flocking to buy tickets, even now.

Speaking of hip young singers, did anyone catch the controversial singer Jerry Lee Lewis on The Steve Allen Show *the other night? Whew! Lewis worked the piano keys into a fast-paced frenzy. No doubt teens went crazy as the singer kicked the piano bench out of his way to stand up about midway through the song. Not that you could really call it standing. How he could keep his legs moving while raking his hands up and down the keyboard remains a mystery. Truly, no one plays the piano like Jerry Lee. One might argue that he slays it instead of plays it. And how he could see with those unruly curls hanging down over his eyes is anybody's guess. Still, he gave the performance of a lifetime, one that—no doubt—caused mothers and fathers to dial in to the show's sponsors.*

Here's a thought: Maybe Johnny Hartmann and Jerry Lee Lewis could team up for an appearance on The Ed Sullivan Show. *Now, wouldn't that be a treat! One has to wonder who would garner the most attention—the newcomer with the boyish good looks or the wild-eyed church-boy-turned-rock-n-roller with the magic fingers.*

I'm putting my money on the new kid.

— Reporting for Hollywood Heartthrob *magazine, "Jukebox Jive" columnist, Hepcat Harry*

* * * * *

On Monday afternoon Debbie raced around the soda shop waiting on customers. She had one thing and one thing only on her mind—Johnny's visit. Jim would be dropping him off at noon so they could talk through the plans for the fundraiser this coming Saturday.

Talk about a miraculous turnaround. The girls of Laguna Beach—and all of Orange County, for that matter—were suddenly on board, ready to welcome Johnny with open arms. Oh, what a fool she'd been! Why, she'd hardly given Johnny a chance to prove himself before doubting him. And how wrong she'd turned out to be. Now everyone in town had witnessed his incredible talent. Debbie wondered how she could keep him to herself until the day of the event. It was likely Martha Lou and Cassie would drop by this afternoon, as soon as they heard Johnny was coming.

Unfortunately, at twelve o'clock straight up, Everett Anderson dropped in for lunch with his wife. Debbie deliberately seated them at a table about midway back in the restaurant. She and Johnny could sit at the counter to talk about plans for the fundraiser, far from listening ears. She still wondered what Mr. Anderson thought about the turn of events.

As Debbie handed Mr. and Mrs. Anderson their menus, she was distracted by the jingling of the bell at the front door. She almost over-filled Mrs. Anderson's water glass as she watched Johnny approach.

"Careful, dear," Mrs. Anderson said. "You almost got my alligator handbag wet."

"Oh, I'm so sorry."

Debbie studied Ginny's mother as she handed off the menu with a forced smile, noting her expensive dress and shoes. After the most recent threats from the bank, the last thing she wanted to do was upset Mr. or Mrs. Anderson. Besides, the Bible said to turn the other cheek, and that's just what she planned to do.

After a moment's glance at the menu, Mrs. Anderson looked up at Debbie. Her question was loud enough for everyone within hearing distance to notice. "Are your mashed potatoes instant or the real thing?"

Debbie quickly answered, "They're very real, I can assure you."

"Well then, I'll have the meatloaf, with mashed potatoes and peas. Oh, and a cup of coffee."

"I'll have the same." Mr. Anderson shoved his menu across the table and glanced at his watch. "Try and make sure the coffee is hot. Last time it was lukewarm. And don't make me wait all day for a glass of water, either. You really need to beef up your service."

"Yes sir." Debbie kept her smile firmly in place until she turned back toward the kitchen. Only then did she allow it to wilt. Until she saw Johnny, anyway. She couldn't help but smile when she clapped eyes on him.

She gave him a playful wink. "Take a seat at the counter, and I'll be right with you."

Debbie walked toward the kitchen. "Blueplate special, draw one!" she hollered back. "Double that." She wanted to add, "For the king and queen," but resisted. No point in allowing her mouth to take over where her heart left off. Besides, expressing anger at the Andersons wouldn't pay the mortgage.

Really, only one thing could cheer her up right now, and he happened to be sitting across the counter from her. Debbie turned and faced Johnny, suddenly feeling like a shy kid. She owed him an apology. A big one. But would he accept it? One look at his beautiful eyes convinced her that he would.

"Glad you could come," she managed, giving him a shy smile.

"Me, too." He stared at her, his gorgeous green eyes hinting of joy.

"I…I need to say something. What I said on the beach the other day was so stupid. So hurtful. I need to—" She'd just opened her mouth to begin the apology when he put his finger over her lips.

"You don't need to say anything," he whispered.

"But Johnny…" A lone tear made its way down her cheek. He wiped it away.

"Nope. It's behind us. We have big plans ahead of us."

She whispered a gentle "thank you" then stood in silence gazing into his eyes.

He stared back, offering a smile so sweet she couldn't look away. Not that she wanted to.

After a few seconds of staring, she chuckled. "You're a man of few words today."

"Mm-hmm." He quirked a brow and traced her cheek with his finger. "I think I've said enough."

She felt her cheeks turn warm. "You have."

The older woman on the barstool next to Johnny turned to face him then let out a squeal.

"Oh, you're that boy from *Talent Scouts*!" A girlish giggle followed. "I watched the show on Saturday night. That 'Dear Debbie' song took my breath away. My name happens to be Deborah. Deborah Snee." A wink followed.

Johnny's cheeks turned all shades of pink. He thanked her for watching the show then reached for a menu, hiding behind it.

Debbie tried not to chuckle but couldn't help herself. She leaned close to Johnny and whispered, "Looks like you've won over ladies of all ages."

He lowered the menu and shrugged. "I guess."

"That's a good thing," Debbie added, trying to keep her voice as low as possible. "Because we need the folks in that age group to support the fundraiser. The teens will love it, but they won't have a lot of money to donate. Older fans will help."

Johnny still looked embarrassed.

After a moment, Debbie came to her senses. She walked to the Andersons' table, dropped off two glasses of water, and assured them their food would be out shortly. Then she made her way back to the counter to visit with Johnny.

"What's up with those two?" he asked, gesturing to the middle-aged couple. "Not the nicest pair."

"I know." Debbie sighed. "He's the banker. I, um, well, he's the one who holds the mortgage on this place. And we've been struggling to make payments ever since Pop's heart attack."

"I see." Johnny gave him a pensive look. "Seems like the banker would be a little nicer, with your father's situation in mind."

Debbie shrugged.

Becky Ann approached to fill a couple of soda glasses. "You two talking about you-know-who and Mrs. you-know-who?"

"Yes." Debbie couldn't help the sigh that followed.

"He kind of reminds me of Yul Brynner in *The King and I*," Becky Ann said.

"What do you mean?"

Becky Ann put on her sternest voice. "'When I sit, you sit. When I kneel, you kneel. Etcetera, etcetera, etcetera!' Don't you remember?"

Pop came out of the kitchen with Mom on his heels. They were just in time to hear Becky Ann's dramatic impersonation.

"Yul Brynner, eh?" Pop grinned. "He's one of my favorites. Folks often tell me I look like him."

"You look nothing like Yul Brynner, dear." Debbie's mother gave him a kiss on the cheek. "For one thing, you have hair."

He laughed. "Not as much as I used to have, thank you very much."

"For another thing," she added., "you're not bossy. The king was always bossing Deborah Kerr around."

"Yes, but he truly loved her," Debbie's father said. "Secretly, of course."

Mom gave him a knowing look. "Of course."

"They were an unusual pair, no doubt about that, but talk about onscreen chemistry!" Debbie watched as her father wrapped her mother in a warm embrace and gave her a tender kiss, right there in the soda shop.

"Nothing secret about that," she said, feeling a little embarrassed that Johnny had witnessed her parents' public display of affection.

"I think it's great." Johnny gave her an empathetic look. "Reminds me of my mom and dad. I love that."

"Anything we can do to entertain the troops." Debbie's parents began to do a funny little waltz as her father sang "Shall We Dance." He only changed keys three times. Not bad.

When they stopped, Debbie's mother caught her breath. "Maybe you're more like Yul Brynner than I thought." She gave him another kiss.

"You two are better than any movie," Johnny observed.

"Oh?" Debbie's father gave him an inquisitive look. "How so?"

"You're the genuine article." He gave Debbie's mom a smile. "A real-life team."

"That we are!" Debbie's father said with a smile. "Through thick and thin."

"I still love the movie, though," Debbie's mom said. "It's one of my favorites."

Somehow this led to a discussion about everyone's favorite movie. Pop voted for *Giant*. Mom went for *The Ten Commandments*. Junior hollered out the word *Casablanca* from the kitchen. Becky Ann, of course, preferred Pat Boone's performance in *April Love*, and Johnny surprised everyone with his answer: *Rear Window*.

"Oh, I loved that movie," Debbie's mom said. "Kept me on the edge of my seat. I wasn't sure if Jimmy Stewart was going to catch the killer or not."

"I liked it, too," Debbie said. "But not as much as the romances I've seen. Give me a love story any day."

"Like what?" Johnny asked.

"Oh, I don't know." She paused. "*Sabrina* is near the top of the list. Audrey Hepburn is gorgeous. And I love all of Elvis's movies. But those Rock Hudson, Doris Day movies are my favorites."

"Wait. Why are we talking about love stories all of a sudden?" Becky Ann looked back and forth between them. "Something I need to know?"

Debbie flashed her a warning look, not wanting to share the original tidbit about how Mr. Anderson reminded them of Yul Brynner. Thankfully, Pop switched gears. He gestured to the Peppermint uniforms Becky Ann and Debbie were wearing. "Hey, Johnny."

Johnny gave him a curious look. "Yes sir?"

"You know how to keep a Peppermint in suspense?"

Debbie braced herself for the answer. Looked like her father was up to his tricks again.

When Johnny shrugged, her pop held off on responding. After an exorbitant amount of time, he slapped his knee and said, "Nah, I'll tell you later."

Debbie couldn't help but roll her eyes. Pop and his jokes.

"You still have your sense of humor, after all these years." Debbie's mom linked her arm with his. "Just one more thing I love about you."

"I can think of a thousand things I love about you." He gave her a kiss on the nose, and the two disappeared into the kitchen together.

Debbie turned to Johnny and shrugged. "They're obviously still in love."

Johnny grinned. "Hey, that's better than most of the people I've been reading about. Seems like marriages don't last long out here."

"Well, they're as different as night and day," she explained. "Mom has always said that's why it works. She thinks it helps to marry someone different from yourself."

"Ah."

When Johnny's lips turned up in a smile, she felt her cheeks warm.

"Guess we'd better get busy talking about the fundraiser." She paused then dove right in. "Okay, here's what we're going to do. I've called Mr. Davies at the *Laguna Beach Times*. He's stopping by at two o'clock."

"Great." Johnny nodded.

"He saw you on *Talent Scouts*, so he's really excited to write an article. The new posters went up last week, so everyone knows the particulars. And you're doing three sets. I guess we just need to decide what songs, and in what order."

"I've already done that. It's all taken care of."

"Great. One less thing to think about." Debbie paused and then an idea hit like a lightning bolt. "Oh, I just thought of a way to promote the event! Maybe we can get Louella Parsons and Hedda Hopper to come."

Johnny gave her a curious look. "Who are they? Singers?"

"Singers!" She laughed. "No, silly. They're only the leading gossip columnists in the world. And they're archenemies."

"Wow. Why is that?"

"Not sure. They were one-time friends, I understand, but then parted ways. Now they always try to outdo each other by coming up with bigger, better stories. Maybe I can get them both to come at the same time. Talk about drama. And I'm sure they would do a terrific write-up about the fundraiser when it's over, which could generate some interest in the soda shop for months to come."

"You're filled with great ideas." Johnny gave her an admiring look.

"Thanks." Debbie smiled. "I'm a little upset about one thing. I haven't heard back from Cinema Cindy or Hepcat Harry yet. Jim was supposed to be checking to see if someone from the magazine could come."

"Oh, that's right," Johnny said. "Well, it sounds like this Head-hopper lady would be just the ticket."

"*Hedda* Hopper." Debbie giggled. "I wonder if she'll come on such short notice."

"You never know unless you ask."

Someone put a nickel in the jukebox and "Mr. Sandman" came on. Debbie paused, unable to speak as the words saturated her heart.

"Everything okay?" Johnny looked concerned.

"Yes." She did her best to hide the shy smile. "I, um, well, I like this song."

"Me, too."

"Guess I'm just a dreamer," she said. "I was never the kind of girl who dated a lot of boys in high school."

"She had plenty of boys to choose from," Becky Ann chimed in as she walked by. "But none of them met her very high expectations."

"I've been waiting for that fairytale ending." Debbie shrugged. "Probably sounds a little silly."

"Not at all. You don't have to come from the West Coast to dream. I've had a few of them myself."

"Well, you've come to the right place." Becky Ann's eyes sparkled. "Hollywood is the place where dreams come true."

"Or the place where they're crushed," Debbie added. "I've seen both."

"Here's the problem that I've noticed." Johnny paused. "And I've been guilty of this, too. Seems like most everyone I've met out here is so busy trying to prove himself. Or herself. I guess we want people to think we're something special. But the Lord is all about showing us that it isn't about us at all. It's about Him. It's been a bit of a journey for me, to be honest."

"I guess you're right." Becky Ann shrugged. "Never really thought about it."

"Boy, I have." Debbie nodded. "Especially over the past week. In Hollywood, people are always buying bigger, better houses and bigger, better cars. It's like they think people will be more impressed if they have bigger, better stuff."

"Exactly," Johnny said. "The way I look at it, it's a huge balancing act. Wanting to make a living doing the thing you love—in my case, singing—but not letting pride and selfishness get in the way. It's tough."

"How tough could it be for you, Johnny?" Debbie smiled. "You're not the selfish type. Not at all."

"I do my best, but please keep praying for me. I have a feeling the next few weeks and months are going to bring a few temptations. And having an agent on board…"

"What about it?"

"Well, sometimes I wonder. Jim is so driven, and who can blame him? This is his livelihood. It's how he puts food on the table for his family. So I want to be successful, in part, because I know it will benefit him. But I'm not like a lot of people. It's not really about having my name up in lights or being noticed. It's just…" He paused.

"Just about getting to do the thing you love?"

"Yes." He nodded. "To me, it's as much about giving as getting. More, in fact."

"That's what sets you apart, Johnny," Debbie said. "People who are selfish and prideful are just the opposite. They're all about getting, not giving."

"Yes, and I'm sure that temptation will rear its ugly head as I go along. But I've got to remember all the things my father has taught me.

He's the best preacher you've ever heard, Debbie. I wish you could hear some of his sermons. They're really life-changing."

"I wish I could."

"He preached a great one on vanity last year. God wants us to empty ourselves of, well, ourselves, and to live for Him and others."

"Wow. That's really deep, Johnny. I would imagine it would be a tough sell in Hollywood, where everyone is out to prove they've got more than the next guy."

"Yes, but there's no better place to present that message than Hollywood, where it's needed. Bigger homes, pools, sports cars...none of those things will fill the God-sized hole in the hearts of those people. They want folks to think they've got a great life—a great story—but really, they're just tacking on all of the 'stuff' to make themselves look better. It won't take long before the house of cards falls if they're not rooted and grounded in Christ."

"I agree." She gave him a look of admiration.

"Like I said, my dad's a preacher." He grinned. "I guess I come by it honestly."

"I'd say." She wondered if Johnny might turn out to be one, as well.

"Our story might be big in our own eyes, but God has a bigger one," he said. "The only way we'll ever discover it, though, is if we empty ourselves of the desire to have more. And I've made up my mind that having the Lord is still the better choice, even if I lose it all by worldly standards. We're destitute apart from Him, even if we live in a Hollywood mansion."

Debbie stared at him, feeling like he'd just delivered the State of the Union address.

"What?" he asked.

She shook her head. "You can sing, you can act, you can preach. Is there anything you can't do?"

He laughed. "I'm not very good at cooking. My mom tried to teach me, but I was a lousy student. So, don't ask me to make anything. I'd probably ruin it."

"As long as you're cooking up there on that stage next Saturday, I'll be a happy girl," she said. "So leave the stuff in the kitchen to us. You just get ready to face the crowd with your music. I'll face them with the cheeseburgers and fries."

"Deal." He extended his hand and she took it. "You must really like working here."

Debbie paused. How could she explain how much the family's business meant to her and how much she loved being with the people she loved?

"I do like it," she said at last. "In fact, I like to think I'll still be here when I have kids of my own." She paused and shook her head. "I guess I'm getting ahead of myself. Maybe, by the time my kids are grown, folks won't even eat at family-run diners like this. Maybe they'll be a thing of the past. But while this dream lingers, I want to enjoy it to the fullest."

Johnny reached to take her hand again and gave it a squeeze. "I think that's nice. And you're a hard worker, Debbie. I see you—waiting tables, carrying trays, putting up with a lot from the kids. I've watched you take on extra work so your mom and dad don't have to. You're a blessing to your parents. I know they must be grateful for your hard work."

Debbie wasn't sure how to respond to such glowing praise. There were days when she didn't feel like working. But even then, the soda shop was as much a part of her as the blood that flowed through her veins. She ate, slept, and breathed it. Every nuance was familiar. The clatter of dishes. The ever-present smell of food. The bell above the door. The sound of the cash register drawer closing. Sticky tables with wads of pink Double Bubble stuck underneath. The sound of voices raised in joyous conversation. Teen boys arguing over the latest ball-game. Girls chattering about their latest crushes. Those amazing songs coming from the jukebox in the corner. The flashing sign outside. If she closed her eyes, she could still see everything. If she plugged her ears, the sounds would go on in her imagination.

Oh, but how she longed for them to go on in reality, too. She couldn't bear the thought of anything happening to the business her father had worked so hard to build. And nothing would happen to it... if she could help it. But that meant she and Johnny had to get busy. They had to convince the teens of Laguna Beach to attend the concert.

As Debbie's thoughts drifted, she heard Johnny clearing his throat.

"Oh, sorry." She glanced his way. "Did you say something?"

He shook his head and for the first time, Debbie realized he was still holding her hand. A warm tingly sensation eased its way from her neck to her cheeks. She thought about pulling her hand away, but didn't. Looking up into Johnny's eyes, she realized that having him here—in the soda shop—felt as normal as the sound of the music overhead. Comfortable. That's how she felt with Johnny around. At ease. Herself.

They sat there, hand-in-hand, until Debbie nearly lost herself in Johnny's smile. The sound of a man clearing his throat startled her.

"I've been trying to get your attention for the last several minutes," Mr. Anderson called out. "We need more water and our food should have arrived by now."

"Oh, yes sir." Debbie turned away from Johnny, embarrassed at having been seen holding his hand. "I'll be right there."

"You'd better be."

Debbie did her best to still her rapidly beating heart, then she turned her attention back to her work.

* * * * *

Johnny watched the exchange between Debbie and Mr. Anderson with some degree of curiosity. The fellow really was like Yul Brynner, clearly huffing and puffing. Only, in this case, he had the capability of actually bringing the house down…and not with applause. No, Everett Anderson was a force to be reckoned with.

Not that Johnny had a clue where to begin. Still, he would do whatever it took to protect Debbie and her family from the unfriendly banker. A thousand thoughts went through his mind at once. He wanted to take the fellow down a notch or two, to tell him that he needed to treat people better. Instead, Johnny closed his eyes and drew in a deep breath, trying to imagine what his father would suggest.

Turning the other cheek felt a little wimpy, to be honest, and yet that's exactly what Dad would tell him to do. Johnny sighed, realizing just how tough this balancing act could be. For, while he wanted to turn the other cheek, he wanted to protect Debbie even more. He paused, reflecting on his words to Toby: "Sing now, fight later." Looked like that was exactly what the Lord was calling him to do. Focus on the singing now. Let the Lord fight the battle on Saturday during the fundraiser.

Out of the corner of his eye, he kept a watchful eye on Debbie. The lyrics and melody to "Dear Debbie" rushed over him, and he felt himself more drawn to her than ever. It wasn't her physical beauty, though that wowed him, too. No, he felt a deeper connection with Debbie

Carmichael. Last Wednesday, on the beach, he'd intertwined his heart-strings with hers. And now, one week later, he found himself unable to breathe whenever she came near.

He decided right then and there that breathing was highly overrated.

Chapter Fourteen

BEHIND THE SCENES

I love music as much as the next girl, but there seems to be an epidemic of Hollywood big-screen musicals over the past few years. Have you noticed? Gone are the days of people talking to one another on camera. These days, they sing their dialogue. It's an interesting concept. Picture an actor and actress in the middle of a tender love scene. He interrupts the kiss to sing her a song. She doesn't seem to mind. Stranger still, she doesn't think to ask where the orchestra is hiding or how her sweetheart learned such beautifully choreographed steps. She simply smiles and joins in, somehow knowing the words to verse two. And three. Then she joins the dance, never missing a step.

As I said, strange concept. And yet it seems to be winning over audiences. Teens and adults alike are flocking to theaters to watch Hollywood's latest and greatest sing their stories to life. If we're going to be completely honest, we have to admit that some of the songs are rather lame. Still, every now and again, a masterpiece leaps off the silver screen and makes the transition to radio. Elvis's " Love Me Tender," for instance. Pat Boone's "April Love." Bobby Conrad's "First Kiss." As I've pondered this phenomenon, I can only draw one conclusion: people prefer fiction to fact. They'd rather trade life's troubles for a song-and-dance number.

Since watching Johnny Hartmann on Talent Scouts *last Saturday night, this reporter has been trying to figure out what sort of life he leads when the cameras aren't rolling. I've also spent a little time wondering what sort of movie he could star in that would feature his hit song, "Dear Debbie." The story of a wayfaring stranger, perhaps? A man in search of a new life in a new place? Maybe something really simple, like a small-town waitress falling for a handsome traveling salesman.*

Nah. That last one's probably a little overdone. Still, I love to see reality and fiction merge, even if a musical comedy is the inevitable conclusion.

Join me next week, when I'll be singing and dancing my column. (Kidding!) Thinking about escaping from life's woes sure has been fun, though. Till next time!

— Reporting for Hollywood Heartthrob *magazine, "On the Big Screen" columnist, Cinema Cindy*

* * * * *

Johnny awoke early Tuesday morning, thoughts about the fundraiser tumbling through his head. He discovered Toby already gone from his bunk. Strange, since the sun wasn't even up yet. Johnny went into the kitchen, still dressed in his pajamas, and found the youngster sitting on the kitchen counter, holding a jar of peanut butter and mouthing something indistinguishable.

"Toby?" Johnny rubbed his eyes.

"Oh, hey." Toby held up the jar. "Choosy mothers choose Jif."

"Toby, have you been reading *Variety* again?"

"Maybe." Toby shrugged. "There's an audition for Jif peanut butter next Thursday. I'd be perfect. They're looking for an adorable little boy with a freckled face and red hair."

"Kid, I hate to break this to you, but your hair is brown, and there's not a freckle on your face."

"Yes there is." Toby pointed to the tip of his nose. "See? Right there. I have a freckle."

Johnny rolled his eyes. "Okay, if you say so. But you're not going into television or movies till you're grown."

Toby put the jar of peanut butter on the counter. "Who made you king?"

"No one. I'm just saying that you should wait until you're older."

"I don't like peanut butter, anyway," Toby muttered under his breath. "Gives me hives."

Johnny roughed up the youngster's hair. "Sorry about that, kid. One of these days you'll get to make your own choices. Until then…"

"Yeah, I know. Until then, no show biz for me." His shoulders slumped forward.

"Let me ask you a question, Toby." Johnny took a seat at the table. "Why are you so set on becoming famous?"

For a second, Johnny thought he saw a hint of tears in the youngster's eyes.

Toby took awhile to respond. "I just want to, is all."

"Because…?"

Toby jumped off the counter, landing on his feet. After a few seconds, he spoke. "Maybe my dad thinks I don't have any talent."

"What?"

Toby walked to the table and plunked down in a chair. "I mean, he's always going out and discovering people. Then they move in here and share my room. He's so busy thinking about how talented everyone else is. I wonder if he'll ever discover me."

Johnny pondered the boy's words. When he spoke, his words were calculated. "Toby, I want to tell you something, but hear me out, okay?"

Toby shrugged.

"Your dad loves you. I know he does. He told me all about you that first night on the way here."

"He did?"

"Yes." Johnny nodded. "I heard all about how smart you are. How great you are at sports. How funny you are. How you make him laugh and keep people entertained. He thinks you're very talented, trust me."

Toby's eyes misted over. "How come he never tells me?"

Because he's worried your talent could thrust you into a world you're not yet ready for?

Johnny shook his head. "I don't know. I just know your dad loves you, and he's very proud you're his son."

At this point, tears erupted. Toby quickly brushed them aside with the back of his hand and rose. He put the jar of peanut butter back in the cupboard. "I'm not hungry anymore."

Johnny's heart tightened as he watched the pained expression on the youngster's face. "If you ever want to talk, I'm here. And I still owe you a guitar lesson. I haven't forgotten, I promise."

Toby left the room mumbling, "Never mind."

Less than a minute later, Jim entered the kitchen, rubbing his eyes. "What's going on in here? I thought I heard talking."

"Oh, sorry. Didn't mean to wake you," Johnny said. "Toby and I were just talking."

"Toby?" Jim looked around, his brow wrinkled. "Did he pull a disappearing act?"

"Just one of my many talents, Dad." Toby popped his head back in the kitchen door. "One minute I'm here, the next I'm not!" He jumped inside the room and hollered a rousing, "Ta-da!"

"Always performing, my boy. Always performing." Jim ran his fingers through Toby's hair and pulled him close. "Gotta love it."

Not quite *I love you*, but close. And from the smile on Toby's face, it was certainly enough to turn things around for today.

* * * * *

Debbie awoke early on Tuesday morning. She showered and dressed then walked through the living room, headed for the stairs. She paused as she saw Pop sitting on the divan, reading the paper. Out of the corner of her eye, she caught him grimacing and rubbing at his chest. She paused to ask the obvious. "Not feeling well this morning?"

He looked up from the newspaper. "G'morning, Sunshine. I'm okay. I'd probably feel a lot better if we stopped taking this paper."

"Oh?" She sat next to him on the divan. "What is it? The Communists, again?"

He shook his head. "Don't get me started on the Communists or my blood pressure really will go up. I don't know what this world is going to be like when your kids are grown." He shook his head and a sad look settled over him.

"What do you mean?"

"Things are just moving so fast. And a lot of things don't make sense to me."

"Like what?"

"It's hard to put my finger on just one thing. But I have a sneaking suspicion that the world is going to be a lot different by the time you have children and grandchildren. I'm not sure we're headed in the right direction."

"Don't worry, Pop. Even if the world changes, I won't. I promise."

He smiled. "I know you won't, honey. You're the most level-headed girl I know." He chuckled. "Unless we're talking about Bobby Conrad. Then you get as silly as the others."

"Not anymore." She shook her head, determined to prove him wrong.

"Oh?" He gave her a curious look.

"I know my crush on Bobby was just that...a crush. It wasn't reality. I'm ready for reality now." She felt a smile tugging at the edges of her lips as she thought of Johnny. Yes, he was certainly a nice reality. And all the more as they got to know each other better. Before long, she'd forget that she ever dreamed of Bobby Conrad.

Hmm. Better change the subject. Pop's suspicious look would lead to questions if she didn't shift gears.

"So, what else is going on in the world?" she asked. "What are today's headlines?"

His expression soured. "Well, for one thing, folks in Washington are talking about raising the minimum wage to a dollar."

"A dollar!" Debbie gasped. "Really?"

He sighed. "I'm afraid so. Don't know how small businesses like ours are going to be able to afford to hire anyone, especially with..." He paused.

"Everett Anderson breathing down our necks." She finished the sentence for him.

"Yes." Her father lowered the paper. "I don't know why he feels like he's got to put added pressure on me this week, of all weeks."

"Johnny says he's like the big bad wolf…huffing and puffing."

"And trying to blow our house down?" Pop grinned.

"Yes, but we're not going to let him. He's filled with hot air."

"Not so sure about that, Sunshine. We are behind on the mortgage, you know."

"Just a couple of months. He can't do anything until after the concert. We'll have more than enough to pay him then. Watch and see. The mortgage will be paid off and you'll be sitting pretty."

"Sitting pretty, huh?" He began to read from the paper. "'According to the U.S. Department of Commerce and Dun & Bradstreet, the United States is currently experiencing a forty-eight percent business failure rate.'" Pop looked at Debbie and shook his head. "Forty-eight percent." He stressed the words.

Debbie chose her response with great care. "Well, I suppose we could look at it like this. That means 52 percent of all businesses succeed." She flashed what she hoped would look like a confident smile.

He just shook his head and then pointed to another headline. "On a more somber note…"

"Wait. There's something more somber than 48 percent of American businesses failing?"

"Yes. Look at this."

She leaned over and followed his fingertip to the heading above a large column in the center of the page: FOUR FOOD GROUPS NAMED.

"What's that all about?" Debbie asked.

He skimmed a couple of lines with his fingertip then glanced up at her. "It seems the Department of Agriculture has decided to divide food into four basic groups."

"Oh?"

"Yes, look here." He pointed at the paper. "Meats, dairy, grains, and finally, fruits and vegetables."

"Wouldn't that be five groups?"

"Nope. Fruits and vegetables go together."

"Ah."

He shook his head and she could read the sadness in his eyes.

"I don't understand," she said at last. "Why is this such tragic news?"

"Because, honey-bun. Cheeseburgers didn't make the cut." He slapped his knee and let out a laugh that brought a smile—a real, honest-to-goodness smile—to Debbie's face.

"You're funny, Pop," she said as she finally caught her breath. "But think about it. A cheeseburger is all of the food groups in one: meat, dairy, grain, and vegetables. If you add pickles and lettuce, I mean."

"Hmm. Guess you're right." He frowned. "Still, the doctor says I need to lay off the burgers and fries. Have to eat more salads. It's better for my heart." He rubbed his chest and that odd expression passed over his face again.

"Well then, you're going to do what the doctor says." She gave him a kiss on the cheek. "We want to keep you around a good, long while, so that means you'll be eating a lot of salads."

"I suppose."

She pulled the newspaper from his hand. "And another thing...I want you to stop reading the paper. And watching the news. I think it's bad for you to know what's going on out there in the world. The less you know, the better."

He chuckled. "So, cheeseburgers are out...and newspapers are out?"

"And the evening news on TV, too."

He shook his head. "How will I ever keep myself occupied?"

"Read a good book. Or watch television."

"In the middle of the day?" He looked horrified. "On a workday?"

"No one would mind. Besides, there are lots of great new shows on TV these days. You might find something you really like. A game show, maybe. Or a variety show."

"I miss my old favorite. *Colgate Comedy Hour* was the best." He sighed and went off on a tangent. Something about Jimmy Durante. Then Bob Hope. Then Eddie Cantor. Just about the time he got to Abbott and Costello, Debbie gave him a kiss on the forehead and headed toward the stairs. She pondered the fact that her father—unlike most in Southern California—actually preferred fact to fiction. He'd choose news over a movie any day. Most people were the opposite. Folks these days wanted to escape by watching television shows or movies, not by watching the evening news.

Minutes later she was deep in thought as she waited on customers. Her parents came down the stairs a few minutes later and joined her. Debbie paused to watch them as they interacted. They really were as different as night and day. Mom was slender and tall. Her father stood a couple of inches taller, but his round middle spoke of one cheese-burger too many.

"Pop, I thought you were going to stay upstairs today and watch television," Debbie scolded.

"I promised your mother I wouldn't work," he said. "But I want to be down here with my family. It's where I belong. I'll keep myself busy in the office."

The bell jangled above the door and Clifford entered.

"Morning, Carmichael family." He reached inside his mail pouch and came out with a handful of envelopes.

"Hope you're bringing us good news today, Clifford," Debbie's mother said.

"I just deliver the mail. I'm not responsible for the content." He flashed a crooked grin then passed the envelopes over to Debbie's father, who thumbed through them.

A few seconds later, Pop's smile faded.

"What is it?" Debbie asked, drawing near.

"We got another letter from the bank." He shook his head and smiled, though it seemed a bit forced. "I'll take care of it. I'm heading to my office. I'll be there all morning, if anyone needs me."

Debbie forced back the tears that threatened to erupt. She didn't want to bring anyone down, but every time she thought about that banker and the pressure he was putting on Pop, she got angry.

Debbie saw Junior walk to the jukebox, and a moment later the beautifully blended harmonies of Bill Haley and the Comets resonated around the room, immediately bringing a smile to Debbie's face. Her foot began to tap, and before long she and Junior were both singing "See You Later Alligator," at the top of their lungs. How interesting that music could change the mood in a room so quickly.

Within seconds, Pop stuck his head out of the office, all smiles. He grabbed Mom by the hand and pulled her to the dance floor. As he did a funny little dance, the whole family joined in, singing, "See you later alligator!" And for that moment—that rare, funny moment—the troubles of the world didn't exist.

Oh, if only they would fade away...forever.

Chapter Fifteen

TAKE TWO

We're going to call today's offering, We Never Saw This One Coming. *In this special issue of* Hollywood Heartthrob, *we're talking about some of the most oddly matched couples in Hollywood.*

Take Marilyn Monroe and Joe DiMaggio, for example. Yes, the two were as different as oil and vinegar. Would you have pictured the blond bombshell and the somewhat average-looking DiMaggio a couple? Likely not. And what about Lucy and Desi? Her quirky redheaded ways and his fiery Cuban temper? Talk about an unusual match. But they're not alone. Hepburn and Tracy. Prince Rainier and Grace Kelly. Yes, the relationships of the "unlikely" do seem to catch us off guard. And yet many appear to be working.

A handful of onscreen married couples seem like mismatches, as well. Take Vivian Vance and William Frawley, for example. As Ethel and Fred Mertz, they make us laugh, but I shudder to think of those two married in real life. (Can you imagine?) And what about Jackie Gleason and Audrey Meadows of Honeymooners *fame? As Ralph and Alice Cramdon, their biting sarcasm makes us both laugh...and squirm. Why do we love to see them bicker so much?*

The odd pairings seem to happen in the entertainment industry, as well. Sometimes the most unlikely comedians come together to make us chuckle. Laurel and Hardy. Dean Martin and Jerry Lewis. (Did you ever see two more different people?) And what about Buffalo Bob and Howdy Doody? Yep. Different as night and day.

And yet it seems to work. In most of these situations, the oddly matched duos prove us wrong. They entertain and delight...and remind us that sometimes a perfect match begins with a perfect mismatch! Perhaps there's a lesson here. Maybe we need to stop speculating on who's right for who and mind our own business.

Scratch that. Speculating is my business.

— *Reporting for* Hollywood Heartthrob *magazine, "Star Chasers" columnist, Hollywood Molly*

* * * * *

Less than half an hour after Debbie and the rest of the Carmichael clan finished their early morning dance-a-thon to the Bill Haley song, the bell above the door jangled and Johnny walked in carrying a bouquet of pink sweetheart roses. Debbie took one look at him, and her heart jumped to her throat. Had he brought those roses... for her?

Johnny took a few steps in her direction then gave the bouquet to her. "I, um, well, we picked these up on the way."

"They're beautiful."

"Yes, they are." Johnny's cheeks reddened. "Theresa told me what to get, actually. Hope that's okay."

"Of course."

"She, um, sent me with something else, too."

"Oh?"

Behind him, the door opened again, and Toby came plowing in, wearing some sort of alien costume. "Hello, inter-galactic beings!" the youngster shouted. "I come in peace."

"Well, that's good." Debbie chuckled. "We'd hate to think you'd come to bring some sort of harm."

Johnny smiled. "Sorry about the costume. Toby's on a kick. He wants to audition for a new movie. Something about aliens."

"I see." Debbie chuckled. "Well, he's got me convinced."

"Thank you, earthling." Toby bowed then straightened up and sat on a barstool. "Could I have something to drink, please?"

"It's okay with me if Johnny says it's okay."

"Sure, why not." Johnny sat next to Toby.

Debbie clutched the bouquet of flowers in her hand, realizing she needed to do something with them before fixing Toby's drink.

"Let me put these in some water." She walked to the kitchen and located a large vase, which she filled with water. Lowering the stems into the vase, she drew in a deep breath. "Mmm." A ripple of excitement washed over her as she realized that Johnny had been thinking of her. These roses represented his feelings for her…feelings she hoped—prayed—were growing as fast as hers were for him.

She carried the roses out and put them on the counter where everyone could see them. Then she turned her attention to Johnny.

"Jim and Theresa had plans all day today, so they dropped us both off," he said. "Hope you're okay with that."

"Of course. Glad to have you."

"Am I going to get something to drink, or what?" Toby asked.

"Oh, right." Debbie paused. "Maybe you can help with the customers when you're done. I think you'll make a fine waiter."

Toby rolled his eyes. "Space beings don't wait tables."

"Oh, I see. Well, do they drink chocolate malts?"

"They do." He nodded with great enthusiasm.

Just as Debbie reached for the ice cream scooper, her father came staggering out of the office.

"Pop?" Debbie stared at him, alarmed at his pale face. "Are you okay?"

"I don't know." He rubbed his chest and shook his head. "Might be a good idea to sit out here for a few minutes. The bills can wait."

"Of course they can," Debbie's mother said, drawing near.

"Here." Johnny pulled out a chair at the closest table.

Debbie's father sat, resting his elbows on the table. "Not sure what's up," he said at last.

Debbie shook her head and tears sprang to cover her lashes. "You've been working too hard again, Pop."

"Junior can't handle the kitchen by himself, Sunshine." Her father rubbed his left shoulder and grimaced. "Until then…"

"Until then, we're going to figure out another plan," Debbie's mom said, taking the seat across from him. "I'll work in the kitchen if I have to."

As he reached to squeeze her mother's hand, Debbie could read the pain in Pop's eyes.

"I think we need to go to the hospital," Debbie's mom said, the concern in her eyes evident.

"Absolutely not," Pop argued. "I'll be fine."

"Well, rest a few minutes right here until you feel like going up the stairs to lie down, Frankie," her mother argued. "When you're ready, I'll come with you. The breakfast crowd will be thinning out soon, and the kids can handle it."

"You sure?" he asked, looking around.

"Of course." Debbie, Becky Ann, and Junior spoke in unison.

Her father sat at the table for a few minutes with a pained expression on his face, then rose much slower than usual. As he made his way to the stairs, Debbie noticed that he sounded a little breathless. She tried not to let fear get the best of her, but as he rounded the corner, she couldn't hold back the tears. Slumping down into the booth, she shook her head. "We've got to figure out something between now and Saturday. Pop isn't well enough to keep going until then, and we can't afford to hire someone else to help Junior in the kitchen."

"You don't have to," Johnny said. "I'll do it."

"W–what?" She looked at him, stunned. "You're going to help flip burgers? During the most important week of your life?"

He shrugged and a hint of a smile turned up the corners of those gorgeous lips. "Why not? There's no place I'd rather be than here…with all of you."

Debbie felt her cheeks turn warm at that revelation. Becky Ann looked back and forth between them. "I knew it. You two are sweet on each other."

Johnny grinned. "Maybe. That's for us to know and you to find out."

Becky Ann sighed. "Hope Martha Lou doesn't find out. She's already planning to be your number-one fan."

"Sorry, but that slot is already taken." Debbie winked, feeling her spirits lift. She turned back to Johnny. "What about all of that stuff you said about not being a good cook?"

"I'm not," he said. "But I'm happy to try."

"Let's see what Junior says. It's really his decision." Debbie called for her brother to meet them behind the counter and filled him in on the situation.

Junior gave Johnny an inquisitive look. "So, you want to cook?"

"Me, too!" Toby hollered. "I can cook, too."

"You can watch," Debbie said. "But promise you'll stay out of Junior's way. He doesn't like a crowded kitchen."

"I promise," Toby said.

"Ever flip a burger before?" Junior asked, looking in Johnny's direction.

Johnny's face turned red. "Actually, no. I told Debbie that I'm probably the worst cook in the world."

"Hmm. Looks like you've got a lot to learn then." Junior slapped him on the back. "No problem. You look like an able-bodied student. I'll teach you the ropes."

"Go easy on him, Junior," Debbie said. "We don't want to scare him away."

"Don't go too easy on him," Becky Ann chimed in as she entered the room with an order in hand. "If he ruins the food, it might make the customers sick. We don't need that."

"Gee, thanks for the encouragement," Johnny said with a wry grin.

"Anything I can do to help," Becky Ann said.

Debbie tagged along behind her brother as he led the way into the kitchen. He stopped to point out a couple of pieces of equipment.

"This is our malt mixer," Junior explained. "We keep it out here behind the counter so it's handy. Becky Ann and Debbie usually make the malts—and the sodas." He pointed to the soda dispenser. "We've got everything you can think of in there for regular sodas—from Coca-Cola, Dr. Pepper, 7-Up, and root beer, to flavorings for phosphates."

"Wow." Johnny shook his head. "I hope you don't quiz me on this later. I think I'd fail."

"Set it all to music," Becky Ann said, as she rang up a customer nearby. "You seem to be really good at remembering lines when they're in a song."

"Good idea." He nodded.

"Let's talk about ice cream." Junior paused in front of the ice cream case, which was next to the soda dispenser. "We've got chocolate and vanilla, of course. And strawberry. Sometimes folks like to have all three in their banana split. And speaking of banana splits, how are you at making sundaes?"

"Sundaes?" Johnny shook his head. "About as good as I am at making Mondays and Tuesdays."

Becky Ann let out a snort and punched him in the arm. "Good one, Johnny. I think I'm going to like having you work here." She batted her eyelashes at him, and Debbie realized that her younger sister enjoyed having Johnny here for more reasons than one.

Hmm. She might have to remedy that. Soon.

"I'll help you with sundaes and shakes later," Debbie said.

Johnny gave her a smile so warm it threatened to melt the case of ice cream right on the spot. Debbie felt her heart shift into overdrive and turned her gaze to the ground to avoid sharing it with everyone in the place.

The next few minutes were spent familiarizing Johnny with the various pieces of equipment. Debbie giggled her way through Junior's burger-flipping demonstration, and the laughter only increased as Johnny took his place behind the stove. He managed to drop the first burger on the floor, and the second split in half as he flipped it. Toby made fun of him at every available opportunity, but Johnny seemed to take it in stride.

"Don't worry," Debbie said. "You'll get better with time."

"Hope so." He chuckled. "Good thing the restaurant's not crowded."

"There's always a bit of a lull between the breakfast crowd and the lunch crowd," Junior explained. "So we have time to go through this. We'll tackle hot dogs, fries, and onion rings next."

"Working with all of this food makes me hungry," Johnny said.

"You'll get past that," Junior explained. "When I was younger, I couldn't make onion rings without eating three or four. And I've probably consumed more hot, salty fries than a person should be allowed by law."

"Now I'm hungrier than ever."

Just as they started a basket of onion rings in the fryer, the bell jangled, and the first of the lunch customers entered the shop.

"Okay, hang on for the ride," Junior said. "We're about to get really busy."

Debbie gave Johnny a you-can-do-it smile, one she hoped would see him not just through the lunch crowd, but through the rest of the day. After all, it looked like Johnny Hartmann was here to stay.

* * * * *

As the lunch crowd poured in, Johnny swallowed hard, hoping Debbie couldn't read the fear in his eyes. He watched through the kitchen window as Becky Ann took the first order.

"I'll have a burger, no mayo or mustard, to go," the man said.

"Burger high and dry," Becky Ann called back. "Let's take it for a walk."

"Got that?" Junior asked with a twinkle in his eye.

"High and dry. That means nothing on it?" Johnny asked.

"No condiments. But you're catching on."

Johnny took a raw burger and dropped it onto the skillet. He felt Debbie's eyes on him, which only made this process even more nerve-wracking. Not that he wanted her to leave. Oh no. She could stay all day if she liked. Right beside him. Somehow, knowing she was there made all of this okay.

"Got another order coming up in a couple of minutes," Becky Ann said as she headed off to a table in the back with a new customer. Minutes later she returned. "He wants to know if we're still serving breakfast. I told him we might make an exception."

"Breakfast?" Johnny looked at Junior, panic setting in.

"Sure. Why not." Junior nodded.

"Okay. I'll be right back with his order," Becky Ann said. A couple of minutes later, she hollered out, "Eggs, wreck 'em. Noah's son in the side-car. And draw one!"

Johnny looked at Junior, unable to move. He felt like a stranger in a foreign land.

"Deep breath, Johnny," Debbie said. "He just ordered scrambled eggs and a slice of ham on the side. And 'draw one' means he wants a cup of coffee. See?"

"Um, sure." Made sense. Sort of. Johnny reached for the eggs and tried to crack one. The slippery mess slid through his fingers and missed the bowl altogether, landing on the floor. "Oops."

"I'll get it," Debbie said. "You keep working."

After a couple more attempts, he gave up.

"Make you a deal," Junior said at last. "You do the burgers and hot dogs. I'll take care of most of the other foods. That way we can split the workload down the middle."

"Got it." Johnny wondered what he'd gotten himself into.

"By the way"—Junior pointed to a package of hot dogs—"these are bow-wows."

"Bow-wows."

"Yes. And hot dog buns are called bun pups."

Over the next few minutes, the diner education continued. Turned out, salad was known as cow feed, crackers were dog biscuits, and to eighty-six something meant, "Don't sell to that customer." Who'd have thunk it?

Johnny continued to work, every burger blurring into the next and every hot dog an exact duplicate of the one before. Toby came in and out of the kitchen, helping Becky Ann deliver orders. He also refilled drinks for customers. The youngster seemed to be having a good time. Gone was his sadness from earlier this morning. In its place, a happy grin. And Debbie's mom gave him a smile when she joined them once again. In fact, Sweet Sal gave him several pats on the back and spoke many encouraging words as he worked.

Before long, Johnny looked at the clock and nearly fainted. "Two o'clock?" He shook his head. "It's not possible."

"Oh, it's more than possible." Junior slapped him on the back. "Welcome to the world of the culinary arts, Johnny, where time flies when you're having a good time."

"Guess so." Only one problem with this scenario. Jim and Theresa would be here to pick Johnny and Toby up at five, and he hadn't even talked to Debbie yet about the fundraiser. He hadn't showed her the new song he'd written just last night—the one about walking on the beach with her, hand in hand.

Finally the crowd thinned. Johnny felt like he'd lost ten pounds from sweating so much. Still, the satisfaction of knowing how much he'd accomplished felt good. Really good. And the idea that he'd been helping Debbie and her family only made it that much better.

"Whew." Becky Ann sat at the counter. "My feet are tired."

"Mine, too," Johnny threw in.

"At least the Andersons didn't come by today," Debbie said. "That's a good thing." She looked at Johnny. "You ready for Phase Three?"

"Phase Three?" His thoughts scrambled like the egg he'd cracked earlier.

"Breakfast is Phase One. Lunch is Phase Two. Afternoon ice cream-eating crowd, Phase Three. Dinner, Phase Four. Late night sodas and shakes, Phase Five."

"Wow." He shook his head, feeling a little dizzy. "I guess I'm ready to learn more."

"Good." She leaned forward and whispered in his ear, "Because this time I'll be your teacher."

"In that case…" He gave her a wink, his heart racing out of his chest.

Debbie smiled. "Fine. We'll start with malts then work our way to sodas and sundaes. Hope you don't mind that you're stuck with me. Junior's got to get a start cleaning up the kitchen before the dinner crowd arrives."

"I don't mind a bit." *In fact, I prefer it*. He smiled and her eyelashes fluttered, sending his heart in a thousand directions at once.

"Better pay attention," she whispered, leaning in.

"I am," he whispered in response, his lips brushing her hair as he spoke.

For a moment, both of them paused, and he could sense her

closeness. He wanted to pull her into his arms and kiss her like he'd done that day on the beach, but right now they had work to do. If one could call mixing up a chocolate shake work.

Debbie leaned back as Becky Ann walked by. "Okay, this is what you need to do. Put three scoops of vanilla ice cream in the cup and add a little bit of milk. If it's a chocolate shake, add this syrup." She pointed to a round tin can. "And if it's a malt, also add a scoop of the malt powder."

"Mm-hmm." He deliberately reached around her to get the chocolate syrup, which left them so close he could smell her perfume. What was left of it, anyway.

Debbie blushed. "You turn the machine on like this." She flipped a switch then turned the machine off again. "Got it?"

"Got it."

"When you're done, grab one of these glasses and pour the malt into it." Her voice was all business, but he could see that she was trying to hide a grin. "I usually take what's left in the mixing cup to the table. No point in pouring out the leftovers."

"We wouldn't want to do that." He smiled.

Debbie giggled. "Now, for the root beer float. Start with three scoops of ice cream then pour the root beer on top of it in the glass. Add the root beer a little at a time, though, because it gets foamy."

"Foamy." Johnny clucked his tongue. "That would be a disgrace."

They continued to work alongside each other until Becky Ann drew near.

"Debbie, the guy at table seven wants a hot fudge sundae." She gave her sister an inquisitive look. "Think you can remember how to make one of those?"

"Um, yes. I'm pretty sure I can. But I'll get Johnny to help."

"Sure you will." Becky Ann laughed. "Some help he is." She pointed to the dribble of chocolate running down Johnny's apron.

"Hey, you can't fault a fella for trying," he said.

"No, I don't suppose I can."

Johnny looked at Debbie. "So, we're making a hot fudge sundae."

"No, you're making it," she said. "I'm watching. And instructing."

"Well, instruct away." He reached for the scoop and a sundae dish. "Two scoops or three?"

"Three."

He scooped them out, nearly dropping one on the floor. Finally he managed to get all three in the dish. "Now fudge topping, I presume."

"You presume correctly." She pointed to the container holding the hot fudge. He poured a generous amount on top of the ice cream, which started to melt under the heat.

"The rest needs to be done quickly before it melts." Debbie reached for a container of nuts, sprinkling a few on top. Then she grabbed a can of pressurized whipped cream and passed it his way.

When he pushed the button on top, the cream sprayed everywhere. "Oops." Johnny chuckled.

"Oops is right. You got it all over me." Debbie went to work cleaning the whipped cream out of her hair. "You missed a spot," he said, gesturing to the edge of her lip.

"Oh?" Her eyelashes fluttered, melting his heart.

"Yes." Johnny's playfulness got the better of him. He reached down to give her a quick kiss, the whipped cream disappearing from the edges of her beautiful lips. "There. All gone."

Her eyes grew large and her cheeks turned as red as the maraschino cherry she grabbed from a jar nearby. Debbie plopped it on top and raced to the table to deliver the sundae. Johnny shook his head in disbelief.

Did I just kiss her...right here? In front of everyone?

He turned to find Becky Ann staring. Her mother stood next to her, also looking a bit stupefied. None of that, however, compared to the sight of Mr. Carmichael's wide eyes.

Mr. Carmichael? Isn't he supposed to be upstairs...resting?

Johnny gave a half smile and tried to turn this thing around. Thankfully, the song on the jukebox changed and Bobby's song, "First Kiss," rang out. Mr. Carmichael extended his hand in his wife's direction and she took it, scolding that he needed to be resting, not dancing.

"I don't care what you say, I'm going to dance with my wife. It's good for my heart, trust me."

And so he did. Johnny paused from his labors long enough to watch them. Their tenderness amazed him. So did the fact that—different though they were—they clearly fit into each other's arms. They were made for one another.

He glanced at Debbie, trying to imagine what it would be like to sweep her in his arms and dance her across the floor to this particular song. She gave him a little nod. An invitation, perhaps?

Johnny had just taken a step in Debbie's direction when he noticed Toby step out in front of him. The youngster extended his hand. "Could I have this dance, Miss?"

"Why, of course." Debbie took Toby's hand and the two began an awkward waltz.

Junior approached with a sympathetic look on his face. "Lost the opportunity? I know what that's like."

"Oh?" Johnny turned to face him.

"Yeah. I've been there many times myself."

At that moment, Becky Ann approached and extended her hand. "If you can't beat 'em, you might as well join 'em. C'mon, Johnny. Let's show these old folks what the young people can do." She began a funny little dance that left him all smiles. And though he reeked of burgers and onion rings, Johnny allowed himself to be pulled into the dance. Sure, he was with the wrong partner, but that would change. He would make sure of it. In the meantime, he might as well relax and enjoy the ride before Phase Four kicked in.

A shiver ran down his spine as he thought about the dinner crowd. Oh, well. Enough fretting over that. Right now, dancing was far more fun than dealing with all of that.

Chapter Sixteen

STAR STRUCK

Sunset Sam here, out on the streets of Hollywood, chatting with teen girls. I've posed the following question: "If you could meet any Hollywood actor, who would it be, and why?" An overwhelming majority answered with names you would expect: Elvis Presley, Bobby Conrad, Pat Boone, Rock Hudson, James Dean, Marlon Brando, Cary Grant, and Troy Donahue. As for the "why" part, several of the girls responded that they would offer proposals of marriage, many more would be happy with an autograph or a handshake, some adding that they would never wash their hands again.

For most girls, the dream of meeting a Hollywood star in person is really just that...a dream. Still, most cling fiercely to the illusion, willing it to come true. This reporter finds it strange, indeed, that many of these girls shrug off romantic possibilities with real boys as they while away the hours, hoping Elvis picks up the phone to give them a call.

Ain't gonna happen, girls. Elvis doesn't have your number, and Marlon Brando is too busy filming his next movie. Bobby Conrad is happy with his current state of singleness and Pat Boone...well, he's married. His wife would probably frown on the idea.

Here's a thought. Why not turn a fresh eye to the boy right in front of you? Don't let some poor sap end up like Sunset Sam, wondering how he let that gal get away, just because he didn't look like Cary Grant or sing like Sinatra. Do him a favor and glance his way. Better yet, go with him to the school dance. He'll probably buy you a pretty corsage and offer to pick you up in his daddy's car. In other words, he'll do everything within his power to impress you. So why not consider the possibilities? You might just meet the man of your dreams—if you can get the lights of Hollywood out of your eyes.

— *Reporting for* Hollywood Heartthrob *magazine, "Man About Town" columnist, Sunset Sam*

* * * * *

On Friday morning around ten o'clock, Johnny walked into Jim and Theresa's kitchen, grabbed a glass of milk, and took a seat at the table. He pored over the list of songs in front of him in preparation for tomorrow's fundraiser. He'd written a total of three, but planned to cover a few Elvis songs, too.

"Hey, kid." Theresa came in and opened the refrigerator. "What are you up to? Getting ready for the rehearsal tonight?"

"Yes. Thinking things through."

"Don't think too hard," she said. "Let your heart rule you." She poured a glass of water then joined him at the table. "Jim says we'll be leaving in an hour or so to drop you and Toby off at the soda shop. Think you can handle my boy for another day?"

"Sure, why not. He's a great kid. And he had a blast the other day. I wish you could've seen him waiting tables in that alien costume."

"No doubt he kept the customers entertained." She grinned.

"He did." Johnny smiled, remembering.

Theresa grew silent for a few moments as she took sips from her glass of water. When she finally spoke, her words surprised Johnny. "I have a feeling you won't be with us much longer. Jim says a big-name reporter is going to be at the event down in Laguna tomorrow. That should probably do the trick."

"Do the trick?"

"Get you the exposure you need to make the jump from television to movies."

"I can't even imagine it, to be honest," he said. "I pray I'm ready to make the jump when the time comes. I guess I'll know for sure then, but right now, I feel most comfortable singing my songs."

She shook her head. "You'll see, Johnny. It all goes hand in hand. Out here a singer is only as good as his next movie or TV appearance."

Johnny did see. He just wasn't sure he liked what he saw.

"I love this business," Theresa said. "But sometimes being married to it is tough."

"How so?" Johnny took a swig of his milk then swiped his lip with the back of his hand.

"I don't know. Sometimes Jim is so busy working that it takes time away from family things. And other times I'm convinced he has stars in his eyes. He doesn't always see what's right in front of him."

Johnny felt pretty sure she wanted to add: "Like Toby." But, she didn't. Instead, she took a sip of her water and leaned back in her chair.

"Funny, that's what Toby said, too."

"Really?" She looked perplexed. "When?"

"Tuesday morning. He woke up before everyone in the house. We had a little talk."

"He's been bitten by the bug, for sure," Theresa said. "But I'm with Jim. I don't want to push him into that world just yet. It's not always a friendly world, and he's just a kid. You know?"

"I do. And I think it's admirable that you're trying to protect him. That's what parents do." At once Johnny thought of his mother and father, who were probably already hard at work in Topeka. "They do what they think is right. They raise their kids in the way they should go." The rest of the verse almost slipped out: *"And when they are old, they will not depart from it."* He wondered, though, if Theresa would understand the scriptural reference.

"Jim's got his mind made up that his son isn't going into show business and that's that. Talented or not." Theresa shrugged. "It's not my place to change his mind. I'm not sure I'd want to, anyway. I want the best for my boy. I always have." At once her eyes brimmed with tears, which she dabbed away.

"I know you do, Theresa," Johnny said. "And Toby will figure it out, too."

"Well, if you want the truth, Jim is trying to protect him. He grew up with a father in the business. Don't know if you knew that."

"I had no idea. Who was he?"

"Butch Williams. Folks called him 'Uncle Butch.' He was really famous back in the thirties. Quite a charmer. On-screen, anyway. But not the best father, from what I understand. He presented one image on the screen and another off. Whenever he would come home at night…" She shook her head. "I'm sorry. I probably shouldn't be telling you all of this. It's not my place."

She rose and made her way to the sink with her half-empty glass. After dumping out the rest of the water, she turned to face him. "Can I ask you a question?"

"Sure."

"You've been going to that church with Bobby for a few weeks now. How do you like it?"

Johnny paused a moment before answering. "Well, it's a lot different from my father's church back home. Much bigger. But I love the music, and the sermons are great, too. The pastor is young… probably about your age."

She blushed. "Well, that was an unexpected compliment." After a pause, she said, "I've thought about going for several weeks now. And I think it would be really good for Toby. Do they have a Sunday school?"

"Yes." Johnny nodded. "And I think it would be good for him, too." He snapped his fingers. "Oh, I just thought of something. They're doing a play with the kids. A back-to-school thing. I saw a write-up in the church bulletin last week about auditions."

"Ironic." She drew in a deep breath. "I wonder if Jim would consider that."

"Wonder if Jim would consider what?"

Johnny turned as Jim's voice rang out.

Theresa's cheeks flamed pink. "Oh, Johnny and I were just talking about a little play they're having at his church. Something he thought Toby might like." She gave Jim a pleading look. "Might not be a bad idea to check it out, Jim. It would be a safe way to let him do the thing he's dying to do."

Jim shrugged. "You know what the great Fred Allen said about performing at church, don't you, Theresa?"

"No." She pressed a loose hair behind her ear. "But I feel sure you're going to tell me."

"I am." Jim winked at her then pulled her into his arms. "He said, 'The first time I sang in the church choir, two hundred people changed their religion.'"

Theresa chuckled. "That's funny." She grew more serious. "But I'm not asking anyone to change their religion." After a pause, she said, "Or maybe I am."

Jim gave her a curious look. "What do you mean?"

"I mean show business has been like a religion to us. That's why Toby's so star-struck. Maybe…" She shrugged. "Maybe it wouldn't hurt if we all considered a different religion. One where I could get out of this house and meet a few nice people. Make some friends who, for once, aren't talking about how famous they want to be. Normal people."

Johnny listened to her little speech, his heart now pounding in his ears. He couldn't help but hold his breath until Jim responded. In the lapse between her words and his, Johnny ushered up a quick "Lord, be in control" prayer.

For a minute, Jim didn't say anything. When he did, his words stunned Johnny. "I guess we could give it a try."

Just eight little words. But Johnny had a feeling they would change the course of history for Jim, Theresa, and Toby.

The telephone rang. Johnny used it as an excuse to step out of the room and give Theresa and Jim some privacy. However, before he could make a step into the living room, Toby's voice rang out.

"Johnny, phone!"

"Phone…for me?" He looked at Jim, as if Jim could somehow predict who might be on the other end of the line.

"It's Bobby," Toby called out. "He wants to talk to you. Says it's important."

"Coming." As Johnny made his way to the phone, his thoughts

shifted, once again, to his earlier conversation with Theresa. He wondered what Bobby would say once he found out that Jim and his family might visit his church.

He never had a chance to bring it up. Looked like Bobby had something big on his mind. Something that clearly couldn't wait for another day.

* * * * *

On Friday afternoon, Debbie buzzed around the soda shop trying to ready the place for tomorrow's concert. She was glad Pop had closed down the diner for the day in preparation. Johnny and Toby arrived just as she and Mom finished a baking spree for the event. As always, her heart could not be stilled when Johnny came in. She still marveled that so much had happened so quickly.

He took one look at her and laughed. "Um, did you know you have flour on your cheeks? And your nose? And in your hair?"

She giggled. "Yeah, sorry. We've been baking all afternoon. Mom wants to have plenty of cakes on hand. And breads. And...well, everything. We've been working like crazy." She gestured to her messy uniform. For once, the apron was anything but crisp and clean. "Hope I don't scare you away, but what you see is what you get today. I'm too busy to do anything about it."

"Scare me away?" He pulled her into his arms and gave her a kiss on the nose. "Never."

Debbie heard her father clear his throat. She took a step back, heat rising in her cheeks. As much as she longed to remain in Johnny's embrace, they had work to do...and lots of it.

"We're going to work straight through until time for the rehearsal," she said. "Mom and me. And Junior and Becky Ann, too, of course. Oh, and Martha Lou is helping."

"It's the least I can do." Martha Lou's voice rang out from the kitchen. "You're doing all of us such a big favor, Johnny."

A smile lit his face.

Something in his smile piqued Debbie's curiosity. "You're up to something," she said. "Out with it."

"Maybe."

"Well, don't keep us in suspense."

"Fine. Well, I have a little surprise," Johnny said. "Something I've been keeping under wraps. I've known about it for a couple of hours, ever since Bobby called me."

"Oh?" Debbie brushed her messy hair out of her face. "What is it?"

"Bobby's coming."

"He's…he's what?"

"He's coming."

"Here?" She paused, unable to breathe. "To the soda shop?"

"Yes. He found out yesterday that the filming of his new movie has been postponed because Brenda Valentine broke her leg. They were going to try to work around it, but the whole thing's been put off for several weeks. So, he got the official word a few hours ago and called me to say he's able to come to the fundraiser tomorrow, if you still want him."

"*If* we still want him?" Becky Ann squealed. "*If* we still want him?"

"Are you kidding?" Martha Lou came running from the kitchen. "Seriously? I mean, do you think we would turn down Bobby Conrad? Oh, just wait till I tell the other girls. They're going to flip. They're going to absolutely die." On and on she went, singing Bobby's praises and talking about how the girls of Laguna Beach were going to respond to the news.

The idea of finally meeting Bobby Conrad face to face brought an excitement to Debbie, as well, but she couldn't let go of one troubling thought. "Johnny, it's not fair."

"What do you mean?" He gave her an inquisitive look.

"It's not fair…to you or to the public. We told everyone you would be singing. I think you need to be the one to do the concert, not Bobby."

"Are you kidding?" He shook his head. "This is Bobby Conrad we're talking about here, Debbie. Movie star. Hollywood big-name. Besides, he's already coming. When I got the news, I told him to come on down."

"Just like that? Without asking me?"

He gave her a blank stare. "You're serious?"

"Very." Debbie shook her head. "I have to think about this. I want to do the right thing." She began to pace, her thoughts tumbling. "I think it's admirable that he wants to help, but we've shifted gears. If we shift again, people will think we're unreliable."

"No they won't," Martha Lou argued. "Once they get the word that Bobby Conrad is in town, everything else will be forgotten."

"Martha Lou's right," Becky Ann said. "The girls are gaga over Bobby Conrad."

"Is someone looking for me?" A male voice rang out from behind them. Debbie turned and, much to her surprise, found the one and only Bobby Conrad standing directly behind her. Bobby Conrad? Bobby! Conrad!

At once, she felt faint. Her knees gave way and she started to tumble.

"Oh, watch it." Bobby reached to grab her and led her to a chair.

From the corner of her eye she saw her sister and Martha Lou standing in frozen silence.

Shock. They must be in shock.

For that matter, so was she. In all the times Debbie had dreamed of meeting the famous star, she'd never once pictured it like this. She had cake batter all over her uniform and flour in her hair. Her apron was twisted and her makeup had worn off. Her usual Pollyanna Pink lipstick was long gone, and the scent of her day lily perfume had faded hours ago, during round three of the baking extravaganza.

In short, she was a mess.

And strangely, that part didn't matter. Not one little bit. For, while the star of all stars stood before her, the picture of televised perfection, the only opinion she cared about...was Johnny's.

He swept in behind her to make sure she was okay.

"I think my girl here is a little star-struck," Johnny said.

Debbie shook her head. "No." She gathered her wits and stood, extending her hand. "I'm not. I'm fine. Bobby, it's nice to finally meet you. I...well, obviously I had no idea you were coming."

Bobby laughed, his gorgeous white-toothed smile lighting the room. "Just the way I wanted it. I always love the surprise factor."

"Speaking of the surprise factor..." Debbie pointed to Martha Lou and Becky Ann, who were both still frozen in place, eyes wider than the salami on the submarine sandwich. "I think these two might need medical attention."

"Should we call for an ambulance?" Bobby asked, his eyes twinkling.

"Oh no!" Martha Lou squealed. "Please don't. They might medicate me, and I'd miss the most amazing moment of my life. Please, please don't call for medical help."

She clutched Becky Ann's hand and the two approached together, timidly at first, and then garnering courage. Before long, they were babbling non-stop. Debbie could hardly make sense of their chatter and knew Bobby must be confused by the pair, too. His head bobbed back and forth between them as their words overlapped.

Ginny stood in the background, a perplexed look on her face. She let the other girls go on for a few minutes before finally interrupting them.

"Bobby, please excuse these two." She stepped forward and extended her hand. "They're…" She never managed the final word. As Bobby took her hand in his, she clammed up and looked a little green around the gills.

"She's going down," Martha Lou whispered. "I'd bet my allowance on it."

Debbie watched to see if Ginny would faint. No, the twenty-year-old held her own. While she continued to hold Bobby's hand.

Not that he seemed to mind. Not at all. "Oh, it's okay, I…" Bobby paused, staring at Ginny. He continued to grip her hand, and the two of them stood frozen in time and space.

Johnny cleared his throat. "Um, Bobby?"

"Oh, yeah." Bobby startled to attention, releasing his hold on Ginny's hand.

"Let me introduce the girls of Sweet Sal's."

"Starting with Sal herself, I hope!" Debbie's mom pushed her way through the crowd. "I don't believe it! Finally! We get Bobby Conrad to come to Sweet Sal's in person, and I look a fright."

"You look perfect," he said. "Just as I pictured you after all of Johnny's glowing descriptions."

"Oh?" Debbie's mom looked a little shaken. "What has he told you?"

"Oh, a thousand things, and all of them good." Bobby smiled. "He told me about the food, of course. And the people. And the photos on the walls. And about your family. I've heard about Sweet Sal's so much that it's been real to me all along. So I figured it was about time I came down for a visit. I'm sorry to say it took this long. My life has been, well, crazy."

"No doubt." Debbie's mother smiled. "Well, we're so glad you're finally here. The girls have been dying to meet you for ages."

That was putting it mildly. Debbie shook her head, still not quite believing this.

"Hope you don't mind, but a deejay friend of mine for a radio station in L.A. is coming tomorrow," Bobby said.

"Really?" Debbie's thoughts twirled around in her head. Having a radio deejay here was an amazing opportunity. Still, she couldn't get over the fact that Johnny—her Johnny—had suddenly been pushed from the foreground to the background. She didn't like that feeling. If anyone deserved his moment in the spotlight, he did.

She glanced his way, noticing the kindness in his eyes as he spoke with Bobby. Looked like he didn't mind a bit. Still, Debbie did. And she wished she could figure out a way to turn this thing around while there was still time.

The phone rang and Pop came down the stairs just in time to catch it. Debbie could hear his voice as he spoke to the person on the other end.

"No, you've got that wrong," he said. "Bobby Conrad's not singing here tomorrow, after all. Johnny Hartmann is."

Debbie's mother rushed to her husband's side and tried to relay the message that Bobby was, indeed, singing.

Debbie watched as her father's head turned toward them, his jaw dropping as he took in the young star. "I, um…" He spoke to the person on the other end of the line. "It looks like I was wrong. Maybe Conrad is singing after all."

Bobby nodded.

Pop continued to stare. And stutter. He managed to speak a few more words to the person on the phone then ended the call. He filled them in, his gaze never leaving Bobby. "That was a reporter from the L.A. Times. Says he's coming down to do a feature story on Bobby Conrad singing at Sweet Sal's Soda Shop. Someone want to let me know what's going on around here?"

"Bobby's going to be able to do the concert after all, Pop!" Becky Ann let out a squeal that caused their father to put his fingers in his ears. He removed them, albeit slowly, and his gaze traveled back and forth between Johnny and Bobby.

"What about Johnny?"

"Exactly my question," Debbie said. "What about Johnny?"

They all turned to face him, and his cheeks lit up like the flashing red neon sign outside.

Before anyone could give an opinion, Bobby spoke up. "Well, I'm glad you asked about Johnny. I think I've got a solution that everyone might agree on. Hear me out, okay?"

He began to share his heart…and his plan. And by the end of his upbeat monologue, everyone was on board.

Looked like they were going to have a fundraiser that no one in Orange County would soon forget!

Chapter Seventeen

THE NEXT TEEN SENSATION

In Hollywood, appearance is everything. And stars of today will go to all sorts of effort to impress, changing their hair, wardrobe, makeup, and even the way they speak. They're revamped, readjusted, and re-educated. Then they're reintroduced to a watching world, where folks clamor to see the changes. And, indeed, they are different...on the outside. One has to wonder, though, if the image they put forth is really as perfect as it seems, if the transformation runs deeper than appearance.

Call me tainted, but I've been in this business awhile now, and have started to question many things, including the advice I've been giving in this column. Sure, it's great to look nice. And being fashionable is fun, as we've discovered. But, what about the child who has no money for new shoes, or the teen who can't afford that great new leather jacket? What about the man who can barely keep food on his family's table, let alone spend money on expensive suits? What do we say to him?

Stars of today are just that...stars. We look to them to razzle-dazzle us. Perhaps that's why we hope to see them wearing the best and looking their best. We want them tweaked and polished, the very picture of perfection. In a sense, we've pressed them into a mold, asked them to lift us out of our dreary lives with their sparkle and shine. If we were honest with ourselves, we would do better to ask them to present who they really are—with all of their flaws, scars, and imperfections. Only then could we truly know them.

Maybe that's why we don't. Maybe the image in our minds is far better than the reality of who that star is when the makeup comes off.

One has to wonder.

— *Reporting for* Hollywood Heartthrob *magazine, "Glamour Girls" columnist, Fashionable Frances*

* * * * *

The next few hours were a whirlwind for Johnny. Outside, the men of Laguna Beach worked together to construct a huge stage on the south end of the parking lot. Local officers looked on while sipping coffee and sodas, provided by Frankie and Sal.

With Debbie's help, Johnny and Bobby came up with a solid plan of action for tomorrow's event. Bobby would start the show at noon. He'd sing three songs in the first set then pass the microphone to Johnny, who would sing three: "Dear Debbie," the new song, and then an Elvis tune. After Johnny's songs, the microphone would go back to Bobby, who would wrap up the show. The media would eat this up. They'd love writing about the two guys performing together. No doubt about it.

And the soda shop. Johnny made up his mind that any story he gave would be about the shop, first and foremost. Surely when people outside of Orange County got the news, they would pitch in, too. He hoped so, anyway.

At nine o'clock, with most of the patrons gone and the plan solidified, Bobby took the inside stage for a rehearsal. The acoustics wouldn't be the same in here, but they didn't dare move outside yet. Not with so many people milling about.

Johnny couldn't help but notice that Bobby had spent most of the afternoon in quiet conversation with Ginny Anderson. Interesting. He had to wonder how her father would take to that idea. Still, no one could blame Bobby for being attracted to the beauty, with her dark brown hair and bright blue eyes. And Ginny—who rarely blushed or giggled—did little else when Bobby was around. Truly, they were both transformed.

As Bobby stepped onto the stage, Martha Lou approached, a gleam in her eye.

"Bobby, Becky Ann and I had an idea. We want to run it by you."

"Oh?" He gave her a curious look.

"Yes, we're both singers, too. We're in choir at school."

"And?" He quirked a brow.

"Yes, and we're great at harmonizing. Debbie is, too. So we were thinking we could back you up on one of your songs. We've been practicing for days and know all of the harmonies to 'First Kiss.'"

Johnny looked at Debbie, whose face blazed red. "I didn't put them up to this, Bobby, I promise. And I have never—repeat, never—sung in front of anyone. Other than playing around when the jukebox is on, I mean. It's not the same thing."

Johnny could have guessed as much. Still, he wasn't sure how Bobby would respond.

After a few seconds, Bobby said, "It won't hurt to try. Come on up on the stage, girls. Let's see how you sound."

Becky Ann and Martha Lou practically leaped onto the stage. Debbie sat glued to her seat.

"You might as well join them," her mother said. "You might never get a chance like this again."

Bobby stepped down off the stage and extended his hand. Debbie flinched and didn't move. For a moment, anyway. Then, finally, she took his hand and stood. The strangest feelings washed over Johnny as he watched Debbie's hand slip so easily into Bobby's. And that feeling only increased as Bobby strummed his guitar and sang the opening verse of "First Kiss." When he reached the chorus, the girls began to sing along. Interesting. They sounded pretty good. Martha Lou and Becky Ann had both chosen to sing alto and blended nicely with Bobby's voice.

And Debbie... Wow. She sang a lovely soprano, adding the nicest touch of all. Of course she looked terrified, but Johnny knew the fear would pass. In time. He also wondered what it would be like to sing with her himself. Hmm. Something to think about.

As Bobby wrapped up "First Kiss," everyone in attendance— the Carmichael family, Ginny, Jim, Theresa, Toby, and Johnny—all responded with cheers and applause.

"Great idea," Jim said, standing. He gave the girls a pensive look. "So, you girls call yourselves the Peppermints, huh?"

"Yes." Becky Ann pointed to her red-and-white-striped uniform.

"Well, that's it, then." Jim nodded. "Bobby and the Peppermints. We'll pull you up onstage to sing that song tomorrow, if you're up for it."

The girls began to squeal, and Martha Lou again looked like she might faint. For that matter, so did Debbie. She could barely make it off the stage. Johnny rose from his chair and helped her into a seat. She was shaking so hard her words barely made sense.

"I—I—I can't do that tomorrow. I can't."

"Sure you can." Her father gave her an encouraging smile. "You're a Carmichael. We Carmichaels go the extra mile. It might be hard, honey, but you can do it. And I dare say, you'll be proud of yourself when it's over."

"I'm proud of you now." Johnny squeezed her hand. "I had no idea you could sing."

"I—I didn't e–either." Her face turned red.

Bobby ran through a couple more songs then turned over the rehearsal to Johnny. He made it through "Dear Debbie," with everyone in the place looking back and forth between him and Debbie as he sang. Surely by now everyone in the place knew he'd fallen for her. Hard. No denying it. As he sang the song this time, Johnny focused all his attention on her. Sang it straight from the heart. When he finished, the object of his affections had tears in her eyes. She mouthed the words, "Thank you," and he smiled in response.

Now for the hard part. To sing the new ballad. The one he'd written after kissing her on the beach. Johnny settled back onto the bench and strummed the first few chords of "Oceans of Love" then dove in. The words rippled forth, telling the whole story. They conveyed the beauty of her smile. The sun in her long strands of blond hair. The freckles on her nose. The playful way she ran along the ocean's shore, kicking up water. They told the joy of wrapping her in his arms. Kissing her for the first time. Standing in solitude with the waves crashing around them. They offered up his praise to the One who'd brought her to him, and his inexplicable joy at the thought of spending more time with her, of making her his own.

In short, "Oceans of Love" expressed the sentiments of his heart.

And when the song ended, there wasn't a dry eye in the place. An eerily silent crowd stared at him, and he felt his heart begin to race. Did they like it? Had he said too much?

His eyes sought out Debbie's. She gazed at him with the most beautiful, blissful expression on her face. If he'd been an artist, he would have captured it in paint or pen. Instead, he opted to write it on his heart, to file it away for a future song.

Finally, Toby broke the ice. "Johnny, that's the dumbest song I ever heard."

A gasp went up from the girls, and before long everyone in the soda shop entered into a rousing argument. He was thankful no one agreed with Toby, but Johnny still couldn't get a feel for where they stood. Not that he really cared. Only one opinion mattered to him—Debbie's.

Toby continued to ramble, stating his case. "I'm so sick of all these songs about kissing. Why does everything have to be about kissing, anyway? Can't somebody write a song about aliens or dogs or best friends or something? Maybe a song about show business? Being famous?"

Bobby laughed. "You can write those songs someday, kid. I hear Johnny's been giving you guitar lessons."

"Yeah," Toby said. "I know three chords—D, G, and A. I guess that's enough to write a song."

"Well, if you want to win the girls, you're better off writing a song like the one Johnny just sang," Bobby said. "Because I'll tell you the truth, that's a Billboard hit if I ever heard one, and I've heard a few in my day."

"Do you think so?" Johnny took a step down from the stage.

"Yes, I do," Bobby said.

"And I second that." Jim shook Johnny's hand. "Kid, I knew you were good, but I didn't know you were that good."

"Thank you." Now the embarrassment kicked in.

"Johnny, it was…" Debbie rose to meet him. "It was…" Her eyes filled with tears. "It was the most beautiful thing I've ever heard in my life, and Toby is a nut for saying it's anything but." She turned back to the youngster. "Sorry, kid, but you're way off base. Bobby's right. That's the best song I've ever heard, bar none."

"Worthy of *American Bandstand*," Jim said. "So that's where Johnny's headed next. I'm going to make it happen." He paused and looked at the girls. "You've been watching the show, haven't you? What do you think?"

"Oh, I love it!" Martha Lou gave him a dreamy-eyed look. "That Dick Clark is so handsome."

"He is," Becky Ann agreed.

"I'm asking what you think of the music," Jim said. "Not the emcee."

"Oh, the music's great," Martha Lou said. "And that song Johnny just sang would be perfect."

"This new show has the power to seriously jumpstart careers. If we can get Johnny on there with "Oceans of Love," he'll be an overnight sensation. We're talking about something much, much bigger than *Talent Scouts*. This could very well be the best thing that ever happened to him. First *American Bandstand*, then…the ends of the earth!"

Johnny listened to this conversation about his career in silence. He was too exhausted to argue, but if he'd had the strength he might've told Jim that he didn't really care to go to the ends of the earth…unless he could take Debbie with him.

Toby shrugged and yawned. "Are we gonna stay here all night and listen to these dumb songs? I'm tired."

"No, we're all done." Jim patted him on the back. "It's going to be a long day tomorrow, so I think we'd better head back up to L.A. and get a good night's sleep."

As everyone said their good-byes, Johnny slipped back onto the stage to grab his guitar. Debbie met him there, her face awash with joy.

"Johnny, thank you." She smiled. "I thought 'Dear Debbie' was great, but that song…" Her eyes filled with tears. "It's the sweetest thing I've ever heard."

"I meant every word," he whispered. Johnny drew her into his arms and gave her a soft kiss on the forehead. He wanted to be swept away, like that moment on the beach, but not with so many people looking on. There would be plenty of time for kisses later.

The other girls clustered around Bobby, giggling and sighing as they wished him a good night. Martha Lou erupted in tears, and Becky Ann looked as if she might cry, too.

And Ginny…he watched as Bobby reached to give her a shy hug. She responded with pink cheeks and a broad smile.

Bobby headed off to Malibu in his convertible, and Jim led his family to their car in the parking lot.

"We'll be back tomorrow morning by ten," he called out to Mr. Carmichael. "See you then."

Johnny gave Debbie another quick kiss on the forehead then climbed in the back seat next to Toby. He watched out the window as they pulled away, feeling as if he was leaving part of his heart behind. In fact, he was.

His thoughts were a jumbled mess all the way back to Los Angeles. In the seat next to him, Toby chattered endlessly, setting his nerves on edge. For once, Johnny just wanted quiet. Peace. Time to think. To gather his emotions in hand and examine them. For what he could no longer deny—to himself or anyone else—was the love he felt for Debbie Carmichael. Blissful, terrifying love.

He would find a way to tell her…tomorrow. With spoken words, not sung. In the meantime, he had to calm his mind. Had to rest.

In the seat next to him, Toby continued to talk a mile a minute. "Hey, Dad, are you in a good mood?" the youngster asked.

"Good mood?" Jim chuckled as he steered the car north on the highway. "The best ever. Why?"

"Because I want to ask you something important," Toby said. "I really, really mean it this time."

"What is it, son?"

"CBS is doing a new show in October and I want to audition."

Johnny braced himself in preparation for Jim's response.

"Son, we've talked about this a thousand times."

"No, Dad, listen. I really mean it this time. This is different. This is the opportunity of a lifetime. It's a brand-new show, and I could audition for the lead. They're looking for a boy just my age, and the whole show is going to be about him."

Jim glanced back over his shoulder. "And just what is this show you're talking about?" He shifted his focus back to the road.

"It's called *Leave It to Beaver*."

"Beaver?" Johnny laughed and soon everyone else followed suit.

"Is the main character building a dam, by chance?" Jim asked.

"No, Dad. His real name isn't Beaver. It's Theodore, but everyone calls him Beaver. I read all about it in *Variety*. He's the youngest brother, and he's always getting into trouble. And his older brother"—Toby glared at Johnny—"is always getting him out of trouble."

"Sounds like type casting," Theresa said, turning to Jim. "Maybe you'd better let him do this one, Jim."

"Yes, Dad, please!" Toby began to bounce up and down in his seat. "CBS is auditioning boys this coming week and I know I'd be perfect. Absolutely, totally perfect."

Jim changed lanes, preparing to exit the highway. "Son, I'm tired of arguing with you about this. You don't seem to be listening, anyway."

Toby's voice grew more animated. "Are you saying I can audition?"

"No." Jim shook his head. "I'm just saying that I'm tired of arguing with you." He chuckled. "Listen, kiddo, any show about a kid named Beaver is doomed to failure. Trust me on this. I've been in this business for years and I know what I'm talking about. You'll be glad I didn't let you waste your time auditioning for this one."

Toby sighed. "I suppose."

The rest of the trip was made in silence. When they arrived home, Johnny trudged through the living room, so exhausted he wondered how he could possibly put on the show of a lifetime tomorrow.

"You okay, son?" Jim asked.

"Just worn out. I'm sure tomorrow will be great."

"It's going to be the best day of your life." Jim smiled. He reached to take Johnny by the arm. "Oh, and by the way…"

"Yes?"

"I don't think you need to worry about Bobby being any sort of competition," Jim said. "I think it's safe to say you've won Debbie's heart."

"With my voice or my face?" Johnny asked with a grin.

"Neither, son." Jim shook his head. "This time I'd have to say you've done it with your heart."

* * * * *

Debbie practically floated up the stairs. This whole day had been like a dream. She'd finally met Bobby Conrad—that part was exciting enough—but hearing the song Johnny had written for her had been the icing on the cake. She could hardly breathe, even now, as she thought about it. In one song, he'd captured every emotion they'd both felt that day on the beach. She marveled at his ability to write something so—perfect.

After showering, she dressed for bed. She heard the television and knew Pop was watching *Alfred Hitchcock*. She pulled on a robe and tiptoed to the living room.

"You're up late," she said.

"Just thinking." He gave her a smile. "Lots to think about today."

"There is." She couldn't hide her smile. Debbie settled onto the divan next to her father. He reached to take her hand.

"You're growing up."

"Y–Yes."

"Before long, you'll be married and have kids of your own." His eyes filled with tears.

"Oh, Pop! Don't!" She rested her head on his shoulder.

"But I'm right. You'll see. You'll have children, and life will move on. This world will change, but you'll still be little Debbie Carmichael from Laguna Beach. That will never change...in my eyes, anyway."

Debbie couldn't manage the words over the lump in her throat. For, while she wanted to say otherwise, she knew Pop was right. She was growing up, and things were changing.

Mom walked into the living room, saw Debbie and Pop in tears, and came straight to the sofa. "What's happened?"

"Our daughter is growing up," Pop said.

"Ah, so that's it."

"Yes." He sighed.

"And it would appear she's falling in love," Mom added.

Debbie nodded, feeling a little embarrassed. She whispered the words, "I am."

"With Johnny," her mother added.

"Yes…with Johnny." The lump in her throat disappeared at the mention of his name.

"It's so obvious that you care for him, honey." Her mother's eyes twinkled. "There's no hiding it from me. I see it, plain as day."

"I do, Mama. I care for him…a lot."

"And he's crazy about you. We'd have to be blind not to see it."

"Especially after hearing that song," Pop said, reaching to give her a hug. "Though I kind of wish I didn't know all that stuff about you two kissing on the beach."

"Sorry. But it was bound to come out sooner or later." She paused a moment, embarrassment kicking in. "I just feel so silly."

"About what?" her mother asked.

Debbie shook her head. "So many things." After a moment's reflection, she decided the time had come to share her heart. "Do you remember that scene in *Love Me Tender*?"

"Which scene, honey?" her mother asked.

"You know, the one where Elvis's brother went off to war, and he stayed behind and married his brother's girlfriend."

"Ah." Pop nodded. "A lot of conflict in that scene."

"Yes." Debbie released a deep breath. "All that stuff about the two brothers. I can relate so well."

"What are you saying?" her mother asked. "You've been torn between two brothers?"

"Well, not literal brothers," she said. "But I guess Bobby and Johnny are brothers in the Christian sense. And I have been torn, Mom." She paused. "When I think of Bobby, I think of someone strong and loving, someone romantic. He's so…" She paused again. "So…"

"Ideal?"

Debbie pondered her mother's words. "Well, yes. He seems so perfect."

"Honey, everyone on the silver screen appears perfect. Ideal. But I can promise you that life in the real world doesn't match up. Bobby is an illusion of perfection, but I guarantee, he's flawed, just like every man." She was quick to add, "And woman."

"I see that now." Debbie sighed. "I just had this picture in my head of how it would be if Bobby loved me back. It was…"

"A dream?"

"Bobby Conrad fever," Pop said. "It's a hopeless malady."

"Not hopeless any longer." Debbie smiled. "It's so funny, because I always accuse the younger girls of being unrealistic. Seems a little strange that I almost fell in love with the image of someone I'd never met."

"Not terribly unusual, honey," her mother said. "Did I ever tell you I was once in love with Clark Gable?"

"W–what?" Debbie shook her head. "I don't recall ever hearing that one before."

"Oh yes," Pop said. "I knew all about it."

"Wow."

"It was back in 1934, I think. Clark had just filmed *It Happened One Night* with Claudette Colbert and I was star struck. Your father and I were next-door neighbors, so he knew me pretty well. I didn't know it at the time, but he'd fallen for me in high school. I was too busy swooning over Clark to notice."

"Oh, mom." Debbie shook her head. "I guess we Carmichael girls come by this honestly, then."

"More than you know." Her mother laughed. "I actually went to the Academy Awards that year because Clark was nominated for best actor. Of course, I didn't get to go inside and watch the actual event. But I was there, waiting when his limousine pulled up. I could barely catch a glimpse of him through the crowd, but finally, there he was, in all his splendor." Her eyes took on a faraway look, and Debbie did her best not to giggle. Looked like she and her mother had more in common that she'd thought.

"What happened next, Mom?"

Her mother sighed. "I called out his name, but he walked right by me. I hollered it again, and even told him I loved him, if memory serves me correctly."

"You didn't!"

"I did." Her mother sighed. "Not that it mattered. He never even saw me. Or, if he did, he didn't turn around. At any rate, it broke my heart. Shattered my dream of living a happily ever after with him, that's for sure."

"And Pop?" She turned to face him. "What about you?"

He grinned. "I was there, waiting for her when she got back home."

A smile lit Mom's face. "He took me in his arms and kissed away my silly tears and finally 'fessed up to his feelings for me."

"I'm a little slow to the punch, but I made it just in time," her father said.

"Wow." Debbie took a moment to let all of this absorb.

"My mama used to say, 'Sometimes you can't see the forest for the trees.'" Debbie's mother gave her a knowing look. "I suppose you could say that Hollywood is full of trees."

"Tall, handsome, debonair trees," Debbie responded. "With great singing voices."

She and her mother sighed in unison.

"Still sorry you settled for the boy next door?" Pop's voice rang out.

"Are you kidding?" Mom gave him a tender look. "You think I would trade in this"—she gestured to the tiny apartment—"for a mansion in Beverly Hills? Of course not!"

He rose and took her by the hand. She stood and kissed him soundly. This led to a couple more kisses and a few whispered words between them. Debbie finally decided she'd better scoot. She needed time to process all of this.

Minutes later, curled up in bed, she thought about her mother's story, how she'd fallen for the wrong guy. Thought about the idealistic picture she'd painted in her head about Bobby Conrad. Then, finally, she allowed her thoughts to shift to the one person who truly brought a smile to her face, the one whose very name caused her heart to flutter and her heart to sing in tune—Johnny Hartmann.

The reality of her feelings swept over her like the lyrics in his song had done just a short time ago. Yes, Johnny Hartmann was the forest. And Bobby Conrad? Why, he was simply a tree.

Chapter Eighteen

HERE'S LOOKIN' AT YOU, KID

Stage fright. This reporter understands it firsthand, having suffered a serious bout of it during a second-grade play. I wore a great costume (a Pilgrim suit, if memory serves me correctly) and had my lines memorized. But when my teacher tried to push me out onto the stage, I heard the voices of audience members and panicked. Not only was I frozen in place at the idea of performing in public, I have remained thus for over twenty years.

Yes, stage fright is a problem, even for those who are exceptionally gifted. And though they may not show it, many of today's stars enter the stage or set with knees knocking. Take Elvis, for example. Here's what he had to say on the subject: "I've never gotten over what they call stage fright. I go through it every show. I'm pretty concerned, I'm pretty much thinking about the show. I never get completely comfortable with it, and I don't let the people around me get comfortable with it, in that I remind them that it's a new crowd out there, it's a new audience, and they haven't seen us before. So it's got to be like the first time we go on."

And lest you think Elvis is alone in his jittery state, ask those who've worked with the gorgeous Marilyn Monroe. Her classmates at the Actors Studio would attest to the fact that stage fright was one of her biggest obstacles.

And these two stars are not alone. During a live production of Hamlet, *the great Laurence Olivier once completely blanked out in the middle of the infamous "to be or not to be" soliloquy. His solution? He took a seat on the stage, where he remained until the lines came to him.*

Yes, stage fright can do strange things to a person, even one who is completely prepared. When you walk onto the stage and the lights hit you squarely in the face...when the audience cheers and your name is hollered from the rafters...chances are you're going to forget...just about everything.

— Reporting for Hollywood Heartthrob *magazine, "On the Big Screen" columnist, Cinema Cindy*

* * * * *

Debbie awoke early on Saturday morning. Still exhausted from her work over the past few days, she found herself wishing she could sleep in. Then, as she came fully awake, she remembered: today's the day!

She bolted upright in bed, her thoughts now tumbling madly. There were so many things to do. First, of course, she needed to shower and slip into a clean, pressed Peppermints uniform. Several photographers were bound to be in attendance, and she needed to look her best. For a moment she allowed her thoughts to travel to the role she would play as Bobby's backup singer. A wave of nausea passed over her as nerves kicked in. How had she landed center stage in all of this, when she'd only meant to play a role in the background?

Still, if she could get over the jitters, this would turn out to be a day for the record books, one she would tell her grandchildren about.

Grandchildren. Hmm.

Thinking about the future, of course, brought her thoughts around to Johnny, the one she hoped to be spending it with. With each passing day—with every single breath—she clearly saw what the Lord had been doing all along. While she had been chasing after Mr. Wrong, her heavenly Father had placed Mr. Right directly in her path. Would she have overlooked him if the Lord hadn't been so clear? Debbie shuddered, thinking about it. For, while she didn't even realize she could feel this strongly about Johnny a week or two ago, she now wondered how she could get along without him. She prayed she wouldn't have to.

Thoughts of him brought the usual sense of expectation. He would be arriving at ten. She'd better get busy!

A couple of shouts from outside caught her attention. She peered out the window, stunned to see a sea of girls in the vacant field next door. It was a good thing they couldn't get onto the property just yet. Not without going through the officers, anyway. Still, who would have guessed Orange County's teen girls would turn up this early? She'd better get this show on the road.

By nine o'clock, the Carmichael family was pressed, dressed, and headed downstairs. All the activity would shift outdoors once the show began at noon. For now, Debbie and the others had plenty to keep them busy inside the shop. They weren't serving breakfast customers, as they would usually do on a Saturday morning. They'd changed the diner's hours for the day, canceling breakfast altogether. With such a huge lunch crowd headed in, there simply wasn't time or energy to handle breakfast, too.

They'd modified the menu for the event, too, offering only burgers, hot dogs, fries, onion rings, shakes, malts, and sodas, which Junior had already started preparing in abundance. Several of the local residents—including some ministers and their families—had offered to serve as waiters, carrying food out to the parking lot to guests when the time came. What fun! Debbie could hardly wait to see them decked out in Sweet Sal's hats and aprons.

Buzzing around in happy anticipation, her mother sang along with Patti Page, whose beautiful voice rang out from the jukebox. Debbie smiled as she listened to her mother join in, singing the words to "Tennessee Waltz" in perfect harmony. How come she'd never noticed her mom's singing ability before? Or her own, for that matter. Deciding a warm-up was in order, Debbie added her voice to the fray.

At ten o'clock several of Laguna Beach's finest officers entered the soda shop, looking frazzled. With the help of the mayor and police chief, they came up with a quick plan of action for how they would protect Bobby and Johnny from the expected onslaught of girls. They also set up a plan for the crowd. One of the officers—Sergeant Tompkins—estimated there were already at least three hundred girls outside, waiting in the field next door, with dozens more arriving every few minutes.

"Thank goodness we had the foresight to rope off the parking lot last night," he explained. "Otherwise we'd have a real mess on our hands. We're probably going to end up with over a thousand people here, the way things are going. Maybe more."

Debbie could only manage one word: "Wow."

"What happens next?" her father asked.

"Well, we're about to create an opening where they can come through," the sergeant explained. "Your audience members will have to pass by the folks with the donation buckets to get inside the stage area."

"Hopefully dropping something in the buckets," one of the other officers said then chuckled.

"Yes," Sergeant Tompkins added. "Once they come through that opening, they can find a place to stand near the stage. I dare say the stage will be circled on all sides, mostly by females in their teens and twenties."

"And late forties," Debbie's mother said then winked.

The good sergeant went on to explain that the officers would do their best to keep a path between the stage and the soda shop door so the waiters could come and go, and so Bobby and Johnny could safely move in and out.

"I don't know how we'll ever be able to thank you," Debbie's pop said at last. "It's wonderful, what you're doing."

"All in a day's work, Frankie," one of the officers said. "Besides, this is the best thing to ever happen to Laguna Beach. It really puts us on the map."

The officers headed back outside just as Ginny arrived with Cassie Perkins at her side. Cassie held up a hand-painted bucket with the word DONATIONS on the front.

"We have dozens of these," she said. "The police officers are holding them. So are the firefighters and the mailmen. You should see Clifford. He's having the time of his life out there. The whole thing is... wonderful!"

"We're already collecting money," Ginny added. "Lots of it." She handed her bucket to Debbie, who whistled when she saw the bills inside.

"I'm stunned." Debbie could hardly imagine how this would turn out.

"You're not going to believe this," Ginny added. "But my parents are here."

To keep an eye on us, no doubt. Debbie forced a smiled but couldn't help feeling like a cloud had suddenly swept in. She prayed Mr. Anderson wouldn't do anything to dampen the mood of the patrons today.

"My father actually dropped a ten-dollar bill in the bucket," Ginny said. She laughed. "Can you believe it?"

"Crazy." That was all Debbie could manage, but under the circumstances, it was probably enough.

The girls went back outside, chattering all the way. At five minutes after ten, Bobby arrived in his red Corvette. A crowd of girls immediately swarmed him. He could barely pull the car up to the curb without bumping into them. Only the shrill whistle of the police officer persuaded the girls to back off and let him approach.

When he got out of the car, Bobby was nearly ambushed again. Sergeant Tomkins and the other officers managed to get the crowd under control and ushered him safely inside. Still, Debbie had to wonder how they would manage once Bobby took the stage at noon. She also wondered why Johnny and Jim hadn't shown up yet.

She continued to wonder—and worry—about them as the minutes ticked by.

"They said ten o'clock, right?" she asked her father.

"Yes." He glanced at his watch. "Jim's rarely late."

"Strange. I hope they're okay." Debbie paced the restaurant, her nerves almost getting the best of her.

"You okay?" Bobby's voice rang out, his concern evident.

"Oh, I…" She paused. "I'm worried about Johnny."

"He'll be here soon." Bobby reached to touch her arm and—in spite of her best attempts—she couldn't drum up so much as a tingle. Nothing.

Bobby is a tree.

Now, where is my forest?

She gave Bobby a smile. "I'm just anxious, I guess."

"I can see why," he responded. "It's so obvious that the Lord has done something pretty special by bringing Johnny all the way from Topeka, Kansas, to meet you."

Debbie felt a rush of warmth rise to her cheeks. She managed a little, "Mm-hmm," before heading back to the window to peer outside.

At exactly eleven o'clock, as the crowd outside grew to a near-frightening level, folks from the media began to arrive. The first to set up in the field next door was a camera crew from a television station in Los Angeles. Next came several newspaper reporters. Debbie watched it all, dumbfounded. What would they do if Johnny didn't make it?

Finally, at eleven-fifteen, Jim's car pulled up. She watched out the window as police offered Johnny an escort inside. By the time he made it through the throng of females, Johnny's eyes were wide, and he looked a little pale. Until he saw Debbie. Then a smile as bright as the summer sun lit his face and he drew near, drawing her into a comfortable embrace.

"I thought we'd never make it." He kissed her on the forehead. "The traffic on the Coastal Highway is unbelievable. I've never seen anything like it."

"Well, of course it's unbelievable," an unfamiliar voice called out. "People from all corners of Southern California are coming to see you."

Debbie turned to see an older woman with dark curly hair, dressed in a stylish suit. Another woman stood directly behind her with a not-so-happy look on her face.

The older woman held up a press badge. "Hope you don't mind, but the nice sergeant let me inside. Hedda Hopper. Maybe you've heard of me."

"I saw him first, Hedda. You cover Bobby. I get the new kid."

Hedda turned to face the other woman, the color draining from her cheeks. "Louella. Good to see you."

"Humph." A short response from Louella, but enough to send a little shiver down Debbie's spine.

Within minutes Eddie Jennings—Bobby's deejay friend from L.A.—arrived. Debbie kept a watchful eye out for Cinema Cindy, or perhaps Hepcat Harry. Surely they would get here soon.

She never had a chance to find out. Within minutes, she was serving sodas, malts, and shakes to all of the reporters. Then, at exactly eleven forty-five, the noise level in the parking lot rose to a near-deafening level. Junior worked in the kitchen with Pop at his side. Debbie prayed the strain of the day would not be too much for her father. She was thankful that a handful of his friends from church had offered their services.

Through the plate glass windows, Debbie watched the teen girls grow more frantic with each passing moment. Those closest to the shop pressed their faces against the glass, trying to get a better look inside, a few shouting out Bobby's name.

"They're like a lynch mob," Debbie said. "It's crazy."

"They're just impatient," her mother said. "They'll settle down as soon as Bobby takes the stage."

"I hope so." Debbie watched as several of the teens left lipstick prints on the glass. A couple of them even spelled out Bobby and John-ny's names in lipstick, as well. Backwards, of course. One girl began to rap on the glass, hollering out Bobby's name then chanting, "Come out! Come out! Come out!"

Thankfully, an officer stopped her. In that moment, the whole thing became very real. Overwhelmingly real. Debbie thought she might lose all control of her senses. Then she spotted Johnny, who gave her a little wink. Suddenly, the planets aligned themselves once again and she could breathe normally.

At about that time, Ginny and Cassie made their way inside once more, this time looking a little wild-eyed and winded.

"It's crazy out there," Cassie said. "I think every girl in Laguna Beach is here."

Ginny nodded. "And half of Orange County."

"We got a call this morning from a girls' school in Los Angeles," Debbie said. "They're sending seventy girls for the second set."

"Lots of donations still coming in from the girls," Ginny said. "But I'm going to take a break for a couple of minutes to say hello to Bobby before he goes onstage." She turned toward the office, where Bobby and Johnny were chatting with a few of the reporters.

"I promised Becky Ann I'd help wait on customers once the concert started," Cassie said. "Looks like I'd better get to it." She, too, disappeared from sight.

Debbie headed outside, where she did her best to help the waiters keep up with the ongoing demand for food and drinks.

At twelve o'clock the girls outside began to clap in steady rhythm. Debbie sensed their impatience more than ever. She knew that Johnny and Bobby were safely tucked away in Pop's office. She managed to squeeze through the mob to get inside the shop just before they were escorted out.

Once inside, she saw Ginny and Bobby huddled together in the corner of the room. They appeared to be praying. Jim had allowed a handful of reporters in and they stood between her and the person she most wanted to see.

Johnny. Wonderful, handsome Johnny. Tears threatened to cover her lashes as she caught a glimpse of him. She fought her way through the crowd, finally reaching him. He slipped an arm around her shoulders.

"I see tears. Is everything okay?"

She couldn't keep the waterworks at bay. "Have I told you how grateful I am that you're doing this for us?"

Johnny smiled. "You don't have to tell me. I know you are."

"This is the nicest thing anyone's ever done for my family," she whispered, burying her head against his neck. "It means the world to me."

"Then the feeling is mutual." Johnny's next words nearly took her breath away. "Because *you* mean the world to me."

Debbie gazed up into his eyes, her heart racing. She wanted to thank him with a thousand kisses, but with so many people looking on, she didn't dare. Instead, she whispered, "That was so sweet."

"No," he whispered back, his words soft against her hair. "You're the one who's sweet." His hands began to tremble, and his next words came out a little shaky. "It's easy to love someone as sweet as you."

She almost stopped breathing at those words. Debbie looked into his eyes, noticing he'd gone misty, too. She couldn't help herself. Really, she couldn't. She repaid his words with a kiss that he wouldn't soon forget.

Then, when the clicking of cameras began to sound out across the room, she realized it might very well be a kiss that his fans wouldn't soon forget, either. Not that she cared. No, right now she only cared about one thing—the man wrapped safely in her arms.

* * * * *

Johnny felt like shouting for joy as Debbie responded to his words of love. Unfortunately, so did the reporters, who snapped photos right and left. Many of them let out a whoop or holler. He could sense Jim's eyes on him, but he didn't care. Honestly, the only opinion that mattered to him right now—short of the Lord's, anyway—was Debbie's. And she was apparently happy to share her thoughts through her kiss.

Just about the time Johnny and Debbie came up for air, Jim ushered the media folks out of the room. He quirked a brow at Johnny and let out a whistle.

Johnny laughed. "Sorry, but for a minute there I forgot we weren't alone."

"Obviously." Jim chuckled. "Nothing to be ashamed of, son. You've got people talking, and that's a good thing. Besides, everyone loves a love story, and you two…" He shook his head. "Well, you two are obviously quite the story."

Debbie's cheeks turned pink, but she didn't say a word. Not that she needed to. No, she'd said plenty with her kiss.

From outside the soda shop, the roar of the crowd grew louder. Jim glanced at his watch. "It's ten after. Don't think we can hold 'em off any longer. You boys ready?"

"Ready," Bobby called out from the corner. "Want to lead the way, Jim?"

"Sure."

"Should I stay in here while he sings?" Johnny asked.

"No, c'mon out and let me introduce both of my boys together," Jim said. "Then you and the girls can sit in the reserved section on the stage while Bobby performs so you're close."

"Sounds good." Johnny took Debbie by the hand and whispered, "Are you ready for this?"

She looked for a moment like she might be sick, but nodded anyway.

The next few minutes were a blur. Somehow, Jim, Bobby, Johnny, Debbie, and the other Peppermints made it through the mob. They managed to make it up the steps to the stage. Johnny gave Debbie's hand a squeeze as she took a seat in one of the reserved seats, alongside Becky Ann and Martha Lou. The younger girls teased the audience by blowing kisses and waving, but Debbie still looked like she might be ill. Jim gestured for Johnny to sit in the empty seat to Bobby's right. Then Jim approached the microphone. The crowd went crazy. The screams from the girls nearly scared Johnny witless. He'd never heard anything so loud. If things didn't calm down, his nerves might not be able to take it. A couple of teenage girls rushed the stage, but an officer stopped them and ushered them back to where they'd come from.

Jim's voice rang out across the crowd: "Thank you all for coming to this special event to benefit Sweet Sal's Soda Shoppe!"

Another cheer went up.

Jim said a few more words, none of them intelligible through the shouts, then hollered, "Welcome, Bobby Conrad!"

Again, the crowd went crazy. Squeals and screams filled the parking lot from one end to the other. Sounded like hundreds—no, thousands. Johnny had a feeling folks all the way to Topeka could hear the shouts.

Bobby rose to stand before the crowd looking cool as a cucumber.

Johnny listened in amazement as his friend sang the first song. The crowd seemed to love it. One girl even fainted. She came to moments later and continued squealing with gusto. Next, Debbie, Becky Ann, and Martha Lou rose and joined Bobby, singing backup on "First Kiss." The crowd went crazy. For that matter, so did Martha Lou, who apparently liked being in the spotlight. She blew kisses at everyone as she exited the stage after the number. Debbie, on the other hand, looked like she couldn't get off the stage fast enough. Oh, but how wonderful she had sounded!

As Bobby wrapped up his final number, Johnny's mouth went dry. He took a sip from a glass of water Jim had placed nearby, but that didn't help. In fact, he wondered if his teeth were stuck to the inside of his lips. Would he even be able to sing?

Hmm. No time to ponder that for long. Bobby's set came to an end, and Jim approached the microphone to calm the crowd. Once their cheers died down, the moment arrived that Johnny had both dreaded and looked forward to.

"Ladies and gentlemen, it is now my pleasure to introduce the next Hollywood heartthrob—all the way from Topeka, Kansas— Johnny Hartmann!"

Debbie gave him an encouraging smile, and Johnny attempted to stand. His legs felt like gelatin. Somehow he made it to the microphone and lifted his guitar from the stand.

Deep breath.

In that moment, as the crowd carried on with full abandon, Johnny whispered up a prayer that the Lord would keep him standing aright. Then he lifted the guitar and the crowd stilled. The first couple of chords were shaky, but Johnny closed his eyes, losing himself in the music, as always.

He couldn't keep his eyes closed for long, however. No, this time it only made sense to sing "Dear Debbie" directly to the girl he'd written it for. So he did. Debbie's sweet expression kept him going, not just through that song, but the second, as well. And when he finished "Oceans of Love," the overwhelming response from the crowd startled him. So did the tears. It seemed like most of the girls were crying.

Wow. Now what?

Hmm. Might as well keep the mood sweet and steady. Johnny leaned forward into the microphone. "Ladies and gentlemen, I'm going to sing a song that means a lot to me. It's one you all know, so feel free to sing along. I'm going to ask a very special girl to join me to sing backup."

He could read the fear on Debbie's face as he extended his hand her way. She shook her head, but he wasn't going to give up that quickly. With a tender gaze, he sent out a final request, and she finally acquiesced. Debbie joined him at the microphone, eyes wide and face bright red.

"I don't know the part," she whispered.

"Sure you do," he whispered back. "Just listen close and come in whenever it feels right."

He strummed the first few chords of "Love Me Tender," and the fear in Debbie's eyes quickly faded. By the time he sang the words, "You have made my life complete," she had joined him, her soft soprano the perfect complement. When they added the next line, "And I love you so," Johnny realized he'd not only shared his true feelings with Debbie...but with a watching world.

Not that he minded sharing in such a public fashion. Oh no. From this day forth, he would go on singing about his love for her, and about the One who had brought him all the way from Topeka, Kansas, to find her. A flood of emotions washed over Johnny as the words to the song continued. For, while he had often dreamed of a life in the spotlight, he'd never realized the only light he'd ever needed was the one that guided him straight into Debbie Carmichael's arms.

Chapter Nineteen

THE BOOK OF LOVE

Here at Hollywood Heartthrob, *we talk a lot about who's dating who. Everyone wants to be in the know. We're on the lookout for makeups and breakups, often stumbling across more broken hearts than blossoming romances. In spite of the many romantic pairings, we rarely hear anyone mention the "L" word. Love. It seems everyone's on a quest to discover it, and yet few actually manage to find the "everlasting" love they hear about in song lyrics.*

So, what is everlasting love, anyway? A fluttering sensation in your heart when that special someone walks in the room? A dedication or commitment to each other? A promise that your affections will never change?

Sure, we've heard it sung about, and even preached about, but what is this elusive thing called love? As I've examined the relationships of Hollywood stars over the past several years, I've found myself trying to get specific about what it is we're actually looking for. Maybe, if we could define it…we could find it. At least, I would like to believe so.

In my quest to find answers, I stumbled across an interview Bobby Conrad gave a few months back, just before the release of his movie, First Kiss. *When asked how he defined love, he responded that love should be patient and kind. That it's not jealous or proud. That it doesn't seek its own way. Conrad went on to say that love bears all things, believes all things, hopes all things, and endures all things. He closed by stating that love never fails.*

Interesting. Especially that "love never fails" part. Makes me wonder if we might be capable of discovering everlasting love, after all. If we could, I suspect it would change a lot of things, both in Hollywood...and across the globe. I, for one, am bound and determined to locate it. And I won't stop trying until I do.

— *Reporting for* Hollywood Heartthrob *magazine, "Star Chasers" columnist, Hollywood Molly*

* * * * *

As the fundraiser drew to a close late Saturday evening, Debbie was both elated and exhausted. It would probably take days to process all that had transpired over the past few hours. Right now, she knew one thing: the Lord had come through. So had Bobby Conrad. And so had the man who now held the key to her heart— Johnny Hartmann.

Around nine o'clock that night, just as the last of the guests were ushered out of the parking lot, Debbie made her way back inside. She plopped down into a chair, every joint aching, every muscle crying out in pain. Oh, but it had been worth it. And she would do it all over again, if it would save the soda shop.

Just outside the door, dozens of neighbors and friends worked to clear the debris. What a mess the teens had left behind, but what wonderful memories, too!

Ginny took the seat across from her. "Did you hear the news?"

"No, what?" Debbie asked.

"Mr. Banning, our church treasurer, has just counted up the proceeds from today's event."

Debbie's heart raced. "Did we raise enough to pay off the mortgage?" she asked.

"Well, not quite," Ginny said. "But we did raise nine thousand dollars, so we're well on our way. And it's more than enough to keep my father humbled, to say the least." She squeezed Debbie's hand. "He won't be bothering you anymore, I promise."

"Oh?"

"Yes, it's the strangest thing. Ever since he met Bobby, he's like a changed man. Seems like all he wants to talk about now is red convertibles." Ginny giggled. "But I like it."

"I'm so glad," Debbie said. Her thoughts shifted back to the money. "I guess I was dreaming to think we could really raise eighteen thousand dollars in a day. But at least we can get caught up on the mortgage now and even pay ahead. That means Pop can take it easy for a while. The rest of us can run the shop while he works in the office. Or retires, even."

"I'm not retiring." Her father's voice rang out from across the room. "I'm only forty-nine. You can't put me out to pasture at forty-nine."

She sighed. "Anyway, he can take it easy, and we can keep the place going."

Bobby came up and placed his hands on Ginny's shoulders. She gazed up at him with such tenderness, it almost took Debbie's breath away.

"I thought maybe we could go for a walk on the beach," Bobby said. "If you're not too tired."

"I…I'm not too tired." Ginny smiled. "But I'm a mess. Look at me, Bobby. Are you sure you want to be seen in public with me? What if there's still a photographer hanging around out there?"

"Then he'll get a photograph of me with the prettiest girl at the concert." Bobby turned to Debbie. "Sorry, Debbie. All of you girls are beautiful, but…" He shook his head and a shy smile lit his face.

"Oh, no offense taken." Debbie gave him an encouraging smile.

Ginny rose, her eyes now bright with excitement. "In that case, I'd love to go for a walk. Just let me call my parents to let them know I'll be a little later than I'd planned."

Minutes later, the two disappeared out the front door, and Debbie found herself lost in her thoughts. A song began to play on the jukebox, then a familiar voice startled her back to attention.

"Could I have this dance, Miss?"

She looked up at the sound of Johnny's voice. He extended his hand, and she paused for a moment, feeling a little guilty because the soda shop was in such a state of disarray. Who had time for dancing right now?

Johnny's pleading green eyes finally convinced her. She tossed her dishrag onto a nearby table and wiped her hands against her apron. "Sure, if you don't mind dancing with someone who looks like something the cat dragged in."

"Mmm." His gaze narrowed. "If this is what the cat dragged in, then the cat has excellent taste."

Debbie couldn't help but chuckle as he swept her into his arms and pulled her out onto the floor to dance. As the words to Elvis's familiar song played overhead, she forgot about the work, forgot about the crowd, the mortgage, everything.

No, in Johnny Hartmann's arms, she could only think clearly about one thing: him. And right now, that's really all that mattered.

She rested her head against his shoulder and drank in the moment, the words to the song now taking root in her heart. Love me tender.

That's how Johnny had won her, wasn't it? He'd shown the same kind of tender love to her—and her family—that Pop always showed.

Interesting. Debbie's thoughts reeled back to that earlier conversation she'd had with Pop about *Father Knows Best*. She thought about the differences between her own father's parenting style and, say, Ginny's. Then she began to think about what a great father Johnny would make one day. He had the same father-heart that Pop did.

Hmm. Perhaps that was because both had such a close relationship with the real Father, the one who loved with the most tenderness of all.

"For my darlin', I love you...and I always will." Johnny added his voice to Elvis's, giving him a run for his money. He stopped dancing and gazed into Debbie's eyes.

"What is it?" she whispered.

"Oh, just thinking about those words."

"Oh?"

"And I always will." He kissed her on the cheek. "They describe how I feel perfectly."

Debbie's heart came alive at this revelation. She was just about to respond when she noticed the sound of someone talking to her left. Two someones, actually. She looked over to discover Junior dancing with Martha Lou. He was whispering something in her ear. Whatever it was caused her to grin with delight.

About halfway into the song, Mom and Pop joined them on the dance floor. Debbie had seen them dance before, but tonight there seemed to be something rather magical in the air. They held each other close and turned in slow circles, their conversation quiet.

Next came Jim and Theresa. Right behind them, Toby entered the floor, dancing with a mop. Nothing like adding a little humor to the mix. When the song came to an end, the youngster gripped the mop in one hand and stared his father down.

"Hey, Dad, can I ask you a question?"

"Sure, son." Jim shrugged. "What's up?"

"I look like a natural dancing, don't I?"

Jim gave him a curious look. "Never really thought about it. Why do you ask?"

"Oh, no reason. Only, I think I look pretty good on the dance floor."

"Son, have you been reading *Variety* again?"

Toby sighed. "Yeah. I know, I know. No son of yours is ever going to be in show business. I've heard it all before."

"Actually, that's not what I was going to say this time." Jim placed a hand on his son's shoulder. "Your mother and I have been talking about visiting the church that Bobby and Johnny attend. I understand they're having auditions for a children's production in a week or so. We thought it might be a good way for you to get your feet wet."

"Really?" Toby's face shone with excitement. "Really truly?"

"Well, don't get your hopes up too high," Jim said. "I'm sure there will be a lot of talented kids auditioning."

"Oh, I don't care," Toby said. "As long as I get a part." He reached over and hugged his father, a smile lighting his face. "Oh, thank you! Thank you, thank you!"

"You're welcome, son. I guess it's about time."

Debbie watched this exchange in silence, saying a gentle "Amen." Looked like the Lord was really doing a work in Jim's heart. She couldn't help but think that Johnny had played a role in this one. Yes, Toby would end up on the big stage at the church…and she would be in the audience, cheering him on.

For now, however, only one person needed her attention. She rested her head against Johnny's shoulder...and continued the dance.

* * * * *

Johnny circled the dance floor, his eyes closed. With the fundraiser behind him and his future as bright as a new copper penny, he couldn't help but feel contented. When the song ended, he and Debbie took a seat at a nearby booth for a quiet conversation. They didn't have much time alone, however. Jim stopped by with a broad smile on his face.

"Johnny, such great news. A good friend who directs for Paramount Studios was in the crowd today. He was scouting you out."

"H–he was?"

"Yes." Jim nodded. "After hearing you and Bobby perform so close together, he came up with a great idea for a beach movie starring the two of you with Brenda Valentine as the love interest. It's going to be a romantic comedy about two brothers who are both in love with the same girl. They're calling it *A Tale of Two Brothers*."

"Really?" Johnny's breath caught in his throat. Was it possible? "How much does it pay?"

Jim gave him a curious look. "Well, you get right to the point, don't you."

"I have my reasons." He did, indeed. Johnny had overheard the news about today's fundraiser. He knew they hadn't raised the full amount. As much as he wanted to celebrate, he wouldn't rest easy until he knew the Carmichaels owned the soda shop, free and clear. He would only take the part in the movie if the money was enough to pay off the balance of the existing mortgage. If not, he would just take singing gigs. They were more his speed, anyway. For that matter, he might consider singing here, at Sweet Sal's.

Why not? He loved the food. He loved the people. He loved—Debbie.

Johnny smiled as their eyes met.

He loved Debbie. And he would go on loving her—from now until eternity.

Chapter Twenty

BOX OFFICE SMASH

Stop the presses! I've got the story of the decade. Maybe the story of the century! Just two days ago at a small soda shop in Laguna Beach, Bobby Conrad and Johnny Hartmann put on a concert that fans are sure to be talking about for years. The event served as a fundraiser for Sweet Sal's Soda Shoppe, which happens to have the best chocolate malts a girl could ask for.

As I watched Conrad and Hartmann share the stage, as I listened to the genuineness of their songs, I was reminded once again that there truly are some great people in show business. And talk about working a crowd! Most would assume that Bobby would win the hearts of audience members, but watching Johnny Hartmann at work was pure bliss, as well. The kid can sing. And, wow! That new song of his…"Oceans of Love." Really a winner with the ladies.

And speaking of ladies, the fellas incorporated some new singers into the act—three girls, waitresses at Sweet Sal's Soda Shoppe, who call themselves the Peppermints. Cute. Their voices were the perfect blend, adding the cream on top of the coffee for this listener. In short, I had the time of my life.

What's next for Bobby? As soon as Brenda Valentine's leg heals, filming will begin on Oh, My Romeo! Until then, my sources tell me that Bobby has a new love interest—a small town banker's daughter from

Laguna. (Can you imagine the dollar signs rolling around in daddy's eyes right now?) As for Johnny, we understand he has been offered a potential visit with Dick Clark on American Bandstand. *No doubt teen girls will swoon. And better still, my sources assure me that a movie deal is in the works, featuring Johnny's new song.*

For now, this reporter's going to pray that Johnny makes it to the studio to record "Oceans of Love." No doubt it will be an overnight sensation...just like he is.

— *Reporting for* Hollywood Heartthrob *magazine, "On the Big Screen" columnist, Cinema Cindy*

* * * * *

Late Monday afternoon Debbie ran all the way from the drugstore to the soda shop with a copy of *Hollywood Heartthrob* in her hand. She still couldn't believe the fundraiser had made Cinema Cindy's column. Just wait till she told everyone.

As she approached the diner, she paused to catch her breath and then smiled as Jim's car pulled into the parking lot. Debbie waved then straightened her apron and cap, wanting to look her best for Johnny.

From the moment he stepped out of the car, she felt like they'd entered a scene in a movie, one that appeared to be moving in slow motion. He flashed a smile that caused her heart to race. She lifted the magazine and waved it. "Johnny, you've got to see this!"

No sooner did he get out of the car, however, than girls came from out of the woodwork. Within seconds, he was swarmed by females on every side. Jim and Theresa managed to distract the teens with the promise of autographed photos, and Debbie ushered Johnny inside.

"Not sure I can get used to that." He shook his head, appearing a little overwhelmed.

"Looks like you have no choice," Debbie said. "Just one more thing you'll have to deal with on the road to stardom."

He groaned. "Let's skip the whole 'stardom' thing, okay? I just want to sing my songs."

"Looks like you're going to get to," she said. "Everyone loves you, Johnny."

"I hope a certain someone loves me more than all the others," he whispered, drawing her close.

She wanted to throw her arms around his neck and share several sweet kisses, to tell him that she'd dreamed of him on Saturday night after the concert, and again on Sunday night. But she didn't. There would be time for romantic exchanges later. Right now, she had to show off the magazine. Probably everyone would flip!

"Mom!" Debbie hollered across the restaurant. "Pop! Come and see what I've got." She gestured for Mr. Jangles and Johnny to join her at a table near the front of the restaurant. Holding up the copy of *Hollywood Heartthrob*, she asked the obvious question. "Have any of you seen today's edition?"

"Not me," Johnny said. "I'm clueless."

"Oh, I can't wait!" Becky Ann ran from the kitchen. "I've been dying to see it. Is there anything in there about the concert?"

"*Is* there!" Debbie opened up the magazine and began to read Cinema Cindy's column aloud. Before long everyone looked as stunned as she felt.

"Wow. Talk about some great publicity for the shop." Pop's eyes misted over. "We owe her our thanks."

Debbie closed the magazine and shook her head. "I can't figure out for the life of me how Cinema Cindy did a review when she wasn't even here."

"Maybe she was," her mother said. "Maybe she was just one of the faces in the crowd."

"But here's what confuses me…" Debbie opened the magazine and pointed to another section. "Sunset Sam did a write-up of the event, too. And so did Fashionable Francis."

Becky Ann grabbed the magazine and thumbed through it. "I'm pretty sure I met all of the people who were here with the press, didn't you?"

"Yes," Debbie said. "I met Hedda Hopper, Louella Parsons, that deejay friend of Bobby's, and a ton of other people, but none of these folks from *Hollywood Heartthrob*. Strange, right?"

"Maybe they want to protect their identity," her mother said. "Think about it, Debbie. If you were always writing articles about famous people—sometimes getting it right and other times getting it wrong—wouldn't you want to protect your identity?"

Debbie shrugged. "I suppose. Still, it seems weird. And all of the articles are good. Really, really good. It's almost too good to be true."

At this point, Jim cleared his throat.

Debbie looked his way. "What is it, Jim?"

"Oh, well, I, um…" He shook his head. "Is it warm in here?"

Debbie narrowed her gaze, growing suspicious. "What do you know about this? Did you sneak these reporters in without us knowing?"

"Sneak them in?" He paused and released a slow breath. "I guess you could say I had a little something to do with it."

Toby chuckled. "Better spill the beans, Pop," he said. "They're all gonna find out, anyway."

"Spill the beans?" Johnny gave him a curious look. "What are you talking about?"

"What is it, Jim?" Debbie's mom asked, looking the nervous agent squarely in the eye. "You might as well tell us."

"I know you're not going to believe this," he said at last. "And I can't believe I'm actually saying this out loud, either. But there is no Cinema Cindy."

"What?" Every mouth dropped open.

"Of course there is," Debbie argued. "I've been reading her column for years. She keeps the girls hopping with her stories about who's starring in which movie."

Jim shook his head. "Nope. And there's no Sunset Sam, either."

"You mean, there's no *real* Sunset Sam," Johnny said. "It's some guy using that name. And the same with Cindy."

"No, you're missing my point." Jim smiled. "I mean, *Hollywood Heartthrob* magazine only has one reporter and she writes all of the columns, using different names."

"W–what?" Debbie stared at him, dumbfounded. "That's...that's impossible. Why, every column in that magazine is completely different from the others."

"Exactly." He nodded. "That's the idea."

"You're telling us that Cinema Cindy is the same person as Sunset Sam?" Becky Ann asked. "I don't believe it."

"You can believe it." Jim nodded. "And he—actually, it's a she—is also Hepcat Harry, Fashionable Frances, and Hollywood Molly, too."

"I can't believe you found this out," Debbie said. "How in the world do you know all of this? It's got to be top secret information."

He laughed. "I know, because that person who's running herself ragged keeping up with it all…is my wife."

At this proclamation, every eye in the place turned to Theresa, who gave a little grin. "What can I say?"

"But, how is that possible?" Johnny looked confused. "I had no idea."

She pulled up a chair and sat down at the table. "Five years ago, Jim and I started the magazine in an office off Sunset to help promote some of Hollywood's up-and-coming talent," she explained. "About two years ago, the publication nearly cratered when teens stopped reading. We couldn't afford to keep our staff, so they disappeared on us, one by one, and we moved the operation to the house. I kept the columns going."

"Wow." Debbie shook her head. "Sounds like a lot of work."

"Yes. But we already owned the names—Cinema Cindy, Hepcat Harry, and so forth. They belonged to the magazine. So, why not? And besides, once we met Bobby, the teens started reading again, so it made writing the articles more fun. The readership grew."

"And grew," Jim said.

"And grew!" Becky Ann said, holding up the magazine. "This is the most popular gossip magazine in the state. Maybe even in the country."

"Pretty close," Jim said. "The circulation is in the multiplied thousands each week, and that's just in Southern California. We've done really well with it."

Debbie shook her head. "I guess this explains why I was told Cinema Cindy was too busy to come."

"Yes." Jim chuckled. "Though, technically, Theresa here *is* Cinema

Cindy. And Fashionable Frances, etc. And she was here the whole day, which is how she pulled off the columns you're reading now."

"You must've been up all night Saturday night," Debbie said.

Theresa shook her head. "No, actually I wrote them while you all were singing on Saturday. Didn't you notice I carried a notebook?"

"Now that you mention it." Debbie nodded. "I figured it had something to do with Jim's agency."

"In a sense it does," Theresa said. "Getting the word out about Bobby—and now Johnny—has been important for their careers. And it's been good for businesses like yours, too, because we can promote their various events. I've had the time of my life writing these columns. And it's given me a chance to see some pretty famous people up close— Elvis, Doris Day, Marlon Brando, and dozens more."

"Wow." Becky Ann's eyes grew wide.

Johnny gave Theresa a knowing look. "Well, I guess this explains why you're always on the typewriter. I wondered what you were up to."

"Jim and I always called the magazine 'our little project.'" She gave her husband a wink. "Though, to be honest, I'm getting a little tired of it. And now that…" She paused and her cheeks turned pink. "Well, now that I'm going to be busy redecorating that spare room, I won't have much time to write."

"Redecorating the spare room?" Debbie's mom gave Theresa a curious look. "Thinking of turning it into a sewing room?"

"No." Theresa's cheeks flamed even pinker. "A, um…a nursery."

At this proclamation, the place came alive. Toby let out a whoop, followed by a whistle from Johnny. Debbie watched it all, mesmerized. What would it be like, to decorate a nursery? To have a husband and child to care for?

"So, the infamous agent is gonna be a papa again." Debbie's father slapped him on the back. "That's great news, Jim. Congratulations."

"Thanks." Jim grinned ear to ear. "I've known for a few days. Couldn't wait to tell everyone. We're happy as two kids just starting out in life. It's going to be a new adventure."

"No doubt about that," Theresa said then chuckled.

One question still raised Debbie's curiosity antennae. "Still gonna keep the magazine going?" she asked.

"Funny you should ask." Jim flashed a smile. "Theresa and I have been talking about that. We'd like to get some help from the younger crowd."

"Oh?" Debbie's curiosity was piqued.

"We wondered if you and Becky Ann might be willing to work part-time for the magazine. You girls could assist Theresa by covering Hollywood Molly's column," Jim said. "If you like, you can even start a *Dear Debbie* column, too. Let folks know who you are. It's fine with us."

Becky Ann managed one word: "Wow!" Looked like she'd otherwise been rendered speechless.

"Really?" Debbie could hardly fathom the idea.

"Yes, but you would have to come up to Hollywood on occasion to stay up on the action."

Debbie suddenly had trouble catching her breath. "Are you serious?"

"Sure." Theresa gave her an encouraging nod. "You girls know as much about Hollywood as I do. More, even. And besides, you've got the inside scoop on at least one of Hollywood's major players." Theresa looked Johnny's way.

Debbie smiled as she watched Johnny's cheeks flash pink. He looked even more adorable when he was embarrassed. And when she thought about all the things she could write about him, her mind came alive with ideas.

"I guess I do have the inside scoop," she said.

"Funny, the only scoops we had before today were chocolate, vanilla, or strawberry," her dad threw in.

The laughter that followed resounded across the room.

"Debbie, we should do it," Becky Ann said. "I won't tell a soul, I promise. It will be our secret." Her brow wrinkled. "Not that I'm the best writer in the world."

"Don't worry about that," Theresa said. "You just come up with the information and I'll help you write it all down. You have no idea what a relief it will be not to carry the load all by myself anymore."

"You don't think it would be a…conflict of interest?" Debbie asked.

Jim shook his head. "No, because we treat every star fairly. Always have and always will."

Debbie felt her curiosity rising. She looked at Theresa. "Can I ask a question?"

"Sure." Theresa nodded. "Ask me anything. I'm an open book."

"Well, I've noticed that the magazine articles have changed a little over the past couple of weeks. They're a bit more…"

"Reflective?"

"Yes," Debbie said. "That's the word."

Theresa remained silent for a moment before responding. "I feel like I've been on a journey for the past several months," she said at last. "And all the more when I found out we're having a little one. I enjoy my work, but it's always felt like something was missing. When Bobby came to stay with us, I caught glimpses of what it might be. And then, when Johnny came along…" Her eyes filled with tears. "When Johnny came along, I knew something was…" She shook her head. "I guess you could say something was stirring inside of me."

Johnny took a seat across from her. "Really?"

"Yes." She paused. "Johnny, I know you think you came to L.A. so that your life could be changed. But I honestly think the Lord brought you here so that you could help bring about change in others. I know I'm different after knowing you, anyway."

Debbie felt the sting of tears in her eyes as she gazed at Johnny. He reached out and took Theresa's hand, giving it a squeeze. "Thank you for telling me, Theresa. I'm so glad."

"No, I'm the one who's glad." Theresa turned her attention back to Debbie. "So, you're right. My articles have been changing lately. And I have a feeling the whole layout of the magazine is eventually going to change. But for now, I just know that I can't do it alone anymore. I need help from someone who understands and appreciates the things that readers really need to hear, and I think that person is you." She turned to give Becky Ann a smile. "And you, too, honey."

Debbie could barely speak. She finally managed three words: "I'd be honored."

"M–me, too," Becky added.

Everyone in the group went back to chatting, but Debbie's thoughts had already shifted to Johnny. She wanted to absorb Theresa's news… and she needed to do it with Johnny at her side. As the noise level around them grew, he looked her way, extending his hand.

"Want to go for a walk on the beach?"

Debbie smiled, feeling a little awkward about leaving. Hmm. No one appeared to be paying attention anyway. Mom and Pop were chatting with Jim and Theresa about the magazine. Becky Ann was flipping through the pages of *Hollywood Heartthrob*, squealing over the various articles. And Junior....

Wait a minute. Martha Lou had sidled up next to Junior at the bar, and the two were sharing a quiet conversation. And a chocolate malt. With two straws.

Suddenly, Debbie felt like laughing. She grabbed Johnny's hand, gave it a squeeze, and looked up into those gorgeous green eyes. "I would love to go to the beach."

They made their way outside. A throng of teen girls had gathered, though two police officers who happened to be stopping by for lunch did a fine job of holding them at bay.

"It's Johnny!" several of the girls screamed as Debbie and Johnny passed by. Suddenly, they were surrounded by a swarm of teens, and she could barely breathe.

One of the police officers blew his whistle while the other shouted a warning for the girls to back off. A few did, but a handful remained close, one clutching at Johnny's sleeve.

"Oh, Johnny, you're the cat's meow," she crooned. "You can sing for me anytime."

"Can I have your autograph?" one of the other girls asked.

Instead of getting flustered, Johnny took the offered pen and paper and scribbled his name on it, along with the words JOHN 3:16.

"What does John 3:16 mean?" the girl asked, looking confused. "Is it some sort of code?"

Johnny chuckled. "Look it up. It's in the Bible."

"The Bible?" She shrugged. "Okay."

As he handed back the pen, she clutched it in her hand and sighed. "I'm going to keep this pen till the day I die."

The girls began to chatter excitedly to each other, and Johnny took Debbie by the arm, gently leading her through the boisterous crowd to the sidewalk near the highway.

"Well, *that* was frightening," he said, once they were free from the throng of giggly girls.

"They're your fans, Johnny. Better get used to it. With a voice like yours, you're bound to have girls following you everywhere you go." Even as Debbie spoke the words, a possessive feeling came over her. She didn't want other girls following him, but what could she do about it?

He paused and gazed into her eyes. "There's only one girl I want to follow me everywhere I go, and she's right here."

Debbie felt her heart swell with joy, and all the more as Johnny slipped an arm around her waist to guide her across the street to the beach.

She would follow him, all right. To the ends of the earth.

Or at least to the edge of the Pacific.

* * * * *

When they reached the water's edge, Johnny instinctively reached down and pulled off his shoes. His thoughts shifted back to the day he'd first walked barefoot in the sand with Debbie at his side. He could barely believe only a few short weeks had passed. My, how his life had changed. When the Lord moved, He really moved.

Johnny left his shoes and socks on the sand and raced for the water. Debbie followed along behind him. Together, they splashed and played, just as they'd done the first time. Off in the distance, the sun dipped low and evening's shadows crept over the horizon.

Johnny decided to take his cue from the skies. He slipped his arms around Debbie, drawing her close. She rested her head against his shoulder, and the two stood cradled together for some time, completely silent.

Not that Johnny's mind was silent. Oh no. He longed to tell Debbie his secret…that he only planned to take the movie deal so he could pay off the soda shop for her parents. But this wasn't the time or place.

"You're being really quiet," Debbie said after a moment. "Everything okay?"

"Are you kidding?" He gazed into her eyes. "I've got the Pacific, a gorgeous sunset, and the prettiest girl in the world. What else could a guy ask for?"

She grinned. "Well, when you put it like that…"

"Actually, there is one more thing," he said at last.

"Oh?"

"Yes. I still haven't seen Bobby's movie, *First Kiss*. You promised me that if I hadn't seen it by the time the fundraiser ended, we could have a date."

"Wow. I can't believe you remembered that."

"You bet I remembered." He kissed the tip of her nose. "So what do you say?"

"I say yes, of course. It's still playing at The Palace on the weekends."

"Perfect. Because I plan to be hanging around on the weekends…a lot."

"Mmm. Sounds lovely."

He draped his arms around her waist, and she sighed. The waves pounded the shore, the tide rolling out for the evening. With it went all of his fears and inhibitions. He was finally free to speak his feelings openly and without hesitation.

"Debbie, I love you with all of my heart. I thank God every day for you." The words came out so softly he wondered if she could hear them against the backdrop of the mighty Pacific.

Apparently so. She gazed at him with joy radiating from her eyes. "I love you, too. And I'm so grateful He brought you here from Topeka. It's like a miracle, really."

Johnny leaned in and his lips met hers for a whisper-soft kiss. She pulled back, and for a second he thought he'd lost her. Just as quickly, her lips met his once again for several light, feathery kisses, tender and innocent, yet filled with emotion.

When the kisses ended, she rested her head against his shoulder. They both stared at the skies overhead, which were layered with myriad colors—red, orange, yellow, and even a hint of purple. Johnny found it nearly as breathtaking as the woman in his arms.

Still, there was one lingering question. It wouldn't leave him alone. He finally worked up the courage to ask it.

"Debbie...are you disappointed?"

"Disappointed?" She looked at him, clearly confused. "What do you mean?"

"I mean, are you sorry you ended up with a guy from Topeka instead of with Bobby Conrad? Do you feel like you've been cheated?"

"Are you serious?" The edges of her lips curled up in a delicious smile. "On the contrary."

"Are you sure?"

"Yes." She gave him a gentle kiss on the cheek. "The way I look at it, I was shooting for a star, and lassoed the moon instead."

He chuckled, pulling her close. "Reminds me of Hey, Diddle, Diddle."

"I'm not jumping over this moon, Johnny Hartmann," she admonished. "You're not getting away." She gave him a playful grin. "I mean, if you'll have me."

"If I'll have you?" He kissed her forehead, not once, but four times. "If I'll have you?" The kisses worked their way down onto her cheeks and she giggled with delight. By the time their lips met, Johnny's heart pounded against his chest, the reality of the moment overwhelming him. When he leaned back, she flashed a shy smile and he kissed the tip of her freckled nose once more.

In that moment, he wanted to share even more of his heart, to tell her that every mile he'd traveled on that Greyhound bus had been worth it, just to find her, that he'd fallen in love, not just with her, but with her family, the soda shop, and the glorious waters of the Pacific.

Instead, he wrapped her in his arms again.

Why waste time talking, when a kiss could say a thousand words?

Epilogue

FROM HERE TO ETERNITY

Hollywood Heartthrob *readers will notice some changes to the publication over upcoming weeks and months. We will be featuring a new column called* Dear Debbie. *Readers are encouraged to send letters to me, Debbie Carmichael, care of* Hollywood Heartthrob *magazine. I hope to answer your questions about today's stars. We will also post several letters from some of Hollywood's finest singers, actors, and comedians. I look forward to hearing these fine people share on issues of faith, family, and friendship.*

Update on Bobby Conrad. Teen girls across America are in mourning this week, ever since receiving word of Bobby's upcoming nuptials to Ginny Anderson, of Laguna Beach, California. Sorry, girls, but the gorgeous brunette has won his heart. Word has it the bride-to-be's father, a prominent banker, is springing for a honeymoon in Acapulco. We wish the happy couple our best.

Readers have also asked for an update on Johnny Hartmann, so here it is…at last. Hartmann has signed a deal to appear in a new musical titled A Tale of Two Brothers, *alongside Bobby Conrad. Filming will begin after Conrad returns home from his honeymoon in March. In the meantime, Johnny stays busy in Laguna Beach, where he currently spends his days singing on the stage of Sweet Sal's Soda Shoppe. Hartmann is looking at a home near Laguna Canyon so that he can remain close to Sweet Sal's…and the people he loves. Speaking of the people he* loves, Johnny is expecting a visit from his parents and younger brother later this month. When asked about his romantic life, Hartmann stated that big things are in the works. He wouldn't offer any more information, and this reporter dares not speculate (though she has her suspicions).

On a side note: Jim Jangles, agent to Conrad and Hartmann, has taken on a new prodigy, a young woman from Laguna Beach named Martha Lou Walters. Jangles recently informed me that she is set to appear on television within weeks. I have it on good authority that Jangles's nine-year-old son, Toby, also has the acting bug. He recently carried the lead role in a children's production at a local church. His parents couldn't be prouder.

So, there you have it, folks. We'll continue to keep you in the know, bringing you love, laughter, and happily ever afters...Hollywood style.

— *Reporting for* Hollywood Heartthrob *magazine, "Dear Debbie" columnist, Debbie Carmichael*

About The Author

 **JANICE HANNA** (also published as Janice A. Thompson) has published more than sixty novels and non-fiction books. She has also written and directed several musical comedies for the stage, including "Johnny Be Good," a fifties soda shop extravaganza. Janice is proud of her four daughters and six darling grandbabies. She makes her home in the Houston area.

Read more at www.janicehannathompson.com.

summerside
PRESS™

When I Fall in Love™
ROMANCE WITH A NOSTALGIC BEAT
Available Starting September 2010

Do you remember the song that was playing during your first kiss? Can you still sing the lyrics to the tune you and your first love called "our song"? If so, you are going to love Summerside's newest fiction line—WHEN I FALL IN LOVE. Each book in the WHEN I FALL IN LOVE romance line, to be set in the 1920s through the 1970s, will carry the title of a familiar love song and will feature new, original romance stories set in the era of its title song's release. Watch for six new releases in the WHEN I FALL IN LOVE romance line in 2011.

I'll Be Home for Christmas
BY JULIE L. CANNON

Bing Crosby's "I'll Be Home for Christmas" provides the backdrop as Maggie Culpepper and William Dove proclaim their undying love to one another. But with the U.S. at war and Maggie's personal home front under attack, the Southern belle impetuously joins the WAVES (Women Accepted for Voluntary Emergency Service). When Christmas draws near and Maggie finds herself miles and miles away from her Georgia hometown, and her beloved William, will she realize that, no matter where she spends Christmas, home is where her heart is?

ABOUT THE AUTHOR

Julie L. Cannon is a multi-published author as well as a speaker and entertainer. She travels across the country serving up helpings of down-home humor and warmth described as "Southern-fried soul food." She lives with her husband and three children in Georgia.